NOV 16 2018

D0440847

SKETCHTASY
MATTILDA BERNSTEIN SYCAMORE

NO LONGER PROPERTY OF
SEATTLE PUBLIC LIBRARY

ARSENAL
PULP PRESS | VANCOUVER

SKETCHTASY

Copyright © 2018 by Mattilda Bernstein Sycamore

All rights reserved. No part of this book may be reproduced in any part by any means—graphic, electronic or mechanical—without the prior written permission of the publisher, except by a reviewer, who may use brief excerpts in a review, or in the case of photocopying in Canada, a license from Access Copyright.

ARSENAL PULP PRESS
Suite 202 – 211 East Georgia St.
Vancouver, BC V6A 1Z6
Canada
arsenalpulp.com

Arsenal Pulp Press acknowledges the xʷməθkʷəy̓əm (Musqueam), Sḵwx̱wú7mesh (Squamish), and səl̓ilwətaʔɬ (Tsleil-Waututh) Nations, speakers of Hul'q'umi'num'/Halq'eméylem/hən̓q̓əmin̓əm̓ and custodians of the traditional, ancestral, and unceded territories where our office is located. We pay respect to their histories, traditions, and continuous living cultures and commit to accountability, respectful relations, and friendship.

This is a work of fiction. Any resemblance of characters to persons either living or deceased is purely coincidental.

Cover and text design by Oliver McPartlin
Edited by Shirarose Wilensky
Copy edited by Doretta Lau
Proofread by Alison Strobel

Printed and bound in Canada

Library and Archives Canada Cataloguing in Publication

Sycamore, Mattilda Bernstein, author
     Sketchtasy / Mattilda Bernstein Sycamore.

Issued in print and electronic formats.
ISBN 978-1-55152-729-1 (softcover).—ISBN 978-1-55152-730-7 (HTML)

     I. Title.

PS3619.Y33S54 2018   813'.6   C2018-901416-4

                                                      C2018-901417-2

To Gabriel Hedemann, for walking that runway with me in
Boston, no matter the consequences

To Jennifer Natalya Fink, on our twentieth anniversary as
sisters of the written word

To all the queens who walk, all the queens who walk away
and all the queens who walk out

For JoAnne, 1974–1995
For Chrissie Contagious, 1974–2010
For David Wojnarowicz, 1954–1992

THE WAY YOU'RE GOING TO BE

I'm at the Other Side with Polly, trying to figure out which is worse—straight celebrities who wear red ribbons to show they really care about their dying gay friends, or gay people who wear them instead of actually doing anything—maybe they should all move to the suburbs so we don't have to deal with them, okay? And this boy Andre who Polly knows from BAGLY leans over and says: That's bullshit.

I'm still strung out from coke, K, pot and ecstasy a few days ago—plus, I'm getting over a cold and all I've had is a double shot of wheatgrass and I'm waiting for the waiter to bring me food so I can write in my journal. Of course Andre is wearing a red ribbon. But Polly was wearing one when I met her, and she figured it out quickly enough.

Girl, I say, it's just an empty symbol.

And that's when Andre starts screaming in my face: I'm not a girl—if I wanted a girl, I'd sleep with a girl. I'm a man, a twenty-one-year-old HIV-positive Latino gay man, and I like the suburbs—what's wrong with the suburbs? If I want to move to the suburbs, I'll move to the suburbs—I don't want to live all my life in a ghetto. You can rebel all you want, but there's no way to fight your parents—they're the people who made you. The way you're brought up is the way you're going to be.

And I say: We're brought up to hate ourselves, and we can go beyond that.

But he just keeps yelling: If I wanted a girl, I'd get a real

5

one—a girl with a pussy. If I wanted a woman, I'd have sex with a woman. I like the suburbs, I want to live in the suburbs, I grew up there—what's wrong with the suburbs?

Then he walks off like we're mortal enemies, and I'm thinking: I need food I need food I need food get me food right now where is my food?

I go to the bathroom, and when I get out I'm about to light a cigarette, but then I think: Smoking's disgusting. So I go back to the table and tell Polly I'm quitting, and of course she looks at me like I'm crazy.

My soup finally arrives, but now I can't focus on eating because some straight asshole behind me is saying the stupidest things, I mean I guess he's on a date so he's trying to sound romantic. He just said: I have to confess something—I've never given flowers to someone I don't know before, but I really like you, I do, you remind me of my sister.

Maybe it's time to look for another pair of combat boots, I mean the duct tape on these looks glamorous but it isn't going to last through winter. Polly's too cold so she decides to go home—girl, bring a coat next time, okay?

By the time I get home it's already dark, and as soon as I get inside I hear something awful on the stereo. Are you kidding? It's *Aqualung*. I get to the living room and there's Brian with two of his buddies from the coast guard. Everyone's yelling and there are beer cans everywhere—I feel like I'm in a frat house. Polly, Joey, Bobby and Billy are all drinking with the straight boys like sorority girls—Bobby giggles and says want a beer? Gross. I walk into my room, even though there's nothing in there—everything's still in the living room. That's what I'm supposed to be doing tonight, moving my shit into my room because I'm finally done painting and I got the new carpet and everything.

I call Joanna, who tells me she went over to Jack and Jamie's house and some man turned blue and they were smacking him trying to wake him up and someone else was screaming and crying and Joanna started laughing and said okay, let's get high. She says: I don't know if I can kick—heroin takes care of me.

I want to say come stay with me, but what the hell would she do in Boston with a bunch of coast guard assholes yelling in the other room? So instead I say: You can come here if you know you're not going to get strung out.

Joanna says listen, our relationship can't be the way it used to be, it hurts me too much—I'm getting close to a woman for the first time and you know our connection was fucked up. I say what do you mean? She says I know we kept each other alive—at one point you were the most important person in my life—but you're on the East Coast now and I need space to love women, to feel the fear and get somewhere with it.

But why are you putting me into some distant category, why can't you just talk to me?

So then she starts talking about speedballs: It's the most amazing feeling—all the colors in your head like you're part of the sofa and everything in your body is a door, the lights on and off, on and off. And I say that's not a sofa, it's a broomstick, and then we're finally laughing together—even if her voice still sounds hollow in that heroin way.

Joanna tells me she's going to help Jack kick—Jack told her she'll be shitting and throwing up in bed for seven days. Please call me, Joanna says, and when I get off the phone I need a cigarette, but then I remember I just quit.

Maybe I need a shower, but now I'm thinking about San Francisco and how Joanna wants me to send her the papers I've written for school, but I'm embarrassed because I feel like school is draining away everything I learned when I left school, I mean every time I hear someone say ontology or epistemology or reify or whatever other stupid theory bullshit I want to die.

I call Melissa, who says: What would you do if you thought AIDS was a government plot? And suddenly it's like everything in the room is vibrating, too dark and too light at the same time, and I get that familiar feeling like someone's behind me, my father. I know he's not behind me, but should I turn around?

Melissa's saying something, and I feel like I'm starting to cry so I say hold on. Where am I? Breathe, Alexa, breathe. Okay, this is my room, my new room. In Boston. My father doesn't even live in Boston. There's some annoying classic rock in the background. A few tears. I pick up the phone and say sorry, I was getting an incest flashback, and Melissa says oh, I'm sorry. There's something in the way her voice changes so fast to meet the situation, and then I'm thinking about when we met in ACT UP and how she would never say anything at meetings, but afterward her analysis was so clear, clearer than anyone I'd ever met, and she'd left school too. Melissa says: I had a dream that I had sex with my father, and I wasn't scared—I'm scared now.

I tell her I can lend her money to move out, but she doesn't want me to—why, I say, why? I can't, she says, there's something I still need to figure out.

I hang up the phone and then I'm sitting on the new remnant I put over the old carpet in my empty room because the landlord wouldn't let me tear it out and shag carpet is disgusting—talk about allergies. I make a list of all the people I love, and there are five. Maybe six. The straight boys are yelling in the other room and I'm thinking about the first time I met Polly at Glad Day, or not the first time but the time when I was putting up my roommate flyers that no one ever responded to, too glamorous for Boston, I mean no one here can even deal with the word faggot. Anyway, Polly was the fag behind the counter, and she said guess what, some friends and I found a place in Dorchester and we need someone else to join the lease.

I didn't even know where Dorchester was, but when I arrived I couldn't believe we would have two stories of a Victorian house with stained-glass windows and a whole floor of common areas for $965. All I knew about Polly was that she'd recently escaped a Christian fundamentalist cult run by her father, and she was getting ready to sign a lease with two people she met at BAGLY, the queer youth group, so I figured at least we were all queer. Or something. Siobhan, the pothead dyke, seemed kind of dazed. And then there was Brian, seventeen going on forty—fake tan, frosted hair, overalls with one strap undone. He was some kind of model queer youth so he could hardly even smile at me, but we signed the lease together anyway.

Then Brian from the coast guard moved in—he's Siobhan's friend. Everyone calls him Straight Boy to distinguish him from Brian Marshall, but I think that's tacky. Luckily he's not in town very often. And now Joey, Bobby and Billy are practically living here too—those tacky queens might as well start paying rent, I mean we have at least two more bedrooms.

Gross—Bobby's calling me: Miss One, you're missing the party. She's the most ridiculous person on earth, but I open my door and go in the living room anyway. Everyone's fawning over the straight boys, and what's playing now? Led Zeppelin—"Squeeze me, baby, 'til the juice runs down my leg." One of the straight boys is doing air guitar. I thought it couldn't get any worse than the *Priscilla* soundtrack. I introduce myself, and Bobby says aren't they all so cute? He's disgusting.

Apparently the coast guard boys have been drinking since ten a.m.—I don't even know why anyone would get up that early, but now they're so drunk they look like they're swimming. One of them's cute, I guess, but whatever. His name's Calvin. Everyone keeps saying have some beer, but they're drinking Milwaukee's Best and anyway I only drink vodka. Billy's giggling and Joey and Polly are chain-smoking and Bobby's perm is looking greasier than ever and he's talking about all his gowns. He says: It's hard for me to hang out with anyone who doesn't know the difference between Armani and Versace.

As far as I know, she's never even put on a dress, but she talks like she's the mother of the House of Webstah, Mass.— don't make me reeeeeead you, Miss One. Or, if you ask her too many questions, she'll fling her wrist in circles and then boom: Talk to the hand.

I go in the living room to move my stuff. Brian stumbles in all red-faced, pats me on the back and says can you get me some coke? I say not unless we're in a club. He says can we go somewhere? I say I've got to move my stuff, but you can head over to the Combat Zone and there will be plenty of people selling.

It's kind of a joke—three smashed white straight boys looking for coke in the Combat Zone—yeah, here's some fifty-dollar laxative, sure. But then they're all up and out the door and the music's off. Bobby starts cleaning up the cans and dumping out the ashtrays, saying oh what a mess, Miss One, then sighing like she's the richest housewife in the world, saying: It's what a mother does.

I'm sitting on my futon, trying to focus on unpacking, and Bobby turns on the *Priscilla* soundtrack. She's singing along and I'm about to smack her, then everyone's on my futon and I've got that smile that hurts my jaw. Of course Joey's wearing her raincoat—does she ever take that raincoat off? Whining about how she needs cocktails and doesn't anyone want to go to the Eagle, and Bobby grunts, comes over to pinch Joey's cheeks and says oh, my messy daughter. Bobby shakes her Fendi key chain, looks at me, and says: It's what a mother does.

Joey says meet us there, okay? Polly looks me in the eyes like bitch you betta, and then four kisses for me, luckily three sets of lips and Bobby's cheeks, and they're off.

I'm fantasizing about car crashes and then I realize *Priscilla*'s still on. I think about throwing it away, but instead I just press eject. Back to the living room and I pick up my boxes, one by one—into my room.

I put water on for pasta and wash spinach for a salad and then I hear someone at the door—already? Sure enough, it's the straight boys falling up the stairs. I'm stirring the pasta and it can't be more than a few minutes later when Calvin comes in. He's coked up for sure, looking at my pasta like it's the most amazing thing he's ever seen. I say it's just parsley garlic fettuccine. He says oh, I eat a lot of pasta, you need loads of carbs when you're working out and I'm trying to bulk up, you know—parsley garlic, I'll have to try that.

I'm squeezing tofu over the spinach and Calvin wants to know what that's good for. I say protein, iron, B vitamins. He says are you vegetarian? I say I'm vegan, and then of course I have to explain what that means. He says wow, I never thought of that, wow. Is that spinach? Yeah. Wow—what a great idea, wow—and then Brian's calling him. Brian sounds like he's about to pass out—maybe he didn't do any coke or maybe he's just that drunk. Calvin says okay, well, I'll see you later, okay? He looks right at me. I try not to notice how pretty his eyes are—sky blue and glassy from the coke.

I'm finishing my food and Calvin comes back in the kitchen, he says Brian and Dave went to bed and do you mind if I hang with you? I say as long as you don't distract me. Because Brian Marshall, the tanning salon queen, did you meet him? Calvin shakes his head no, I say well he'll throw a fit if I don't get my stuff out of the living room. Calvin says well I can help you, I mean I don't mind. His eyes are wide and his lip is vibrating, he takes a ball of tinfoil out of his pocket and says do you have anywhere for me to cut this?

I can feel my eyes getting wide. I get Calvin my drug mirror, and he starts cutting the coke. He says you want some? I say is it good? He says yeah it's great blow, fucking great, and there's a lot left, we should split it. I say no, I need to concentrate on unpacking, but he's not listening.

Calvin cuts the coke and I wash the dishes. When I'm done, he's got two huge lines on the mirror. I say I just want a little. He does his line and I'm not breathing. Hands me the rolled-up dollar bill and I snort the other line, oh it burns I fucking love it. I can feel my eyeballs in the back of my head, lids closed and when I open my eyes I'm high. I say you're right, that stuff is great. I can't believe it.

Calvin's looking me in the eyes again and I'm looking away. We go into the living room and everything feels slow but frantic, in twenty minutes all my shit is in my room and we're doing another line. I lean my head back and wow. Calvin's on the bed and I'm unpacking boxes. The phone rings and it's Joey saying bitch it's almost one, you better get your ass down here, everyone's waiting. I say all right, just a few minutes, all right.

Calvin says what's up. I say they want me to meet them at the Eagle. He says can I come. I say it's a gay bar. He says I don't mind. All right, I say, and we do some more coke.

Damn these straight boys are generous—Joey always has coke, but she'll never even give you a bump unless you trade her something for it. I check my hair in the mirror and, yes, every strand of flamingo pink and pillar-box red is in place. Calvin says he'll drive—sounds like a good idea to me.

Calvin's got this tiny little red sports car and we're both wired. I lean my head back and think I shouldn't have done that coke, I shouldn't have done that coke. But then I think fuck it, I might as well enjoy it, and Calvin puts on "You're So Vain"— more classic rock, gross. He says is this okay—I'm nuts about Carly Simon. Did he really just say nuts? Nuts and blow.

We get to the Eagle and there's our little youth corner in the back of the bar. Everyone's screaming for me and I'm actually happy to see them. Polly's got his ass against the bar and he's holding Bobby and swaying—they better break up soon, gotta get that bitch out of my house. Billy pokes me and grunts, her usual thing. Joey's eyes get big and he says: Oh. You brought the straight boy.

Of course Calvin's the wet dream of everyone in the bar: preppy blond boy in jeans and a flannel, so Boston. The Eagle's all middle-aged South End guppies and then us. I get a drink and Jack the bartender looks me up and down: Well, I bet you've got a big dick, huh. He does that every week. But he never cards. I'm twenty-one and Bobby's twenty-three, but everyone else is underage.

Billy wants some of my drink—I grab him a cocktail from nearby and say drink this and he acts all shocked, but then he drinks it. Bobby's over touching Calvin's ass and giggling. Calvin's totally into it. I'm wired. Polly's trying to keep her eyes open—she says oh honey I'm messy. Joey's pacing the bar and some queen comes up to me, says is that Mizrahi? I say no, Dollar-A-Pound, and Billy grunts—I'm laughing and the queen doesn't know what to say.

I get another drink and then I motion to Calvin, we head to the bathroom. He's about to take out the coke but someone comes in, takes out his coke—I say can I have a bump? He scrunches up his nose at me, and then leaves. I finish my cocktail while Calvin gets out the coke—he says do you have a dollar. I say put it on my hand and he pours a pile on. I snort it up then lick my hand, tasty. He snorts the rest from the foil and then I lick that too, his eyes are bulging. I say thanks. Then I study my hair in the mirror—the magenta matches the stripe in my plaid pants and it all contrasts so well with the green sweater, I'm on fire tonight.

Someone opens the bathroom door, stares at my hair and says you look like a parrot. She thinks she's reading me—I lick my lips and say thank you, honey. He's looking Calvin up and down. Calvin's pretending to piss—or wait, he is pissing and I'm just laughing, head up against the wall, loving my rush I could stay here forever. We go back into the bar, Calvin says what are we going to do afterward? I say maybe Billy can get us into the Loft.

Calvin goes over to his buddies at the pool table and I go back to the bar. Polly's getting sad, Billy and Joey are bored. I buy two madrases and hand one to Joey, tell him to split it with Billy. Their eyes light up. Polly's swaying and here comes Bobby sashaying down the aisle to—no way, it's 1995, and they're still playing "Supermodel." Okay, it is the Eagle so we're all up on the runway anyway—no one knows what to do with

us. I'm pushing Bobby aside, cackling and saying you're no su-
supermodel honey. But she actually can walk—even if she's so
exaggerated it's scary, she does work it.

Then the song's over and it's Crystal Waters—usually the
DJ's bad but not as bad as "back to the middle and around
again." Joey's favorite song of course. Polly's still leaning
against the bar, eyes shut and she's kind of nodding—oh no.
Polly, I say, and she opens her eyes. I say honey you're a mess,
and she shuts her eyes again.

It's getting close to two—I ask Billy if he can get me into the
Loft since he's working there, and he looks at me like I'm crazy.
He says it's Friday.

Friday's straight night, but I don't care. Billy says it's scary,
you'll get beat up. I say honey, it's not that scary. He says: I
might get in trouble. The lights are coming up and Bobby's
pulling Polly along while Joey follows. Bobby says: My husband has a BIG dick. And she's grabbing Polly's crotch while
Polly mumbles and shakes her head like she's in a bad dream.

They file outside and I look for Calvin. He runs up and says
you want to go to an after-hours, I say where? He says upstairs.
Sure.

I go outside and it's freezing but nice, Polly leans over and
wraps her arms around me. Bobby says you need a ride? I say
no, I guess I'm going to an after-hours with Calvin. Bobby
smirks and I roll my eyes.

Calvin comes out with two South End tragedies. Turns out
the party is literally upstairs from the Eagle, which is funny at first,
until we go inside and of course it's some bougie hellhole—hors

d'oeuvres on a silver tray, white frilly curtains, plush department store sofas and a bunch of scary South End gays.

I'm too wired. Calvin goes in the other room with one of the guys who brought us and I'm stuck talking to the only queen who will acknowledge that I'm there. I'm crashing hard, just like that—no one's taking out any drugs and I can't stand the idea of another drink. I try to relax, but I keep thinking why am I here why am I here why am I fucking here?

I pour myself a cocktail, but yuck this tastes gross. Some queen with too much cologne is telling a story about how he went to this after-work party and he thought it was just going to be the boys, but then this chick walked in and he looked over and said: Who brought the fish? Everyone's cackling and I feel like I'm going to scream so I go in the bathroom. Run hot water over my hands and sip my Cape Cod and stare at myself in the mirror. I still look okay but I feel worn out. Just want to lie down. I fix my hair so it looks like feathers again, then someone's knocking so I open the door.

I sit down on one of the sofas and stare into space. The whole room smells like cologne and I sip my empty cocktail like it's giving me life. Everyone is talking about this restaurant and that party and oh the shoes I got the other day at Neiman's. And can you believe who I saw coming out of the Fens with her knees all muddy? Don't get too close to her—she'll give you AIDS. But, girl, are you going to South Beach? I can't wait until summer—we are going to own P-town this year.

Some guy wants to know how I got to this party—well, they all want to know that, but one guy asks and I say my friend

Calvin who's in the other room. Someone says oh, the cute one with blond hair—is that your boyfriend?

I say what? I mean no he's not my boyfriend.

Finally the bedroom door opens and there's Calvin—he stumbles out looking like a zombie, collapses on the sofa next to me. I say what'd you do in there? And he says I don't know—I did a bump and then I didn't know where I was. I say oh, you did a bump of K, and I'm kind of jealous.

Calvin rests and I'm suddenly talkative though who knows what the fuck I'm talking about. Then Calvin's finally ready and I'm literally pushing him out the door—thanks—and then we're out in the cold and Calvin looks clearer. We find his car, get inside and turn on the heat 'cause I'm shivering, didn't bring my coat. Calvin's still dazed—I say are you okay to drive? He says yeah, let's just wait a minute.

Calvin says that shit's crazy. I say yeah. He says no I mean crazy—I didn't know where I was and the bed and the ceiling were fighting with me. He pulls the car out of the space and we're off, I shut my eyes and think about sleep but it feels like flying.

A FAMILY PICTURE

Polly and I are in the spaceship on the highway, I never realized the buildings up ahead blink so much like stars and when I close my eyes we're flying through a tunnel of light in the sky until Polly's saying Alexa, look, isn't that the exit?

Oh, maybe I shouldn't close my eyes while I'm driving. But we make it just in time, and then we're gliding through the streets and there's our Star.

Inside it's yes, oh yes, the light flickering my eyes into my head and Polly—do we need anything? Polly gets a Blow Pop, it's already in her mouth so no need to pay, and I get tabouli and hummus and pita bread for later.

We throw our food in the car and step into the Prudential Center to levitate up the escalators, yes we've got the disposable camera and Polly jumps on a cart that says WATCH OUT. But Polly, what are you watching out for?

Polly's modeling her first club outfit, pink T-shirt with a purple heart drawn over one nipple and a red star on the other, smiley-face boxers pulled above the waist of her baggy striped jeans and just the right shade of lipstick to look totally wrong—she pushes her sunglasses down to show off the rest of her makeup, yellow highlighter pressed into her eyelids and then permanent black marker as eyeliner, stunning.

Wait, there's a sign that says MASS HYSTERIA, just behind Polly's head—get a picture of me with MASS HYSTERIA.

Your hair. How did you do it?

I left the dye in.

You're like a present—purple wrapping paper and a big magenta bow. Did the flash go off?

Oh, what about over there by the candy—so many colors. Should we take one together?

Your dress, it's so soft. What's it made out of?

Candy, let's get candy.

So then we're back at Star Market and I could stare at the colors all night long. Polly, what should we get, lemon drops and Sour Patch Kids and Life Savers and what else? Oh—orange juice, let's get orange juice—vitamin C. For later. To bring back the colors. Let's get the big one. With the pulp. Do you like the pulp? What time is it?

Almost 4:30. I don't like the pulp.

We better get to the Loft. I'll get the one without the pulp.

Are you sure?

We go outside to the car and—wait, look at the John Hancock Tower from this angle, all that shimmering glass pushing into the sky and I wish we could go to the top—Polly, the lights, look at all the lights. Should we give her a name?

Jeannine.

Of course. Jeannine Hancockatiel, revealing her true nature, yes nature or nurture, I mean nature and nurture. Are you sure you want to go to the Loft instead of hanging out with Jeannine?

Polly holds my hand and this time I'm looking at her eyes through the sunglasses, blue lenses, your eyes are so blue.

Your hands are so cold.

We glide in the spaceship down a deserted Boylston but

it's so late the door guy at the Loft doesn't want to let us in—everyone's expecting us, I say.

Tonight's our night: he actually listens. And oh, that feeling of walking up the stairs in anticipation, just the bass until you open the door at the top and oh, wow, I forgot it would be this crowded, but there's Billy's head peeking up in the corner. She's working her new platforms that don't taper out at the bottom so she's having a hard time balancing, sucking on a lollipop while attempting to throw some kicks—she holds out her arms: Fierce, she says, your hair looks fierce. Fierce!

Joey's actually on the dance floor so I know she's really coked out and these beats yes these beats and that boy over there his eyes into my eyes I twirl around into jump rope, feet bouncing up and up and down, down, our feet together and turn, flip the floor, his eyes, give me more. And there's Billy through the lasers yelling fierce and Joey bouncing, I turn again pull breath up to arms swaying now I'm so close to this boy, his breath or mine, back around and when he moves his hips I rotate the bounce to move my moves into the space between his breath and the beat and maybe he can join us afterward, maybe we can drive over the Mass. Ave. Bridge for the sunrise, holding hands in the back seat oh the light yes these lights. There's purple in this red, turn, there's red in this purple, turn, and Billy's really kicking now Joey's on the sidelines and Polly stumbles over, where did she go, and I do my almost-falling move toward the queen next to me, who throws up her arms like help so I dive down to the ground and flip around, but then Polly's waving me over. So I twirl off the dance floor still dancing, even though Polly's standing still, eyes almost closed, leaning against the wall for support, she must have found K in the bathroom and she's saying something to me, what did you say?

I love you. Alexa, I love you.

And I know it's her first time on ecstasy so I close my eyes to feel it, but also I know it's love so I open my eyes to look more closely, Polly's curly hair fluorescent in this light, her skin purple like a pretty alien and she holds out her hand so I kiss it while I keep dancing a little with hips into feet and Joey looks over with big eyes and says Traci Lords was here.

Traci Lords? The porn star?

Traci Lords is fierce.

And how did Billy get over here, now she's taller than all of us, yelling something, what is it?

Joey put Traci Lords in a K-hole. It was fierce. Fierce!

And then the air-raid sirens like a drumroll getting louder and louder until the whole room is shaking and listen, "10,000 screaming, 10,000 screaming"—Joey says that's Traci Lords, but is she really saying 10,000 screaming faggots? Whatever it is we're all on the dance floor now—Billy's working her patent leather tank top with Lycra bike shorts and the lasers are blasting past our heads and Juniper and Sage are hugging the speakers in shiny silver outfits with silver body paint and glow-in-the-dark lipstick and their newest Day-Glo wedding cake platform sneakers and then all of us, all of us together, the whole room shaking but wait, oh no, the music's slowing down.

Billy starts giggling at my expression as the lights are coming up and then we're both laughing and I lean my head back, let my eyes roll while Billy holds my hand and I'm saying something about after-hours at our house, everyone. And then I hear someone spreading the word, but oh, I want to invite that boy, where's that boy I was dancing with and Joey says which one but I don't know, I can't find him. Thank you so much, I say to the doormen, and Joey asks if they want a bump. Joey, don't say that! And the purple sweater coat I found at Dollar-A-Pound, here's my new sweater coat, so soft and furry like a bath mat, oh, warm.

We get outside in the bright of night and I give Joey my keys. Polly's snorting something in the back seat and Billy's giggling about all the refreshments, yes, help yourself to refreshments. Joey says Richie and Michael are coming, and then she says it again like we didn't hear her the first time, they're right behind us, following us to Dorchester all the way on Mass. Ave. so no one gets lost, except then Joey takes the back route anyway, but there are still three cars behind us. Richie and Michael arrive with some blonde woman—that's Traci Lords, Joey says, Traci Lords is in a K-hole.

Then there's Elana with Jon B., and I don't know the rest, but we all make our way upstairs and I arrange the candy in bowls in the living room, bring out the orange juice with glasses. Richie's looking around—how many people live here? Too many. Richie says is it expensive? No, I say, and then I realize he's looking at Bobby, who's coming downstairs in one of Brian's BUM Equipment sweatshirts and a baseball cap—does it really say JOCKS? And then Brian's behind her, wearing Bobby's ridiculous varsity jacket—I guess it's time for Brian to go to work.

Richie says Champagne lives here too? And Bobby giggles like they're best friends, she doesn't even realize Richie is reading her.

Orange juice, I ask, and hold out a glass.

No, Miss One, I've got to get the husband to work.

Work, Polly mumbles.

Work! Billy shrieks.

Michael puts a tape in the boom box and now there are 10,000 screaming faggots right in our living room—really, 10,000, really? Joey says it's a thousand—honey, keep counting.

And I go in the bathroom to take a shower oh yes this is what I needed my skin yes my skin the light this water yes this water oh warm please more warm until, wait, it's getting cold, better dry off. And then my green chenille sweater with burgundy underneath, but then there's that sadness behind my eyes, just a little, and can it be happening already? I go in my room and sit on the futon—I look at my hands and they don't look like my hands, but what do they look like? I'm crashing already, should I take another hit? I bought three this time, thought I would save the others but maybe this is what I was saving them for so then I go in the kitchen for orange juice and stare at the colors in the bowls—do I eat candy?

Polly's in the corner with Traci Lords, doing a bump of something. Polly, I say, I just did another hit of X. I love you, Polly says, eyes closed, but her eyeballs are moving really fast and then the room suddenly feels lighter, yes the vitamin C. And, wait, is that Michael Sheehan on our sofa? Michael Sheehan, I love this mix you made for us.

Michael's laughing and I'm petting the sofa and then I have an idea—wait a second, if we go into Polly's room, we can climb out onto the roof to sit outside in the sun so here we go up the stairs and out the window one at a time and yes the light in my eyes oh I love this light this light give me more light. Just then the landlord decides to come outside and at first I'm thinking oh no, this is the end, because who the hell would be out this early on a Sunday and are we really supposed to be out here anyway, but she just looks up and says it's a beautiful day, isn't it? And we're all nodding our heads—beautiful, yes, beautiful, like spring already.

I lean back and close my eyes and suddenly everything is shooting up into my head, voices too fast and eventually I realize Polly's holding my hand and Joey's talking to us, something about how everyone just left and somehow that's the funniest thing I've ever heard, how long has it been, maybe hours or days or weeks or years and I'm freezing, Polly's petting my sweater and Joey's gritting her teeth but kind of smiling too and then I look at Polly and she still has her eyes closed and I guess my eyes were closed too, right, open or closed it really doesn't matter, nothing matters except this feeling in my head and Joey hands me a glass of orange juice, but how did you get that on the roof? Magic, yes, magic, please.

I take a sip of orange juice and boom it's like the sun is suddenly in my eyes and I'm flying backward through the sky over rooftops toward the light and when I open my eyes I say look, a tree. And I don't know what I mean exactly except then I start picturing the three of us falling off the roof, tumbling to the ground and would anyone help us? Like the guys at the auto repair shop across the street—I don't think so. Or maybe the homophobes at the Irish bar on the corner that everyone always jokes about because it doesn't have any windows and what would happen if we went inside?

But then we're climbing back into the house almost like one motion—Polly taps some K onto her dresser and Joey some coke and then they blend it together and I wonder how long this has been going on, what have I been missing, and Joey says you did another hit of X? I nod my head, and she says do you want some CK One and bitch that's brilliant—I start twirling around in the room, but where's the music? Yes, Michael Sheehan left the tape in the boom box downstairs and now we have it for ourselves, we can play it as many times as we want to. Polly starts shaking her body and making cat noises, and is this really our house?

Polly says something about needing to go to work soon. Work? Work. Work! Joey takes a look at her vial, still half-full— okay, she'll drive. But first I need to take a shower—wait, did I already take a shower? Polly, do you need a shower?

I decide it's time to wash out the dye so then the colors are pouring down my face when Joey comes in to do a bump of coke because she doesn't want Billy to ask for any. I lean my head out for a taste and when I get downstairs Polly's standing in the middle of the living room shaking her head back and forth, still making cat sounds and I'm wondering why I did that coke. Polly, do you want some orange juice?

I tap a little bit of the last capsule into the juice and take a sip: magic. Pass it around, I say, and then we smoke pot and get in the car and I love this day. We get to the Back Bay early so we float over the Mass. Ave. Bridge with the water zooming into the sky and then we're going back over again, I'm cheering and Billy's yelling fierce and Polly's eyes are closed and when we drop her off she looks sad: Come visit, okay?

Joey parks the car and yes, there's Jeannine again so I'm blowing kisses and Billy says who's Jeannine?

Jeannine, I say, and I look up, but Billy's still confused so I say the Tower of Jeannine Hancockatiel, she was just waiting for a better name. Look, she's blending right into the sky and there's a little cloud up top, just a soft little cloud you can almost touch it.

You're crazy.

And I love it.

Back up those escalators, I'm so glad to be back, gliding past WATCH OUT and MASS HYSTERIA except now it really is mass hysteria with all these people rushing around, who are all these people?

But look, a garden: I'm touching all the flowers to see which are the softest—roses or daisies or carnations or lilies. And look at that tiny house, would I like to live in a house like that on a bonsai tree, maybe for a little while if there was a nice view. What are those flowers, the ones my grandmother used to have in her window boxes? Geraniums—they don't look special, but oh, their leaves are almost as soft as the lilies, velvet pants, I'm glad I'm wearing velvet pants.

I never realized the yellow part at the center of a white daisy would be so hard, you could hurt someone with these daisies— stop, stop hitting me with those daisies, but what are these puffy pink flowers like mums but more delicate except when you touch them they bounce right back like sponges with a little water that spurts out and do you think those orchids are real, they feel kind of like plastic and what about that prickly purple flower oh I love this game it's so much fun, but why does Billy keep poking me and pulling my arm and laughing until he says Alexa, we have to go. It's not a garden. It's a flower shop.

Oh, a flower shop.

I pick out the biggest pink gerbera daisy, the one with the longest stem, and the woman working there says I like your earrings. Thank you.

See, she likes us. I like her smile. But Billy drags me away, she wants to get something in the food court.

Oh, the food court—I don't know if I'm hungry, am I hungry? Maybe a juice, do they have juice? Where's Joey? Oh, the bathroom—I'll be right back.

I love this bathroom. It's so—white. There's Joey in the mirror, fixing her hair. Well, hello. My eyes yes my eyes look at my eyes.

Wait, who's that? Oh, do you need to use the sink? We love it here.

Joey, I love this mirror. I can't believe I did three hits of ecstasy. Do you think I'll be okay?

Thank you for the juice, Alexa.

Do they have juice?

The orange juice.

Oh, let's get orange juice. Do you want to go outside together? I don't know if I can handle it alone.

Back into the food court and what on earth is Billy eating, something disgusting—where did you go, she asks with big eyes, but she's just worried we did more drugs without her. My head is racing now, there's too much going on in here—can we go across the street to visit Polly?

Back down the escalators and outside it's so bright if my eyes jump out who will catch them? Across the street through the wind and upstairs into the store oh I love this store, why don't we come here more often? I guess because everything by the counter is *Priscilla Priscilla Priscilla,* but I do like her colors, she might not be as bad as I thought.

Lube and travel guides and postcards. A book about *Ab Fab,* are you kidding? Oh—I do want to read this book by Esther Newton about Cherry Grove, but not now, the words won't stay still. Neil Jordan, who's Neil Jordan? Oh, *The Crying Game,* Neil Jordan wrote *The Crying Game,* and this is his new one.

Joey and Billy go in the back to look at porn, but where's Polly—there are customers around, but there's no one behind the counter. Oh, a familiar snorting sound and then Polly jumps up so I hand her the flower and she starts waving it like a magic wand—Alexa, it matches my outfit. It matches my outfit.

Oh, no—is this really Foucault at the front counter, with all that Jiffy Lube and *Gay Europe* and Herb Ritts's coffee table. What's this music? I love this music.

Alexa, it's the Pet Shop Boys. You hate the Pet Shop Boys.

Maybe I was wrong. Can I borrow your makeup?

I head to the bathroom and do some of Polly's K and then everything slows down, even my hair. I sit on the toilet to relax—my eyes are closed, but there's a lot going on anyway, who needs to open their eyes when there's so much going on and then when I start to stand up I can see the floor on the wall, that's kind of nice, but wait, I never realized there were two people dancing on the toilet paper, yes on every square people are dancing, but sometimes it's just legs or torsos or arms, wait let me take some of this down the hall, don't fall, feet into ground, turn around, lost and found.

Polly's ringing up someone's postcards and *Eros Guide* and Elbow Grease. Thank you for shopping at Glad Day, she says. I hand her the vial and Billy whines so Polly taps some on the counter, good move. Not here, Billy says, and Polly ducks down behind the counter. Yours or mine, I say, and Billy looks both ways and then leans over. When she looks at me she's smiling and I notice she just plucked her eyebrows. But why is she wearing that backward baseball cap like some frat boy, a frat boy with bleached eyebrows and eyes so blue not blue like eyes but blue like the blue on the Elmer's glue label. I brought you something, she says, and hands me a magazine.

Thrust. I open it and there's a cowboys and Indians spread. I'm not looking at that.

Billy hands me another: *Stroke.* Sex with a cop—gross, but his dick is kind of hot—wait, not a cop. What about *Safer Sexy*? This looks good. I open it up and it says, "SLIP on a condom SLAP on some lube SLAM in his arse-hole."

Arsehole, Billy says, and starts laughing. Slam his arsehole.

I hand the book to Polly and she puts it in a bag for me—thank you for shopping at Glad Day, ma'am.

Joey's starting to get impatient because she wants to go to Moka so I hand her a square of toilet paper. Look, I say, two people dancing. Look. Polly ducks back down for another bump, and then she jumps up like a monkey in a box—or, wait, not a monkey, what is it that jumps up like that, a rat? A cat? A cat with its tongue hanging out, eyes open wide, and Polly says wait, do you need to use the restroom, be sure to use the restroom before you leave, and she hands me the vial.

I do a half capful because I can feel myself getting edgy again, I really shouldn't have done three hits of X but then we're on Boylston and I can't figure out which way the cars are going. Are you sure this is the right way? Oh, there's Jeannine so we start walking in her direction. Suddenly there's a gust of wind and everything is so bright it's a good thing we're holding hands because otherwise I would fall over. But why am I sweating so much even though Joey says it's freezing and I hate sweating, maybe if I close my eyes, okay, good thing I'm in the middle but who's that yelling, why is that guy yelling, oh, that car horn, why is everyone so loud, can someone turn it down? Then there's the wind again, this street is a wind tunnel and now I'm freezing too but still sweating, do you think we're close, how much farther, is there somewhere else we can go, can't we just sit down here, are you sure this is the right way, oh, Neiman Marcus, that's right, we're close. Wait, are you sure this is it? Joey opens the door and inside everything is buzzing the lights all shaky I walk down the steps so many steps I don't remember these steps could there really be this many steps and then I fall right into a black hole.

When I wake up I'm collapsed on a sofa and Joey is waving

his hands in front of my face and saying Alexa, are you there, Alexa, this is Dawn Davenport, Back Bay station, Dawn Davenport. I'm trying to say something but I can't. When I look at Joey's eyes I see my eyes but upside down and then everything in the room is dark again, but I can hear people. We're leaving, but how do we get out?

Somehow we're in the car and I'm trying not to look outside, too sharp I might break, where are we going, oh, maybe I said something. I close my eyes—all the keys on a piano are flipping up into my head, hitting the place behind my eyes—can someone else drive? I open my eyes: Joey's driving. I close my eyes and drift off somewhere I'm not sure where I just watch the colors until I hear Joey saying something about stopping at the bar on the corner for some Irish hospitality, and everyone's laughing, and when we get home I'm not sure how I'm going to get up the stairs, but eventually I'm in my room and I look at the clock: three p.m.

I don't know how I'm going to sleep so I snort some doxepin, take a Xanax and throw off my clothes and get in bed and for a while everything zooms past and then I'm talking to Polly about whether we'll ever be able to dream again if we weren't dreaming in the first place until I remember she's not here she's at work so I'm talking to Polly's flower a field of flowers and eventually the clouds start slowing down and then someone's knocking.

Alexa, Alexa—we're going to miss Avalon. It's almost midnight.

I look at the clock, somehow can't figure out how 11:30 relates to midnight but it's definitely dark outside and oh, I'm so hungry. I put on my robe, and everything hurts, especially my back—why does ecstasy always make my back hurt so much, I mean I know what they say about depleting your spinal fluid but no one else ever seems to notice. At least I got my eight hours of sleep, maybe I'll be okay.

Polly's sitting in the kitchen smoking a cigarette—she's wearing the same outfit, including the sunglasses.

Did you sleep?

A little bit.

Are you sure you want to go to Avalon?

We have to go to Avalon.

Why?

The photo booth.

Oh, okay. I need to eat something first, and then take a shower.

Just thinking about walking upstairs I start to feel sad in that way that feels like it will never end—at least I had that Xanax last night, but what am I going to do when I run out of the samples from my father's medicine cabinet—don't worry about that now, I probably still have fifty. I open the refrigerator—oh, I'm so glad I got this hummus and tabouli—Polly, do you want some hummus and tabouli?

I put the pita bread on the table, and we dip it in—oh, this is delicious. Polly's smoking in between tiny bites and I eat pretty much the whole container of hummus, which makes sense because I hardly ate anything yesterday—oh, wait, is that really the same glass of orange juice on the table, I mean I don't usually believe in doing drugs in the morning but this isn't really the morning, is it? An apple a day keeps the doctor away, but a quarter glass of ecstasy-laced orange juice—yes, just the right amount to bring that softness back to my head, okay now I'm ready for my shower yes this shower is amazing I can't believe I didn't try this yesterday it's like a massage with water and then I'm downstairs and I throw together the perfect outfit, quilted polyester paisley housecoats one over the other, pink on top, purple on the bottom almost like petticoats, with my combat boots and pink, purple and green plaid tights—Newbury Street is good for something—but what should I do with my hair? Oh, I know, green rollers, perfect, and now Joey and Billy are downstairs too—Joey is trying to get the last bit of coke out of the vial and Billy's eating my pita bread without asking but at the moment I don't care, I'm just so glad I don't feel disastrous, you girls going out tonight and then just like that we're in the car.

Sure, we don't get there until just before closing and by then I already feel like I'm crashing again and what am I doing going out when I feel like I never want to go out again, but Jason waves us in and right when we get inside they're playing that song that goes "Your hair is beautiful ..." And yes, I'm giving slow runway as we make our way through the endless glitz of carpet and the bar that never ends and the fancy lights and the dance floor full of Boston's finest messes and I lean over to the tired bitches looking at me like they've never seen anything like it and I say yes, my hair.

Turn, stop for the camera, turn again—yes, bitch, my, hair. Yes, bitch, my, hair—speeding up with the beats and Joey starts to sing it, pointing at me: Your hair.

Whose hair?

Your hair, bitch.

Polly's got her Long Island iced tea and she's doing that thing where she hums and sways with her eyes closed and the straw in her mouth and Billy's whining and just like that the music stops.

LIKE I'VE NEVER CRIED BEFORE

I'm on the phone with my father, telling him I know I said I was moving to Boston because I needed to live in a bigger city, I know I said it would only be an hour drive to get to class, I know I said I needed that distance in order to stay in school. But I was wrong, because I can't be there right now. I hate it. I'm not learning anything. It's ruining my life.

I can't believe my father's not screaming at me. All he says is that he and my mother won't be able to support me anymore. He doesn't even remind me that I only have a semester left to get off academic probation, and then I can go anywhere I want. He just says what are you going to do now, and I tell him I found a job phone canvassing. He doesn't ask any more questions. He doesn't even ask for the car back—I thought I might have to drive down to DC. And I don't even want to think about DC. But instead he just tells me I should be in therapy, and I don't tell him I was thinking therapy might be useful while I'm getting ready to confront him. I just say I'll think about it.

So now I'm doing time at the exclusive Copley Place. Not in the mall, exactly, but in those upstairs offices facing the magnificent broken-sun sculpture that pours water onto the hallowed granite Neiman Marcus shoppers tread. But don't get all excited thinking I have that gorgeous view because this is classic office realness so of course my lovely cubicle faces another lovely cubicle, and behind that lovely cubicle I can glimpse another lovely cubicle, facing me, my cubicle, and I.

My highly sought-after position consists of making crank calls for the Uncommon Clout Visa card—you know, the card that gives back to the gay and lesbian community. With every purchase. And when I say Uncommon Clout gives back, honey, I do mean gives back.

That's right—every time you use your Uncommon Clout Visa card, we make a donation of ten cents to the nonprofit of your choice. You heard me right—ten cents. Before you know it, you'll be using that card, honey, using that card and saving our gay children ten cents at a time.

Don't worry, you don't even have to call 1-800-GAY-CLOUT, because you've got this bitch on the phone to set you up with the debt bondage you've been waiting for. But there's absolutely no pressure. I'll just sign you up, and then you can cancel when you get your balance up to $24,999. I'm not working for the collectors, honey, all I need is your name, address and social security number. Or if you prefer, you can just give me your abusive father's name, address and social security number, and we'll go with that. We here at Uncommon Clout are nothing if not flexible, and I would like my two-dollar commission.

Speaking of uncommon irony, Ms Marshall called a house meeting tonight—to discuss Polly's drinking. Are you fucking kidding? Yes, it's true that Polly starts every day with vodka over ice, but can you imagine how you'd feel if your tacky ex-boyfriend slept with your roommate so she didn't have to move back to Webster, Mass.? And now Bobby Champagne Sham-poodle steals from everyone—drugs, money, clothing—I

caught her the other day working one of my black T-shirts—
oh no, Miss One, she said, this is Calvin Klein.

Bitch, a Calvin Klein T-shirt costs twelve dollars.

Now everyone's getting locks on their doors—let's have
a house meeting about that. But not tonight—Polly and I
already have plans to go to Bertucci's for vegan pizza and
cocktails—yes, it's a special occasion, because I'm actually
getting paid. And at Bertucci's, Heavy-Handed Wendy pours
a pint full of Absolut and charges you for one drink—talk
about saving money. But what should we get on the pizza?
Broccoli, spinach, mushrooms, onions—artichokes? I don't
know about artichokes. Okay, artichokes.

And yes, here come those magical cocktails—I don't even
like Absolut, but I do like Heavy-Handed Wendy. Oh, these
artichokes—Polly, you're right, artichokes are the answer. Do
you need another cocktail?

The T is so much more fun after help from Heavy-Handed
Wendy—Polly and I are queening it up on the platform and no
one's even bothering us, or if they are then we don't notice. The
other day I was waiting for the train and some guy came up to
me and said: Your ass stinks, you know what I want to do with
your ass? And then he picked up a discarded beer can from the
ground and stomped on it.

Luckily he got on a different train. But then I was painting
my nails on the platform and this group of kids walked by—I
guess they were getting out of school or something and I don't
know what I was doing out of the house so early but these kids
couldn't have been more than twelve or thirteen and the kid

in the back with crooked glasses and a bowl cut kept staring at me. I couldn't help but remember that when I was twelve I had crooked glasses and a bowl cut so I was smiling at him, trying to be friendly, and he came over and looked at me and asked me the usual: Are you gay?

Honey, I said, I'm a faggot. And he scrunched up his face and said ew, that's GROSS. And then can you believe some old woman sitting there looked at me like I was the one creating a scene—it's a good thing she didn't say anything because I would have read her and that would not have been cute.

Then I got on the train and someone sitting in front of me turned around and said: Stop following me, faggot. At least he didn't ask if I was gay. After a few minutes he got up and changed seats so he was right behind me, I guess so he could punch the seat, over and over again, saying faggot faggot faggot FAGGOT faggot faggot faggot FAGGOT—you know how the Green Line shakes anyway and it was kind of a good rhythm for late-night runway but this was the middle of the day and the point was that I didn't want him to think I was scared so I didn't get up. He kept hitting harder and harder and of course no one on the train said anything and I started to worry he was going to stab me or something so finally I turned around and said bitch I know I'm a faggot, but maybe you need to look in the mirror once in a while. And his face got all red like he was going to punch me, but instead he slammed his fist into the metal part of the seat so hard that his hand started bleeding and I got off the train at the next stop just as I heard him yelling about how that faggot's gonna give him AIDS.

Anyway, tonight there are no incidents, which is a rarity, I mean people stare but at least they don't say anything, and when we get home everyone's already in bed, even better. Polly goes to bed too because tomorrow she's visiting her family and the cult in Bel Air, Maryland, so she has to get up early. Speaking of nightmares, it turns out everyone isn't in bed, because then Sham-bam arrives with Joey and they want to go to the Eagle. After a few bumps of coke I'm easily convinced but the Eagle is as boring as ever and then we're back at home and somehow we all decide to stay up and go with Polly to the airport.

Talk about runway—I mean this is the real thing, blue carpet for days. We're showing off all our best moves, and Champagne says we'll get arrested so she drives us all the way back to Savin Hill and then Joey and I jump right back on the T. We're going to ride every line except the Orange Line. I don't like orange—it's just not good for my complexion.

A few days of runway later, Polly gets home and right away she says let's go to Dollar-A-Pound. Sounds good to me, but of course we get there just before closing, so Polly's busy crawling through the clothes on the floor and throwing so much stuff into a bag I can hardly believe it—dresses, a black purse, even a ratty blonde wig.

I get two pounds and Polly gets thirty-five. That's a lot of dresses. As soon as we get home she's throwing together outfits. She even puts on makeup, full face—where'd you learn to do that?

Kevyn Aucoin.

Kevyn Aucoin's got nothing on you.

Joey calls and she wants to get cocktails, but I tell her I'm not drinking for a week, remember? It's Wednesday, she says, we have to go to Sporters. Which is funny as hell because it's not like Sporters is a particularly glamorous destination. Just that there isn't anywhere else to go on a Wednesday and Polly knows the bartender, who gives us free drinks.

Last week after Sporters, Billy wanted to get coke—really, why do you need coke when we have all this K? But of course she started whining so I said okay, I'll drive, which was a bad idea because I'd done way too much K so at every intersection I started pushing on the brakes from so far away that we kept missing the light, and then it turned out that Billy was getting coke at someone's apartment in the projects in Roxbury and while we were waiting Joey started to say that Billy was really getting crack—who cares, what's the difference? It did take a while, though, but at least that meant the K wore off, but then Joey kept saying maybe Billy's dead and I was thinking about how I used to have a rule that I would never drive on drugs. Not even one drink. Eventually Billy came back with some guy who didn't even know her name and when we got home they went right up to Billy's room and of course Billy didn't offer us anything.

Joey said he was scared to stay in our house and I wasn't sure if it was because the guy was black or if it was because we'd picked him up from the projects, but I told Joey she could take her racist shit somewhere else, and I went upstairs to get ready for bed. When I came back downstairs Joey was already snoring on the sofa, I don't know how he falls asleep like that, and the next day when I got up Billy was in the kitchen scratching at the sink drain with a knife and it kind of smelled like something was burning. I looked around, but the stove wasn't on and when I looked back at Billy I noticed his eyes were bulging out like in a cartoon when someone sticks their finger in a light socket but scarier like someone had put fake eyes in place of her real eyes and she wasn't even wearing her colored contacts. Are you okay? I asked, and she didn't say anything.

So Sporters, all right, sure, I'll drive. Adam, the bartender, thinks it's funny that I'm not drinking so he keeps piling up empty glasses around me and for a moment I start to wonder if he's flirting. At one point he actually leans over and whispers something in my ear, but I can't hear him so I just smile and then he has to close the bar—see you next week.

On our way back, Joey starts going on and on about how we have to drive by the block, we have to. If I see anyone I know, she says, I'll make a whole lot of noise. What are you talking about, I say. And then I get really angry and stop the car in the middle of Newbury Street and get out and slam the door and I'm walking so fast but I don't know where the hell I'm going. Then I realize I left Polly in the car and she didn't do anything so I go back. I say sorry, Polly—Joey, where do you want to be dropped off?

We go to Joey's new apartment in some fancy building and sort of end up talking outside. I'm telling her she always puts on such airs, says all these tired shady things, talking about Billy being on welfare—what's wrong with welfare? And then at Avalon she walks around like a star because all the pointless pompous assholes will talk to her.

Joey says: It isn't classism, I grew up rich. That's your problem, I say, you grew up with that attitude and you still haven't gotten over it. She says: That's just how I talk, I don't really mean it. I say I believe you don't mean it, but that's not how it sounds. And it hurts people—I just want you to think about it, okay? Joey says okay, and then I ask him if he wants a hug so we hug goodbye and then Polly and I head home, what a night.

But get this—three days later, Polly and Joey and I are at home and Joey says let's go to the block. This again? But he says he's serious, he needs extra spending money. I say don't your parents pay for everything, and she holds up an empty vial. I figure I'll suspend disbelief so I put on some tragic outfit to disguise my glamour because I might as well work the block too and we all know tricks don't like glamour.

The boy block is weird because it's right by the Park Plaza—kind of a posh area for hustling, right? There's only one other hustler on the block and he does not look happy about our arrival—whatever, honey, we can share. Cars keep stopping by Joey and she talks to them, but no deal, and then some guy pulls over for me, I say a hundred an hour and he says he lives in Arlington, is that okay?

I've never heard of Arlington except Arlington, Virginia, so I say how far is it. Twenty minutes. As long as you pay me by the hour, including travel, and drive me back, a hundred up front. He says he'd like to see me for a few hours, and I say we can do one-fifty for the first two hours, a hundred an hour after that. We drive a few blocks and he pulls over and counts out eight twenties, I like how you can be more demanding on the street because they assume you're tough.

He tells me he chose me because of my bandana, reminds him of the seventies and am I a counterculture type of guy? Funny since that's what I was trying to hide. It's weird how as soon as we get on the highway we could be anywhere and then who knows where we're going once we get off, past all these big old houses and it feels more like some quaint New England town than a suburb.

His house is at the top of a hill, pretty nice in that rundown sort of way with white paint peeling off red brick, and when we get inside it's still pretty dark, even after he turns on the lights because all the bulbs are red—he really must not like light because he has dark curtains covering the windows and I can tell he never opens them because the plants are trying to push their way through.

He asks me if I want a drink—sure, a screwdriver sounds good, but he says how about a greyhound since I only have grapefruit. I didn't know that's what that was called, and he says do you like music? I always think that's the funniest question, I mean is there anyone who doesn't like music and he wants to know what kind. I tell him mostly I listen to dance music—house, techno, ambient—but I also like blues. Oh, blues, he says—I love the blues. And then he puts on Etta James, who I think of more as jazz, but his sound system is amazing and we just sit there for a while and talk about the music. Maybe a half hour of Etta James and then he starts playing Aretha Franklin and Edith Piaf and Serge Gainsbourg, turns out he lived in

France for a while in his twenties, and then he asks what I think of classical music—I don't know so he puts on Brahms and at first it sounds foreboding but then he's talking about each instrument like it's a person and I guess that's true since there's a person behind it, but also I realize something about how all music is really the same.

I start to feel myself sinking into the sofa like I'm high but all I have is this cocktail and Brahms and now there's a fluffy gray cat—the trick says his name is Karl like Karl Marx. After a while he takes my hand and then we sit there like that, listening to the instruments that somehow sound like voices, it all builds and flies and falls and I'm thinking maybe I could go to a classical music concert like on those billboards by Bread & Circus if it wasn't for all the awful people.

I wouldn't mind another cocktail though I guess I could sit here like this for the rest of the night if he wants to pay me, just close my eyes a little and feel the speakers booming from the corners of the room, my breath in my chest but also how his breath moves his hand, our hands, and then eventually the music ends. I can't remember what he said it was exactly, a concerto or a symphony though what's the difference, maybe I'll ask, but then he says do you want to go in the bedroom?

The bedroom light is blue and he wants to take my clothes off for me, then I'm standing there naked and he's petting my skin— so smooth, he says. I ask him if he wants to take his clothes off too, so then he holds up his arms and I pull off his sweater and his body is all bones. I guess I noticed before that his face looked hollow, but I thought maybe that was just because of dark facial hair and pale skin and the way that sometimes makes people look unhealthy but now his dick looks like it's too strong for his body. I get on top of him in bed anyway and he groans, I kiss him on the lips and he kind of gasps, that stale liquor breath so familiar even when it's not familiar. I can feel his hard-on under my chest—I'm starting to get hard too from the pressure of our bodies, even though when I look at his face in this light I can only really think about death.

Lie down next to me, he says, and then he's touching me way too softly and I'm trying not to cringe. I guide his hand to make the touch firmer but he keeps changing it back—it's funny how I could sit in the living room doing nothing for several hours and it could feel totally relaxing but now it's just a few minutes in bed and I want to run out the door, he moves my hand to his dick while he grabs mine, I spit in my hand and he says oh, that's great, just like that, oh, this is so nice, oh, you're such a nice guy, oh.

Wait, he says, I want to see you come first. Which is fine until I actually come and after that I just want to chop him in half. But I'm massaging his back, touching him softly the way he likes it, and then he wants to turn over, puts my hands on his dick and he shoots just like that. Then he says oh, I haven't felt this way in so long.

I look at the clock: 4:30, that means $350.

He asks if I want a towel, sure. I go to the bathroom and when I get back he counts out the money, $240 more, that's $400, thank you, and he asks if he can call me sometime so I give him my pager number and he says sorry, I forgot your name, and I tell him it's Tyler. His name's Michael, I didn't remember that either, what's the point really unless you need to use it again. The drive back feels shorter than before, maybe because the streets are deserted but I'm starting to wonder about Joey and Polly.

Michael says I can tell you're a really smart guy, are you in school. They always want me to be in school, but at the moment I don't feel like pretending so I say too smart for school, and he says I think I know what you mean. When we get to the block he says are you sure I can't drop you somewhere else, it's awfully late, I can take you home, and I say no, I'm going to meet my friends, and he says I hope we can make this a regular thing.

So now I'm back on the block, which is deserted, though when I get to my car there's a note from Joey saying she and Polly are out looking for me at the police station, area D—really, the police station? And then a second note saying now they're at the Loft, make sure to page Joey—there are pay phones directly behind me. Has it really been that long? I page Joey, and then I wait by the phone, and I realize I'm looking right at Jeannine but I've never seen her from this angle, I don't think—is this the main entrance? No one goes in, or out, but somehow you can see the church reflected in the glass—oh, that's not the church at all, it's another building, kind of like the top of the Empire State Building sitting on the ground. Joey doesn't call, and I'm not wearing this tragic outfit to the Loft, so I go home.

The next day's my date, have I ever gone on a date before? It's this boy Bruno from work who I thought was some clueless straight boy because he was always asking me ridiculous questions about my hair and nails and pretty much every piece of clothing I've ever worn, but turns out he's gay because he asked me out on a date. It's funny how someone I didn't really notice before suddenly seems like the hottest boy in the world. We're at Bertucci's, and I'm watching his big pink chapped lips and the way he keeps looking at me, and I'm not even sure what we're talking about, just glad he hasn't asked me whether I have a new job, since I just told him I'm not going back to work because I can't deal with the surveys. I know everyone else likes the surveys better because we get paid $11.50 an hour and there's no quota, but it's pretty obvious that we're working for Philip Morris, and I know credit card companies are awful, but not as awful as Philip Morris.

Good thing these cocktails are so strong and Bruno doesn't even think pizza without cheese is strange. He lives a few blocks away, so we head over to his place, which must be expensive because it's right on Columbus but there's nothing on the walls except a big mirror behind the sofa with a tacky gold frame. Then of course there's a huge TV, a bed with plaid flannel sheets and luckily we're on that right away it's so soft. When he takes off his shirt his chest is so hairy, kind of a surprise and I love it when he wraps his arms around me and squeezes tight and two of my ribs make that cracking sound.

Now Bruno's biting my neck from behind, which feels great, and then there's his dick poking at my asshole and I start to pull away but he pulls me back and I'm kind of frozen while he's thrusting on top of me, I mean he's just teasing my asshole with his dick but I keep thinking it's going to go in. Then he starts talking like we're in a porn video, saying yeah, you want it, yeah you want my cock, don't you.

Finally I pull away and he says sorry, I'll put on a condom, reaches into his nightstand drawer, pulls one out, opens it and slides it onto his dick, lube, pushes me onto my back and then he's on top of me, grunting and panting and he's not even kissing me anymore, just trying to get his dick in my ass like he's possessed until I pull myself out from under him, stand up and say I think I have to go.

Suddenly he looks like a little kid. What's wrong, he says? Did I do something wrong? I don't even know where to start so I say why don't we talk about it later. I find my clothes in a bundle on the floor and I realize I'm kind of shaking. I'm dressed but Bruno's still shirtless and so cute, the exposed brick on the wall behind his face, faded flowers in the hallway carpet, a vague musty smell.

Outside everything seems faster and the T is so close, good thing I'm not too late for the T.

When I get home I call Joanna and say can I tell you something kind of disturbing? Maybe she didn't hear me, because she starts talking about her relationship with Brenda, who's forty-eight, smokes cigars and wears dirty undershirts with suspenders and slacks. She's my daddy, Joanna says, her eyes get all wild when she sees me. She used to be a mechanic but now she lives off SSI—and, you know.

You know, what?

Cocoa Puffs. With an emphasis on the cuckoo.

They do speedballs together and then Brenda ties Joanna up

and leaves the house, sometimes for hours or at least it feels like it until she comes back and beats Joanna until she's screaming. Sometimes Joanna feels like she's about to pass out from all the pain, but Brenda knows what she's doing so she always unties the ropes at the right moment. My daddy knows how to hurt me without hurting me, Joanna says, so then I can cry like I've never cried before.

SOMETHING SPECIAL

As soon as I start turning tricks again I feel like I never stopped. I don't know if that's good or bad, but we're making out and his breath is awful—finally I can't take it anymore so I start sucking his dick and he keeps saying Tyler, I love you, I love you, I love you, Tyler. And then he grabs my head and pulls me right up to his face and says: Say it, Tyler, tell me that you love me.

There's a lot I'll do for tricks—role play, fantasies, whatever—but I'm not going to say I love you. That's just demeaning.

Then there's the guy who feeds me rails of coke but tells me he doesn't have any alcohol because he's in the program. And I can't even enjoy the high because he's pulling at my dick and scratching my asshole, telling me how beautiful it is. Oh it's so beautiful, he keeps saying, and I'm trying not to fart.

Luckily there's a clock right by the bed, so I give him a few extra minutes and then ask if he wants me to stay longer but he acts surprised that I'm charging by the hour. Obviously that's when I should get the fuck out, but I'm already crashing so then we're doing line after line and I'm so wired it's like my head is going to pop and I can't keep myself from laughing when he grabs my dick. And then whenever I decide to leave I start to crash again so more yes please more but more means his dry mouth back on my dick while I'm making faces in the mirror, sticking out my tongue, opening my mouth all big to see how far I can see down my throat—you, yes, you, bitch, you have the prettiest asshole.

After two more hours of this I finally pull myself together and get in the shower, and then after I'm dressed I ask if I can get another line for the road. Sure, he says, as long as I can get some more action. This must be how hookers get violent.

Can I see you again, he asks when he drops me off, and when I finally get home I'm a total mess. Polly's getting dressed for the girl block—are you okay, she says. She's wearing the ratty blonde wig with the black Victoria's Secret slip dress and those wobbly heels, and for a minute I think about how funny it is that now we're both turning tricks and dammit I need a drink but the T's going to close soon and I'm trying not to drive on drugs anymore.

Polly says she was going to take a cab anyway, it'll be her treat—two cocktails at Luxor and I'm feeling much better, yes in spite of those bitches trying to throw shade—honey, you're going to have to keep throwing because we're not catching it. I go over to Jacques with Polly, and some guy comes right over to me and says how do I know what's in your pants?

He won't leave me alone—I'll give you twenty, he says, I'll give you twenty just to see.

A hundred is my starting point, I say, and he says what are you drinking? A Stoli madras—and one for my friend.

Apparently Jacques doesn't serve Stoli—I can't tell if this guy's lying or just cheap, I mean I know he's cheap but I drink the cocktail anyway, and then he says I'll give you twenty just to see, like he hasn't said that twice already. Oh, well—cab fare, I guess. We go in the bathroom, and then I leave.

The next day I'm rushing out of the house to get to Bread

& Circus, drive a few blocks but then realize I forgot my grocery bags so I go back, run up the stairs to my room and there's Champagne with an electric screwdriver, taking the lock off my door.

Oh, she says, I didn't expect you to come back so soon. I'll put this back on the door.

I don't even know what to say, and I need to get broccoli and tofu because there's nothing in the refrigerator so I leave the house anyway, and then when I get home I look around my room to see if anything's gone—I have no idea, really, so I go upstairs and knock on Sham's door, and when she opens I say I'm just going to look around and see if there's anything of mine in here.

Champagne looks at me like she's some damsel in distress but I start rummaging through her drawers anyway, sure enough there's another one of my T-shirts—look at this, I say, this one has my initials on the label, and I hold it up to her face. She actually looks scared—I can't help thinking that she's been so fucked up by her father that all she can do is put on airs and use people and steal for no reason, and I don't know what to do with this sudden blast of empathy so I just say listen, you can keep the T-shirt if you really want it, it's only twelve dollars, but please stop stealing from me, it's ridiculous.

Then Joey calls and she says you'll never guess what happened to Elana Delano. She got bashed. Right in front of her new apartment. There was blood and everything. She's moving back in with her parents. In Woburn.

Woburn—are you serious? Why is she moving?

Alexa, she just got bashed. In front of her apartment. She shouldn't have moved to Roxbury.

What's wrong with Roxbury? I like the part of Roxbury where she lived.

I'm just glad I live in the South End.

Whatever.

Do you want to get cocktails?

I'm depressed.

Maybe you need cocktails.

What's Elana's number?

You can't call her—she's in the hospital.

What—are you kidding?

No, I told you it was serious.

Let's bring her flowers.

We can't visit. She's not out to her parents.

Are you serious? And she's moving back in with them? I need cocktails.

In the morning someone's causing a big scene in the kitchen— when I first moved in I was worried about living with all these meat eaters, but I'm usually the only one who cooks. But today I can smell the bacon grease from my room, and then I hear Shamboom's giggle and it sounds like everyone is in there together. Sure enough she's saying Miss One, it's what a mother does—oh you bitch you bitch you fucking bitch.

Luckily I fall back asleep but when I wake up I go in the kitchen and it's like every pot in the house is lying on the counter, filled with bacon grease. How the fuck am I going to cook? Finally I take all the dirty pots and throw them in a garbage bag and put them outside on the porch, then I write a note that says clean your fucking dishes, and when Polly comes home I say I can't deal with this anymore, we have to move out.

Polly says she wants to make the roommate flyer so she draws the two of us with the Boston skyline, searching for a place in JP or as far from assimilation nation as we can get—honey, you should make comics.

The next trick wants me to fuck him with a dildo and that's definitely easier than staying hard in a condom—it kind of feels like an anatomy lesson watching how much of this huge thing he can take, and then of course he starts with the porn talk, someone should ban that shit though it's pretty funny the way he keeps saying yeah, fuck me with that big black cock, fuck me with that black horse meat, fuck me with that black monster donkey dick—definitely better than subjecting an actual black person to his racist shit.

Two days later and time for the Four Seasons—I grab a crystal from one of the chandeliers—every lady of the evening needs a crystal collection. So then, just down the street at the Copley Plaza, another crystal. After that, I get that rare trick who's actually hot, a student at Northeastern, or no, not Northeastern, some technical school called WIT. Speaking of wit, he says he's straight. He comes too fast—honey, you'll never hear me say that again.

I go to the Fens. It's really windy, but there's something about how the reeds can become a shelter even if there's so much mud and I almost fall right into the water—whoops, wrong way. But then there's this guy pulling me to him from behind and when I turn around he's got that crazed look in his eyes that makes me crazed too but it's too muddy here so I grab his hand and then we're out in the open and suddenly there's only his tongue, cigarettes and beer and something like vomit if vomit can be soothing, and he stumbles back, I almost fall, but really he's walking me hugging over to one of the trees with multiple trunks, kind of out in the open but it doesn't matter all I want is his body on mine our bodies together, grinding up against the tree it's like we're all one thing and when he zips up his pants to flee I sit down on the bench between trees to catch my breath and try to figure out how even the Prudential Tower looks pretty from here.

The next trick is South End realness—there's a picture of Ronald Reagan in her bedroom. Actually that's beyond South End realness. That's just beyond. Usually I try not to get fucked, but I guess this time I can't avoid it. Afterward I'm walking down the street and suddenly it's like I'm going to shit my pants so I rush into some bar—oh, it's Fritz's, the sports bar, which might be the only gay bar in Boston that I haven't been to. While I'm in the bathroom I get a page, and when I get to the pay phone outside it turns out the guy is staying at the Chandler Inn—where is that exactly?

Upstairs from Fritz's—talk about convenience. I go back to the bathroom to finish shitting and then I grab a cocktail, and when I get upstairs this guy looks shocked. I figure it's because I got there so fast but maybe it's something about my hair because that's what he's looking at. He already handed me the money so I'm undressing him and it turns out he's a good kisser—his mouth is so mentholated that it opens up my sinuses. He's actually pretty sexy for some guppy, sucking my dick right away and I'm starting to think I should have a cocktail right before every trick. Or right before everything.

And then about five minutes later there's someone knocking at the door and the guy jumps up and says oh, I forgot to tell you.

Turns out it's his boyfriend, and we have to get dressed really fast and pretend we just met at the bar downstairs. Are you serious?

His boyfriend looks confused. I'm sure I look confused. But then somehow we're all on the bed together and I get to do that thing where I don't know who's touching me I can just close my eyes and lie back, and when we're done they want to take me downstairs for a cocktail—okay, I can't refuse, even if it is a sports bar, and when I head to the bathroom the first guy follows me and tells me I handled that really well, hands me an extra hundred—and honey, I know it sounds like I'm making a lot of money, I mean I guess I am making a lot of money but we all know it won't last.

The other night I did way too much coke to get out of a K-hole in the kitchen and even after smoking a bunch of pot I was lying in bed gritting my teeth and maybe I was actually asleep when the phone started ringing but I didn't realize that at first so I picked it up. It was Melissa and she was in a panic, telling me she couldn't sleep because at night her father was pacing in the hall, she could hear his breath on the other side of the door. And then she kept almost saying what she wanted to say, what

I've been waiting for her to say, and I was trying to wait a little longer except then she switched topics and started telling me that what hurts her the most is that she knows I don't want the same thing from our relationship as she does.

The irony is that right before that I really felt close to her, so close it was like I was there with her in that hallway, waiting for her father, trying to figure out what to do. But then she started going on about how she wants more from me than I'm able to give, and we've already had this conversation I don't know how many times, but now it's even more annoying since we live across the country from one another so what the fuck am I supposed to do? At some point she asked why I wasn't saying much, and the truth is that I was trying to listen. But then I realized how high I still was, lying in bed feeling my body floating and maybe that was why it was hard to pay attention. So I said I know I should have told you this before, but I'm really high. And Melissa got really quiet, so quiet I could hear the humming of the phone. Then she said: Call me sometime when you're not high.

When I got off the phone I felt like a terrible terrible friend, maybe not even a friend just some drugged-out mess and when the hell was I really going to sleep so I started rummaging through my drawer for Xanax even though doxepin helps more but I'm trying not to take that too much so I don't get addicted. So I snorted half a Xanax, swallowed another one and got back in bed—talk about floating on the ceiling and how can I still be this wired, how much coke did I do last night, maybe I should just get up, oh, wait, yes, finally, yes, thank you.

The next trick kind of looks like Santa Claus except his beard is even bigger and I hate beards because they remind me of my father. I guess if I close my eyes the hair is kind of soft, not scratchy like I expected, and it almost feels comforting in his arms, like I'm a little kid. Except that just when I start to relax he says he wants to fuck me—are you kidding? Then he wants to know if Tyler is my real name.

Speaking of real names, one night when Polly and I were over at Sage and Juniper's, and some ad came on TV for Hooked on Phonics, they revealed a very practical secret. It turns out that if you call the Hooked on Phonics 1-800 number, but don't say anything when they answer, and then stay on the phone after the operator hangs up, you get a dial tone and then you can call anywhere you want for free. For some reason it only works at the pay phones on Newbury Street, in front of the garage just down the street from Urban Outfitters. So here I am, in the ice storm, asking Joanna for advice about where to meet queers with politics in Boston, even though she's never been to Boston, and she says what about a punk show? Are you kidding? I don't even think there would be any queers at a punk show in Boston. Besides, I'm done with punk shows—maybe if they just played "God Save the Queen" over and over, and Lady Dionne was there turning and turning with her fan—did I tell you about Lady Dionne? She's the black queen with a big lace fan spelling out the letters of her name, and all the other black queens at Avalon bow down. And the club kids, or at least the ones who know—I mean we know she's the queen of queens. Oh, I love how she turns so slowly with that fan like you all can just die now, yes, die.

The other day I ran into Lady Dionne on Boylston, and she was like girl, what are you doing out? And I was like girl, what are you doing out? And then I walked her to some bar on the rich end of Newbury, and on the way all these assholes kept yelling nice tits, and I didn't really understand what was going on because why the hell was everyone obsessed with Lady Dionne's tits and then some guy came over and said which one's the man, and which one's the woman? And he really looked like he was going to punch one of us, just like that, until Lady Dionne pulled me over and we stared him down. And afterward she said child, you have to admit it, we do make a stunning couple.

Speaking of turning it out, let me tell you about Joey's heels. Yes, heels. She debuted them on our last visit to Avalon, or not the last visit but the one before—black heels, almost stilettos. They don't exactly make her tall, but they do make her taller. Preppy boy working a raincoat, in stilettos—Boston, watch out.

Then there's the trick who just wants to talk about *Ab Fab*— he says this is his favorite episode so I try to pay attention. He keeps rewinding the part where Edina or Patsy or whoever's in the zebra-print coat leans over to some snooty gay couple and says, "Marlena and Judy rolled into one for you, is it?" I can't tell if he's laughing at the gay couple, or at Edina and Patsy. At least he drinks Stoli.

The funny part is when I walk out on the street in everybody's favorite neighborhood—yes, the South End—and I'm trying to figure out who's worse, the gay people who look at me like I'm trash, the straight couples who look at me like I'm going to steal their unborn child or the straight guys who look at me like they want me dead. Of course there's some baseball cap realness tragedy staring at me and I figure it's just the usual straight boy getting ready to beat his meat so I keep walking but then he keeps saying hey, hey, and it turns out he recognizes me from Avalon. Tells me he just smoked coke out of a TV antenna at Evan Aubergine's house, Evan's in love with him so at least he gets free drugs—he's in business school and he has to get through it somehow.

I'm not sure what this guy wants from me until he says can I suck your dick? Just like that—kind of funny and now I notice he's hot in that tragic way, and then we're upstairs in his apartment filled with puffy tan sofas and Orientalist art.

But did I mention that now that Joey and Polly and I have listened to that Michael Sheehan mix about fifty times, we're not sure if it's Traci Lords saying "faggots" or if Miss Sheehan is just mixing that in, and honey, that would be genius. I'm tempted to say that would be cunt, but can you really say cunt without being a misogynist asshole? I remember when I used to think that any guy who used the word bitch was someone to avoid, but then in San Francisco I realized that when a fag called a straight boy a bitch that was one of the most beautiful reads in the world, and I saw the way when one queen said bitch to another it could be a gesture of love, and could it be that way between fags and dykes too—I don't know if I'll ever figure that one out because dykes in Boston won't even talk to me. But anyway one night after Avalon, Elana Delano was giving me props for my outfit and she said Alexa, you are cunt, and that was like the best compliment in the world—I miss Elana.

Oops, watch out for this K-hole on the stairwell, I'm just going to stay here a while, okay? Yes, it's after-hours at our house again and now the X is the big flat tablets that are literally yellow so you rush to the bathroom to vomit, too much heroin, I mean everyone else rushes to the bathroom to vomit but luckily for me it's just diarrhea though some people actually like the vomiting, heroin for sure, so I only take a half and it just makes me feel like I'm caving in until I do a bunch of coke so then I'm annoyed and edgy until finally too much K so here I am on the stairs. Maybe I'll just stay here for the rest of my life as everyone walks by, seems like they're all in a rush tonight and wait, there's Elana Delano.

Elana, I say, but it's not Elana, it's some guy with her eyebrows who looks over with some blank sneer that I recognize from somewhere, where am I again, oh, this carpet, I love the feel of this carpet, where did we get this carpet? Okay, maybe there is some ecstasy in this ecstasy, my head a swirling tunnel until all the colors pull away into cat's cradle. Then diamond shapes like a video game version of backgammon and that's when I realize I can make it do whatever I want—glow-in-the-dark bouncing balls, rainbow spiral splatter paint, a big field filled with fluorescent-orange trees and pink cats with spider eyes and I'm dancing inside the swirly pattern projecting onto the walls I'm pulsating into tiny spaces and then expanding in light onstage until a black background clears everything and then I'm on top of someone's shiny car in a rainstorm no it's a cave filled with shimmering stalactites the beach in all that sun and my arms flailing around like I'm fitting myself into myself until there's Polly biting her nails and saying Alexa. Alexa. Alexa, are you there, we've got something special.

Oh, Polly's touching me and when I open my eyes there's Elana again—no, not Elana, that awful guy with the plucked eyebrows, but where's Polly? Oh, right next to him except her eyes look so far away, is that really Polly, staring at me like I'm in a laboratory, what's going on?

Polly says it again: Let's go to the bathroom. For something special.

Oh, something special, okay, I guess I can get up, as long as the carpet doesn't swallow me, I'll just hold the railing, wait this is fun, no, slower, okay, you go ahead. And then when I finally get to the bathroom I'm making faces in the mirror to make sure that's me while Polly's sitting at the vanity with Elana who's not Elana cutting lines but I don't want any coke and Polly says Alexa, it's not coke—it's crystal.

And when I look at her eyes again I notice that the blue is sparkling but it's a lake that's been poisoned. So I leave the room without saying anything. And when I get downstairs I realize that's the look in everyone's eyes. Polly catches me as I'm going into my room—she says are you okay? I say I left San Francisco because of crystal—don't wake me up until it's over.

I need to sleep so I cut up some Xanax and snort it, take two doxepin, put on Moby's *Ambient* and get in bed for I-don't-know-how-long, it feels like a roller coaster not a futon and when I get up the clock says 6:12 but I can't tell if it's morning or evening and I go to the kitchen for some water. Polly's still awake but the house is quiet and I say don't ever let anyone bring crystal over again, and she nods her head but I'm not sure she understands, so I say listen, I was serious when I said I left San Francisco because of crystal.

And Polly says it's horrible. I don't know if I'll ever sleep again.

And I say it's everywhere in San Francisco, there's nothing else. It doesn't feel good.

It takes over. It takes over fast. I hope crystal isn't hitting Boston. Who was that guy who brought it?

I don't know.

Someone else will have to host the after-hours from now on, okay?

Okay.

I think about how sometimes I feel so lonely talking to the people I love, and sometimes I feel so lonely talking to the people I hate. And sometimes I just feel so lonely.

LET'S TAKE A BREAK FOR THERAPY

Whenever I go to a new therapist the first thing I notice is that it's kind of like being in my father's office. But then I try to let that go so instead I focus on the details: This furniture has a cherry finish, not teak. This analytic couch looks more like a sofa than my father's. The ceilings are higher. Bigger windows. Way more light. The carpet is kind of plush. There isn't any art on the walls.

Of course Barry has a beard and glasses. Do all psychiatrists have beards? Actually Barry isn't a psychiatrist, but he's a PhD psychologist so my parents will still pay. They don't know that he specializes in hypnotherapy.

I tell Barry I'm getting ready to confront my father about sexually abusing me as a kid so I want to go right to the memories that I'm aware of but can't always feel. I want to figure out everything that happened, I want to know exactly when and where and I know maybe that's impossible so if I can't know then at least I want to feel it.

I tell him about my last therapist, Bryce, who always backed away when I started to approach the deeper memories—I would share something small, like taking a shower as a kid, when my father would unlock the bathroom door with scissors and I would freeze, try to cover my dick with a sponge. And then when I got older I would scream get the fuck out—but he would just laugh and say he needed to piss. He and my mother had their own bathroom, and if my mother was using it then there was a third one downstairs.

And Bryce, who also had a beard and glasses, but lighter hair, almost blond, he said: Maybe that was just horseplay. And right then I froze, almost like a kid, didn't know what to say, couldn't speak. When we had our final session I asked him about this, and all the other times when he moved away from the abuse I was trying to talk about, and he told me I was giving him mixed messages.

Barry says he hears what I'm saying, we can check in about everything, this is an active process. He tells me that with hypnotherapy I always have control. That I'm the one who puts myself into a trance, he's just there to guide me and I can always come out of it.

Barry asks me to close my eyes and lean back in the chair that's kind of like the chairs in my father's office but fancier because of the electronic controls. Uglier too, but more comfortable. Barry asks me to imagine a relaxing place. Right away I think about dancing, the music all around me, the darkness and the lights and oh, that was easy, I'm floating to the sky yes the sky it's so calm here. Except then there's my father in a corner, what's my father doing in this club, and Barry says where would you like him to be? So I put my father in a big cylindrical box but he keeps reaching his hand out of the box and there's my mother too, maybe if I make the box bigger? But it's already time to stop.

Outside Barry's office there's an empty park with grass so green I touch it to make sure it's not fake. This part of Cambridge feels like a suburban office park, even though it's right on the water facing the Boston skyline. Not Jeannine and the skyline I'm used to but all the buildings in the financial district. Oh, there's Jeannine, if I look all the way to the right, somehow a greenish blue against the cloudy sky.

The next time I start hypnosis by imagining I'm on the beach in San Francisco, looking out at the ocean and Barry asks me to write numbers on a piece of clear plastic with wet pink chalk and then erase them, counting down from ten—he says when you get to number one you'll feel completely relaxed and at ease.

And it works—it's like I'm floating out over the water into the sky. Except there's my father again, my mother too and all that panic so I need to put my parents in a cage but they keep getting out, how do they always get out? Maybe something taller, an opaque box with neon lights on the outside, a warning.

What about if you watch everything on a movie screen, Barry says, then you'll have control. So I'm watching *Alice in Wonderland* in black and white, rows and rows of empty seats and my father reaching between my legs and Alice just keeps falling and falling until I start screaming and we have to leave early.

My father says he was wrong, he thought I was old enough to go to a movie. And then I'm trapped in a cave, falling and falling past mushrooms and butterflies until I'm stuck at the bottom, but wait, suddenly all the fear drops away. And I feel so relaxed again, floating like I'm on ecstasy, pure MDMA, and I'm watching the lights flickering though now I need to pull myself out of the ditch with a rope except there's my father running up to me when I get to the top and I smack his face with a heavy metal pitchfork but still he keeps coming back.

I'm hanging from a noose, the rope starting to squeeze around my throat and my head expands until it's a balloon while way down below my father is playing with my penis oh how I hate that word, and it's tiny, he's tickling my balls and then he puts it all in his mouth, looking up at me and I want to poke his eyes out but I can't move. And then pop, there goes my head, that's me, my head way up high and I can't find the rest, chest to thighs, it's all gone. Oh, there it is, hanging from the rope like a piece of meat.

Barry says there's a lot coming up so I could use more time, maybe twice a week. Afterward I go outside and it's like a different planet, everything is darker even though it's the middle of the day—it shouldn't be this dark, should it? I still feel my head way up in the sky, here's the center of my body but can I really feel it?

It's drizzling out but I like the way the air suddenly feels so fresh so I sit under a tree at the edge of the park, listening to the rain as it starts to fall harder. Thinking about my father and his hand reaching toward my crotch and I couldn't get away, not even at therapy—when he fell into a trap door his hand came through and he grabbed my balls. I was trying to take that image onto the screen so I could watch from a distance but it never felt distant. Although by the end of the session I was laughing and crying a bit too, and pop, there went my head again, and the paper towel between my actual head and the chair became a sandwich, time for peppermint tea to bring me back.

I'm sitting under this tree and these guys skate by and suddenly all I can think about is how I need a boyfriend. And what does that mean anyway? Whether everything would be different with someone to hold.

At my next session Barry asks all these questions about my hair and clothes so we end up getting distracted and I'm telling him how I need to have everything in place when I leave the house, every strand of hair, how that's the only way I can exist in the world with everyone harassing me all the time. And Barry asks why I think people are harassing me, which is obvious, right?

On my birthday, all I want is a cool breeze at the ocean like I'm always imagining at therapy, but I can't motivate myself to get out of the house until three p.m. so then I figure I'll just get on the highway and see if I can find the ocean, it can't be that far. I'm thinking about when I went to Bethany as a kid, stumbling around on the beach with the other teenagers when I first started drinking. And then pitcher after pitcher of margaritas with Erik and Kayti at Las Rocas in high school, and we'd always end up asking why do we drink, it just makes us sad? Or La Rondalla with Joanna in San Francisco, where we wouldn't get sad, at least not until the next day. And then I think about Colin because I brought my camera, it's in the same case where Colin's ashes spilled when I drove cross-country. His ashes spilled all over the lenses, and I haven't used the camera since.

Maybe I could do a performance with Colin's ashes—come onstage with the camera, snap photos, tell the audience these are the first pictures I've taken since I drove cross-country. *Flamingo Pink*, that's what I would call it, the color of his hair. My hair too, and I didn't even know him that well. We were friends, but he was much older and there wasn't enough time to get past that.

People passed around his ashes at the memorial, and I took a cupful, thought I'd throw them at businessmen downtown and yell WE DIE, YOU DO NOTHING. Colin died with pink hair, and maybe that was partially because of me. He told me I was brave for dyeing my hair.

I knew Colin was dying when we met—of course, that was true of a lot of fags in ACT UP, and everywhere in San Francisco, really, you went to a club one week and the next week the DJ was dead. I'm sure just as many people are dying in Boston, but it's like no one cares. If I threw Colin's ashes onto an audience here, I wonder if they would believe the ashes were real. Maybe people would discover chunks of bone—what would that make them feel? The ones who are familiar with the deaths of their friends. The ones who aren't.

So I'm driving along and I don't even know where I'm going—I took a turnoff that said Cape Cod but now I'm stuck in bumper-to-bumper traffic. I'm worried I'm not going to get anywhere so I turn around and then I'm back in Dorchester and I don't know what to do. Oh—there's the giant gas tank on the polluted bay, but at least it's water. I park and start walking down a path, but it's too muddy so I walk right by the water and I notice the sand isn't just sand, it's little pieces of bricks and cement and asphalt and old rusty cans and empty bags of Lay's and Cheetos and is that a condom? I jump up on the boulders to walk to the end and somehow it's pretty right now with all the air blowing, the little tiny waves in the water and no one around. There's the highway right there but also kind of not right there and I take off my shirt to feel the sun on my skin even though it's still chilly out and that makes me dance from boulder to boulder and when I stop I notice all these geese up ahead, walking away through the mud and leaving big tracks.

But then it's the next day and I'm worse than I've been in a while, thinking what am I doing with my life what the fuck am I doing I mean why am I living with these horrible people in this apathetic town and can you believe no one has called from the gorgeous roommate flyer Polly made, I mean we put it up all over town. How are we going to find a new place?

Then I realize I have a cold. So I find an acupuncturist in the yellow pages and he uses electricity to zap away my cold while I use hypnosis techniques to float. Then I'm sitting outside at Downtown Crossing and I still have a bad headache, and my teeth hurt too, but I must have more energy because I'm thinking about checking out the bathrooms at Jordan Marsh while I'm waiting for Polly to page me. I'm sitting on a bench with all these old people in baseball caps and sun hats, top-forty soul pumped in from somewhere, and some guy says they always do it that way, why do they have to do it that way, and I'm guessing when he says they he means black people but he doesn't say anything more so I ignore him. And I think this might be the first real spring day, one minute warm but not too warm, and then suddenly chilly but not too chilly.

Then there's Avalon without drugs, and for the first time I'm relieved when the music ends so I can finally go home and get some rest. Then the next day I feel a little better, but for some reason Joey insists that we go to Moka. I can't believe I have to sit in this het-owned, het-run, het-overrun chi-chi gay café with all these South Beach tanning salon casualties carrying Neiman Marcus makeup bags, hetero-wannabe couples spouting a bunch of top/bottom bullshit when they're not comparing couture and throwing shade shade shade. How many times do I have to hear someone say: I saw her on the block. On the block. On the block.

Bitch, what were you doing on the block?

In therapy I'm trying to explain the crash from ecstasy, how all the joy in the world fades away and then there's only sadness and pain. That joy—it isn't possible without the drugs, it's just not a sensation your body can make. You can take more pills to fall asleep, but still there's the next day, you have to deal with the next day.

Hypnosis is kind of like drugs except I don't crash so hard. But every time I leave I think about smoking again. The only addiction I've totally quit is coffee, and that was back in San Francisco. For the first few weeks, whenever I craved coffee I would do a bump of coke, and that really helped.

Barry says he thinks it would be easier without the drugs, and I just feel so angry because he doesn't understand that drugs are the best thing for me in Boston. And yes that's a trap but maybe there's something liberating about it too. I kind of want to walk out right now and never come back, but then Barry says we only have a little time for hypnosis, so I lie back on the chair and suddenly I'm thinking about Jonathan from childhood, lying on his *Star Wars* sheets, kissing and hugging, touching each other, running through the field in his backyard, looking for golf balls.

BRIGHTER DAYS

Maverick Square is kind of cute in an old-town sort of way, even though there's a Store 24 that closes at midnight, which should be illegal. Polly and I do our laundry in the square, which is kind of a hassle but then we get to walk around and look at all the cop cars, why are there always so many cop cars? I start taking photos and after I get them developed I go to Kinko's and print out GET A BRICK, white on black with my mesmerizing Quark-XPress skills, cut and paste and then I'm ready for a wheatpasting adventure but Joey and Polly are scared. Finally I get them to look out while I tape the posters to the cop cars, and that's kind of fun. Not as fun as wheatpasting, but still.

I'm trying to get rid of my acne so I figure I need to sit out in the sun a little bit every day so I put fresh lemon juice on my face even though it burns like hell and then I walk down to the new park by the water. There's never anyone there, maybe because of the rotting fish smell, but that's starting to go away so I lie in the little strip of chemical grass for a few minutes. I guess there's going to be a water taxi, which sounds kind of strange because who would take a water taxi to East Boston?

Anyway, when I get home I put fresh cucumber on my face and that helps for a moment. I'm making oats again, and Polly's smoking—the usual. I'm looking at the train map to figure out where we should go once we save enough money to take our trip cross-country and figure out where to move. My mother's on the phone asking Polly about the weather but I know she just wants to tell me I shouldn't be hustling. I'm not interested in having that conversation again.

Now Polly and I have a three-bedroom all to ourselves, that's the important thing—hopefully we'll never see Sham-poodle or Her Highness Marshall ever again. Now we have a whole extra room for my desk and books and boxes, and Polly's make-up table. Unfortunately there's office carpet in the bedrooms but there's lovely black-and-white checkered linoleum in the kitchen and dining room, and even an empty living room up front with hardwood floors.

Our prized possession is the dining room table—one of those big round metal porch tables courtesy of Au Bon Pain—their salads aren't that great, but I've always liked those tables. Sure, it was a bit tricky to get it in the car, especially driving through the tunnel at three a.m. with the trunk open, but honey it was worth it. So worth it that we went back and grabbed two chairs—figured we better do it right away, because now my car is making some scraping sound on the asphalt so I don't think it's going to last much longer.

There's only one cab company, and they take forever. We're not that far from the Blue Line, and then it's only a few minutes to glorious Government Center and all those screeching Green Line trains, but then the T closes and the tunnel does make it seem like we're in another world. We're right by the airport, but that's not really going to help us get to Avalon, is it?

Every time we go anywhere in East Boston, everyone stares. I mean everyone. At the laundromat it's mostly the kids who talk and point and laugh, until finally one of them comes up to us and says: Are you from Boston?

These kids all have East Boston accents, almost like Southie but maybe a little more nasal. I'm starting to like these neighborhood accents, even if they often come with awful people. And sure, I could point out to these clueless kids that hello, East Boston is really just a neighborhood in Boston—it's not like it's its own town or anything. But instead I just nod my head—sure, we're from Boston.

This kid looks impressed. Meanwhile, Polly and I are using the hot cycle on the washing machines to make sure we don't have crabs again, and while we're waiting we go outside where it's not quite so sweltering and pretend everyone isn't watching. Eventually we head home and while we're walking over the bridge to nowhere someone starts yelling hey, hey, but we're not going to fall for that one. Then a bottle flies right over our heads, bounces off a wall and smashes on the sidewalk a few feet in front of us.

Maybe if we pretend this isn't happening, it isn't happening. Some woman opens her door and I don't know what I'm looking for, but she closes the door anyway. Then some guy with greasy hair comes out of his house up ahead, rubbing his face like he can't believe what he's seeing, and then he starts screaming at us, something about his neighborhood and what the fuck.

Actually it's our neighborhood too, I say, and he says what, what did you just say? What?

I say we live here, honey.

And he spits on the ground, then rushes back inside and you

can hear him going up the stairs in heavy shoes. We keep walking, and just after we pass his house there's a loud noise behind us like maybe he dropped a brick out his window, or not a brick, something bigger, maybe a cinderblock. It kind of makes me jump but I'm still trying to act like I don't notice, though Polly's already turned. Alexa, she says, do you think he was trying to hit us? I'm looking at her and she's biting her lip and we're both holding onto the laundry cart and pushing from different sides because otherwise it starts to collapse.

This is ridiculous, I say, but then I notice Polly's about to cry so I reach over to touch her hand even though I know maybe that's not the safest thing. But it's not like anyone hasn't spotted us spoiling their Italian-American homeland—they're already angry about the Latinos on the other side of the square but we're right next to them. So we push the laundry cart the rest of the way just like that, with my clammy hand on top of Polly's sweaty hand, frosted blue fingernails on top of fuck-me fuchsia. At one point Polly starts to shake like she's really going to cry, so I stop pushing and look over. Her face is all pink, glassy eyes and just a hint of dark eyeliner contrasting her reddish-blonde curls and freckles, and I notice the light is really beautiful right now.

I need a cocktail, Polly says when we get inside and I say there's Stoli in the freezer. Usually I don't drink at home because it's boring, but I guess if there's a time for cocktails it's now. I pour two screwdrivers and Polly snorts a line in her room. Do you want any coke, she says, her voice already different.

No, I say, I have to take the car to the repair shop. Or maybe it's too late. Are you okay?

I'm okay now, she says, and suddenly I feel so sad that I don't know how to speak. Polly comes into the dining room and wiggles her tongue, shakes her hips, and puts the mirror on the table with way too much white powder. I snort a line, and oh, yes, let it begin.

I put on "Brighter Days." Usually I don't like the vocal diva drama, but this song is different, it's Cajmere—yes, honey, those clanking beats rotating into the vocal shaking with the booming bass and they call this the new Chicago sound because it's got that vocal but also it's hard—Polly, if this is what they're playing in Chicago, maybe we should move there.

I sit down with the cocktails, and Polly lights a cigarette and looks at me in that way that means we're here in this mood together, and I say what are we going to do on your birthday?

The same thing we do every day.

Should we go to P-town?

Alexa, we are not going to make it to P-town.

What about Revere Beach?

Revere Beach—that's on the Blue Line, we can make it to Revere. For sunset.

Oh, that's perfect—almost feels like my birthday.

You didn't tell me about your birthday.

I'll tell you next time.

Alexa, you have a page.

Should I call it?

That's up to you.

The way this song takes a cheesy narrative about feeling so blue, that's what the vocal keeps saying, feeling so blue, and then bringing it into something so blue it's bluer than blue, but what does that make it? This cocktail, this conversation right now, our relationship, I mean we're not talking about anything, but somehow we're talking about everything. I don't want to turn a trick right now.

But, sure, I could use the money. He answers on one ring, says I have a sexy voice, wants to know if I do in-calls, tells me he lives right around the corner in Chelsea, he'll be here in fifteen minutes.

I get off the phone and Polly's already doing another line. She hardly even shakes with the burn anymore, just looks at me when she's done and it's her eyes that are on fire, she wants to know if I think my trick will really show up.

I don't know—he said fifteen minutes, is Chelsea that close?

You're the one who's good at geography. Do you want another line?

Oh, yes—feel it, feel it, that's what the music is telling me now—hold that note and shake it, break it, make it into everything I need. Polly, I hope this doesn't ruin my mood. He did tell me I have a nice voice.

You do have a nice voice. Tyler.

Girl, don't call me Tyler.

I guess I better hide and do my makeup.

Maybe I should change my pants. Oh, wait—this is the version of "Brighter Days" that I really like, let's dance. Wait, was that a knock? Polly, was that a knock already?

I rush to the living room, look outside, and sure enough some guy in a brown jacket who actually looks like he's under forty. I open the door. Tyler, he says, and holds out his hand like we just met in the boardroom or at the golf course or—no, where do guys like this meet? The game, right, the game—we met at the game, score! He squeezes my hand way too tightly.

He looks around, but there's nothing to look at in the living room so he asks if I live alone, says he likes this music, what do you call it, do you ever go to Chaps? How come? I bet you'd be a big hit there.

When we get to my room he grabs the back of my head and pushes his tongue all the way back. He tastes like cherry, no not cherry—raspberry?

He lets go and starts to pull off my shirt. He's wearing a lot of layers—one of those brown work jackets, a blue button-down work shirt, wifebeater, Dickies, work boots—actually he's kind of dressed like some of the fags in San Francisco, or maybe he's one of the guys some of the fags in San Francisco are dressed like. Hairy chest, slight tan line right around the wifebeater and his dick is already hard, he pushes me onto the bed. I'm worried I'm not going to get hard because of the coke, but as soon as he starts grinding against me I realize that won't be a problem. Heavy, he says, squeezing my dick.

Heavy? When I look him in the eyes again there's nothing but desire and I wonder if he sees that too. Holding my head while I'm sucking his dick like he wants to make sure I don't go anywhere, and I'm wondering why it can't always be like this— sex, sex work, my life, the music, Boston, the bed, my skin, the air, sweat on his legs, leg hairs, a map, this map, my breathing, hope, close your eyes, eyelashes, pulse, the light, a game, my heartbeat, intimacy—and how can someone's dick in my mouth feel like a hug, but also there's the feeling right in my head, everywhere and nowhere, the weather, what, I even like the weather right now with this guy pumping my face yes the feeling of his hands squeezing my head until I'm starting to choke and right then he pulls my face up to his, so much spit between us and I can feel the places where his lips are chapped.

Now he's rubbing my thighs, yes, exactly like that, how is it that sometimes they know right away, and sometimes they never figure it out, no matter how many times you tell them? And then he's behind me, holding my dick, precome on his finger and he sticks it in my mouth, kind of sweet I mean the taste but maybe he's sweet too. I want to treat you good, he says—don't worry, I'll go slow. Which is what they all say. But I reach over for a condom anyway—it hurts way too much at first and just when I'm about to say let's try something else he collapses on top of me and then somehow it doesn't hurt anymore, the smell of his sweat mixed with Drakkar Noir I remember that smell from high school, somehow I thought the deodorant was sophisticated, that sleek black case.

Hold me, I say, and he does, now just moving his dick slowly and he's saying yeah, yeah, and pretty soon I'm saying yeah, yeah, and he pulls my head around we're pressing tongues like we're both trying to get to the other side a game I like and usually I can't get fucked for nearly this long. Now it's the song I always fast-forward, the one where suddenly it's some straight guy saying whoop that pussy, whoop that pussy, which is kind of funny, now that I think about it, considering the situation, but I hope this guy doesn't notice, no he doesn't notice, probably wouldn't matter if he did notice, he might be straight anyway, don't think about that, there he goes again saying yeah, yeah, yeah, hands on my hips and I move them to my inner thighs, he's jerking my dick but I'm going to come so I pull his hands away, he says what? And then he makes this noise that I can't place, air going into the back of his throat and then coming out right into my ear and he's panting, maybe he just came because he's jerking me really fast and I don't even feel myself coming until I open my eyes and look down at the puddle of white and yellow on the burgundy sheets and just like that he pulls out, just in time for it not to hurt, and when I lie down on my back he's looking at the condom in his hands like it's a mysterious fallen creature smelling faintly or maybe not that faintly of shit so I take it and drop it on the floor. He's already pulling up his pants, counting out twenties. He hands me $220, a seventy-dollar tip, says can I see you again? I'll let myself out.

Okay, I say, even though I'm a little worried he's going to run into Polly, but I lie back and close my eyes anyway, then open my eyes and look at all the dots on the ceiling, the indentations, the different textures of plaster, maybe water damage, mildew covered up, a few brown and green and black specks. I close my eyes again and feel my mouth fall open, still so much saliva, the smell of his sweat, my eyelashes flickering really fast and then I put on my robe and go in the bathroom to wash up.

Now there's the other song I hate on this album, the sample of a man's voice saying, "I ain't fucked all week. I ain't fucked all week. I ain't fucked all week." I guess Cajmere's trying to prove she's a real man or something—you know, with all those faggots making house music about brighter days, he really has to make sure to distinguish himself, right? But still that rattling clap-trap in front of and behind the vocals until the beats take over, except here comes another clever chorus and Polly says it first: I'm a horny motherfucker. And the album says it. And Polly says it. She's talking about me, but I don't even like sex most of the time.

Polly says how was it? It was hot, I say, and Polly laughs and says aren't they all? No, I'm serious—do you want to go to Bertucci's?

I don't have any money. I'm getting ready for the block.

It's on me. He gave me a seventy-dollar tip.

No wonder you thought he was hot.

Then we'll go to Luxor. Call Joey to see if she can get K. I'll take a shower.

How much do you want?

I don't know. Maybe forty. Consider it an early birthday gift.

When I get out of the shower, Polly's staring at a little mound of coke on her mirror. She says Joey can get us a gram of K for fifty.

Perfect. Tell her I'll give her a quarter then.

She already requested that. As a service fee.

Of course she did.

This is all the coke left in the world—do you want half?

Sure.

I notice Polly's using my razor blade, the big one with a fluorescent-pink handle I got in San Francisco to scrape paint off a window—I'm good at saving things, there's always another purpose.

But here's what's pathetic: I'm already starting to wonder whether that guy's going to call again. Even though I know he's not going to. Really I just need to have hot sex with someone I actually care about, but then Polly passes me the dollar bill and I do a line and yes, it's a great day at the office. Coke and carrot juice and cocktails, let's dance to the sound of sirens filtered through the elevator oh I love these beats, and it's starting to get dark out. "U Got Me Up" comes on, and right when the vocal moves into the shakedown we're both out on the checkered linoleum dance floor, drinks in hand and Polly wants to know if she should call a cab. We're dancing close until we're leaning on one another, falling into a kind of balance.

HOW TO LIVE

Melissa says ACT UP meetings keep shrinking, and everyone's getting more desperate. There are these two guys who moved from Orlando and they're totally irrational, they don't want to prepare for anything—they're scaring everyone away. Half the things they want to do don't make any sense—everyone gets irrational when they're dying but it's not like Colin, she says, remember how Colin would say crazy things, but they actually made sense.

And I tell her I still have some of Colin's ashes. What are you going to do with them, she says, and I tell her my idea about throwing them on businessmen downtown, and she says: If I was here longer, we could do that together.

I can't believe Melissa's actually here, I mean we went so long without talking that I thought I was never going to hear from her again. But it turned out she was just busy with activism, in jail a few times and dealing with all the legal stuff—now she's in Boston on the way to her brother's graduation in upstate New York. While she's telling me about activism there's a part of me that wishes I were in San Francisco, and a part of me that just feels so distant, I mean it feels like a whole other world.

I tell Melissa I read somewhere that forty percent of gay men will be positive by the time they're thirty-five, but here no one talks about AIDS except to tell you who to stay away from, and Melissa asks me what I think about the theory that HIV started with the hepatitis vaccine. And that's when I get that panicking feeling like I'm about to have an incest flashback, and didn't this happen before?

Then I realize it's 3:45 a.m. so we're getting ready for bed but actually I'm still scared. I'm trying to figure out how to tell Melissa that I don't want her to sleep with me, that in San Francisco it always made me so tense, that I wanted to share space in an intimate way but her body in my bed made me freeze. It was something about how she smelled like my mother, but I didn't make that connection at first. I'm still worried that if I say something it'll sound misogynist.

Finally I manage to say it's not about you it's about me, it's about my memories, how they're stored in my body and I don't know what to do exactly but would you mind staying in the other room?

And Melissa looks sad, but only for a moment and then she's angry in that way that makes her mouth and eyes move around like they're trying to get off her face. But she's not angry at me, she's angry at my parents and what they've done. She holds out her hands in a shy gesture and then we hug for a while and when we're done I say what about your parents, how are you doing with that? And she says I think I'm getting somewhere, I joined a group. And then we set up the guest room, and I leave a note for Polly since it's after four but I guess she's still on the block.

The next day, Melissa wants to cook a big meal and invite people over, but who should we invite? I call Joey, even though she doesn't eat. Do I have any other friends? Melissa and I go to Bread & Circus to get groceries, and then we're sitting down for a snack from the salad bar and Melissa says you know, you seem calmer here.

Really, I ask. And Melissa says really. And I say I don't feel calmer.

But then I'm thinking about it on the T, and I realize there are things I do here that I would never have done in San Francisco, like go to the park and sit by myself and look at the water. Or just spend time alone or with Polly in the house. Maybe I'm not so manic. Maybe sometimes my head feels clearer.

We get back to the house and Melissa says it's nice to see you here, I can tell you're learning. I ask her what she thinks I'm learning. And she says: How to live.

The next day Melissa's getting ready to leave and she stops and looks at me and says I don't know what I'm going to do when I see my father. And I say what do you mean, don't you see him every day? And she says that's what I mean. We hug for a really long time, and after she leaves I'm sitting in the apartment wondering if I'll ever have friends like that in Boston.

I go with Polly to get cigarettes, and even before we turn the corner I hear one of the neighborhood kids yelling: It's the gays. And then there's a whole group of these kids following us, carrying sticks like they were waiting until we left the house and maybe we're supposed to be scared but these kids are tiny, I mean the ringleader can't be much older than ten. Of course she's a tomboy with ratty hair, food on her lips and dirt all over her hands, and I want to say look in the mirror, honey, but instead I just smile and wave. So then she comes right up to us with her greasy face and says yuck, gays, you're going to burn in hell.

We go in the store, and when we come out the kids are still

there. They follow us all the way to the bridge, and I make sure to smile the whole time like this is such great entertainment but lately it seems like Polly can't bring herself to leave the house without a bump of coke and I hope these kids aren't the reason.

Joanna's back at her mother's house in Issaquah, trying to kick again. I go over to Bread & Circus and borrow the largest container of Rainbow Light multivitamins, a bunch of Emergen-C packets, B complex, digestive enzymes and a few other things that look like they might be helpful. And then a thirty-six-ounce container of Bragg Liquid Aminos, since Joanna loves those amino acids. And then when I'm walking out the door after spending thirty-five dollars, but I have at least $150 of supplements in my bag, I get that rush like yes, I love it here, and I go right over to the post office across the street and mail everything to Issaquah.

Then Polly and I are getting ready for Quest, or not getting ready really, just waiting until it's late enough, and then I get a trick, which turns into another trick, which turns into $350 and I'm worn the fuck out but I make it to Quest to meet Polly anyway, which is fine until we're getting ready to go and I look in my purse and there's nothing there. I mean there's my face powder, my keys and nothing else. I'm so angry I'm shaking—outside I'm yelling I sold my ass for that money, I sold my ass—and everyone's trying to pretend they don't notice. These bitches think they can talk about you like you're trash and then steal your money when you're not looking. When we get home I'm still angry so I decide to make a flyer and hand it out next week—Polly thinks I'm joking, but honey, I'm going to make a flyer, and then we'll hand it out next week, okay?

Then there's a special night at Avalon—Polly and I are dressed as pregnant twins. Of course everyone wants to punch our babies, I mean literally three different guys we don't even know, winding their arms around like we're walking punching bags. Modeling fatherly behavior, I guess.

Good news, though—Polly and I get our HIV tests back, and we're both negative. Back at home, it's time for more laundry—yes, crabs, but this time we have prescription-strength poison, and honey that shit burns. Then we're sitting out in the square with the Latino families because the laundromat is sweltering, and one of the fathers looks over at me and says you have beautiful hair, which is kind of shocking to hear in East Boston and it makes me smile like we're making a pact against everyone in the neighborhood who hates us both.

After laundry and a few bumps to get back out of the house, we make it to Luxor before closing and then I decide it's time for the Fens, I mean it's always time for the Fens as far as I'm concerned but sometimes it takes a little while to convince Polly. But then just when we arrive of course I get a page. When I get to his place, he acts like he didn't realize he had to pay me—he's kind of hot, but the problem is that he knows it—somehow he bargains me down to fifty. Afterward he says my wife is away, so don't tell anyone, but do you want some blow? I love it when straight guys say blow. So then I'm back at the Fens, flying off my ass, trying to smoke pot on the bench but it's too windy, and I get a page from Polly, who says Joey's in jail, he got arrested on the block, will you bail him out?

So I walk all the way over to Berkeley and Tremont, figuring after my walk maybe I won't seem so high, and I hide my pot in a planter outside the jail. It's such a beautiful old building from outside, but inside it's the usual scary hellhole, and I try to act really casual like I'm not coked out of my mind, I mean do you think they can lock you up for that? Anyway, I ask the cop on duty about Joey, and he says no one here by that name, and when I ask again it turns out Joey's been released. I go to White Hen to call Joey to make sure, and when he answers he says what?

Like I didn't just go to the jail to bail her out. And I say I'm just calling to make sure you're okay. She says I'm fine, it wasn't a big deal, they made a mistake, and when I get off the phone I'm definitely ready to smoke some pot, but then I remember I left it in that planter and when I go back I can't find it anywhere.

A few days later I'm back at Michael's house in Arlington, listening to Wagner—I can't believe I agreed to do an overnight, I mean he always wants me to stay but I usually get out of it by telling him I need contact lens solution. Except this time he asked ahead of time, so now he's telling me about his boyfriend George of seven years and how they used to lie in bed listening to this same Wagner opera—they knew they were doomed, but he didn't think George was going to leave so soon, to leave, to leave just like that, and I'm wondering if

Michael is going to start crying. But instead he says: You're only here because I'm paying you.

And I don't know what to say, because actually he's a pretty nice guy, but then he says I'm sorry, that's not fair—I like you because you're not pretending. The last guy I met on the block, he kept telling me he was straight, most of them are like that—he had a serious crack problem, he would show up at all hours asking for money and I could understand, I used to be like that but now it's just alcohol, do you want another cocktail? I tried to stop drinking, but then I couldn't have sex. Now I spend all my time on the internet, do you know much about the internet?

Not really, I say, and he goes in the kitchen to get my cocktail. He says you know I work at MIT, right? I was one of the first people on GayBoston and gaysex and that's where I befriend all these guys who don't know what I really look like, I can be young and hung and on top of the world. But then I get offline, and listen to Wagner.

He comes back with my cocktail: Want to go in the bedroom?

When he starts to touch me, I can feel myself shutting off right away, pulling back, watching the coffee maker on his nightstand, why is there a coffee maker on the nightstand?

But then it's over, and I think okay, that wasn't so bad. But of course I can't sleep, and then I'm delirious at eight a.m. when Michael drops me off at the boy block, I mean he offers to drive me home but I figure this is part of our ritual. Except usually it's not some horrible time in the morning when everyone's rushing to work or wherever and then I'm totally emotional and dehydrated on the T, it's like if anyone says anything to me I'll just break. Then somehow I start thinking maybe I'll call Michael and ask him if he wants to get dinner, tell him I'm an incest survivor, see if he wants to hire me to hang out without sex.

I get in bed as soon as I get home, and when I wake up I don't feel as bad as I thought I would. I unpack all my books, and I go back to that piece by Severo Sarduy where he says, "AIDS is a stalking." And there's that feeling of everything going to my head, the way the silence makes the violence and I know I'm getting ready to confront my father—that's what I'm trying to focus on, that's what I need to do in order to heal, but am I just distracting myself from the violence around me?

Polly and I go to the new Todd Haynes movie, *Safe,* at the Coolidge Corner. It kind of surprises me because I was expecting the shaky camera edginess of *Poison* but instead it opens with a slow drive through gated suburbs and then a het fucking scene—he's thrusting and you see her face, no emotion while her hands move as if to calm him. Big almost-still shots of their empty Southern California suburban lifestyle. Everything moves so slowly you want to gag, and that's what happens to Carol, she gets sick from all the poison around her.

Polly leaves in the middle of the movie—she's bored, she'll meet me at home. She leaves just before Carol passes out at a dry cleaner's because of the chemicals, blood pouring out of her nose. Carol ends up at a retreat center in Albuquerque and it's hard to say which is worse, her life of wealthy nothingness or the vacant positive thinking she searches out. There are so many eerie asides, like a woman who says she made herself sick because she didn't forgive her abuser and I hiss loudly at that, want to leave the theater but I realize that means the movie is working. And then the guru with AIDS who's supposedly living healthfully from positive thinking alone, he sees lesions in a dream and they turn into pansies. In the movie it's the positive thinking that works—Carol says I love you to herself in the mirror as the movie closes.

The most disturbing thing is that there's no allowance for rage as a healing option. Maybe that's what makes it feel so suffocating. Afterward I'm a wreck and I wish Polly were here so we could talk about the movie but I guess to her it was just boring. I'm on the way home and this boy stops me just as I'm getting on the train at Government Center, he looks me right in the eyes and says: You look beautiful.

Thanks, I say, and he says no no sit down. So I sit down with him, and he says: I'm always afraid to dress up on the T, I saw you and I thought I had to say something—I was out with my friend George last night, we were going to Chaps for his drag show, you'd like my friend José, he does crazy stuff.

We get to his stop, and he says sorry, I've got to go. Then he turns around as he's leaving and says: You look fierce. Like he's trying it out for the first time. And I wish I could just stay in this moment, I really do.

Melissa calls to say she's finally moving out, she's moving in with Teresa on Church Street but she still feels scared. Of her father. She says: I keep wanting it to happen again, my whole body wants it—I don't want this body.

In therapy, I'm talking about how I've always been afraid to relax, but maybe that's starting to change, and Barry says why do you think you've been afraid? And right then I get that scared feeling, I can't say anything. I look down at the corner of the armchair cushion, I keep trying to look up but my head is stuck. Eventually I say: I was always afraid my father would rape me, that's what happened when I relaxed. And when I finally get myself to look up I wonder if those are tears in Barry's eyes, or mine. I look back at the shadow in the corner of this armchair, remembering to breathe, but something has changed in the room, is that my father in the therapist's chair? Don't look, don't look up, don't look up at his face. Look at his shoes, oxfords with laces, oh my father never wore shoes like that—but I still can't get past the corner of the armchair.

Lately it seems like Polly's working all the time, or getting ready for work, now that she has a pimp or something—it's the guy who gives her coke for sex so at least now she never runs out of coke. She's been on a trip with him for three days now, and tonight when she gets back we're doing ecstasy for the first time in a while—there was a shortage, and that's when everyone started doing more coke, and no one's really gone back. So it's getting kind of depressing.

I get a trick at the Chandler Inn who calls himself Doug the Piano Player. He's a big fat guy with bleached blond hair, so friendly it feels like I'm doing something worthwhile, but then after I leave I end up getting wired to hell, not sure what to do so I walk down Newbury but I'm not really in the mood for the Other Side or Trident or anywhere else so I take Commonwealth back the other way for the architectural tour and just as I get ready to turn on Dartmouth I look up at Jeannine so sharp against the sky she's like a paper cutout of a building, a huge canvas with shifting parts in yellow and black. Or more like a video installation—if you look carefully you can see that some of the lights are big and white and ominous and probably fluorescent, but some are tiny little yellow dots in the ceiling like jewels, and the rooms with curtains drawn look like they're glowing. And then as I'm heading to the T some kids are commenting on my hair, they want to know what I do.

I tell them I'm a hooker, and they're all excited—Do you have AIDS? Do you have condoms? Are there lots of people like you around here? Do you fuck guys in the ass? Do you stick them in the ass? How much do you charge? How old are you? Will you buy liquor for us? Do you fuck girls? When you have a boyfriend, do you still do this? Were you ever on *Ricki Lake*? What if a girl offered you a lot of money? What do you do all day? What's in your bag? Are you on drugs? What kinds of drugs do you do?

Okay, now I'm ready to go home. Polly's waiting for me, and she's actually in a good mood, not as coked out as I thought she'd be so I make red pepper linguine and when we sit down it almost feels like we're a couple. Are we a couple? How was your day at work, I joke. And she says: How was your day at work?

And then she says she's decided to visit the cult, she already bought a ticket. She's leaving tomorrow at two p.m. but don't worry, she's still going out tonight, that will give her plenty of time. So then we're on our way to Juniper and Sage and Lisa's new place in the South End anyway. Except I'm pretty sure the South End ended a few blocks ago. Lisa opens the door, and oh my she's flying. Her lip ring is vibrating and when she holds out her arms for a hug it looks like she's going to sing. Juniper and Sage are on the sofa in the living room, leaning into one another like they're merging. At first I thought they were watching TV, but the TV isn't on—Juniper starts clapping, and then she runs to her room, comes back with a little glittery box.

I kind of like the way they've decorated, even though it's all earth tones: corduroy sofas and patterned pillows and seventies ceramic lamps shaped like animals on Formica end tables and even a big lava lamp on the orangeish shag rug covering the brown carpet. Juniper hands us two capsules and then sits back down and starts petting Sage like a huge cat, and then Lisa comes in with two glasses and a yellow pitcher of bright pink liquid, what is that?

Yes, Lisa says, yes. Polly and I swallow our drugs with the Kool-Aid—I thought maybe it was a cocktail but it just tastes like sugar. The buzzer rings, it's Joey and one of her most annoying friends. Avery, that's his name. Like an eraser. Or a hole puncher. I look at Polly to see if she wants to go somewhere, but she just sits down on the sofa and closes her eyes. Joey is coked out of her mind, and Avery starts to introduce himself like we haven't met ten times. He's wearing some kind of silky button-down eighties stockbroker shirt that just looks like hi, this is expensive—plus an ascot, in case you didn't get the first part.

Pass the Kool-Aid, Joey says, and then we're all sitting down until Juniper and Sage get up and say they're going to their room for a little while. And then Lisa says she needs a nap—what, a nap on ecstasy, what kind of ecstasy is this? She says oh, we've been up, we've been up for a while—make yourselves at home.

Well, Joey says: Well. Come. Should we go somewhere?

Yes, I'm thinking, yes, but then Polly says let's wait for it to kick in and go to the Loft.

The Loft is closed, Joey says. Shut down. The cops. They weren't paying off the right people. What's in this Kool-Aid, anyway? Tastes like ass.

Somehow Joey's the first one to feel the X, even with all the coke—she's walking around the room saying oh, yes, oh. Then she goes into the hallway and starts telling us how fabulous it is. Music, Polly says, we need music, and when I look at her eyes I realize this is going to be good. Except no one can figure out the stereo.

Wait, listen. There it is, really soft, somewhere deep in the speakers—Avery thinks we're joking, but then he gets closer and we're all holding on until wait, it's slowly getting louder, do you hear that? Yes, yes, and then suddenly it's all around us, oh, the lights, turn on all the lights, yes, the lights.

But when I turn on the lights they're ugly and fluorescent. No one knows what to do except maybe more Kool-Aid, yes, this Kool-Aid, yes, what is this song? And damn this hallway is good for runway. Avery wants me to teach him how to walk, so I give him sassy stockbroker-on-leave—I'm yearning, I'm spurning, I'm burning, I'm turning, I'm learning. And she looks at me. And I say: Investment, divestment. Investment, divestment. And she's watching me close while I'm giving it, eyes wide, and then I lean up against her right arm turn back behind her and she turns with me, yes, bitch, turn.

Feel your body, shake your body, move your body—did I just

say that, or is it in the music? Avery unties her ascot and wraps it around her head. Give it, honey, give. It. Joey says oh, Alexa, I left my heels in the car.

Polly's swinging her arms in a circle in the living room, and Joey gets the pitcher of Kool-Aid and walks around saying welcome, welcome to the Factory. Now Avery's doing jumping jacks, little kicks—wait, wait, wait Jane Fonda wait. And Joey says Gene Simmons. No, Richard Simmons. And we're all doing it, whatever it is, and then I start throwing myself against the wall—it catches me, we tumble together. And then Polly's doing it. And then Avery. And Joey's doing it on the windowsill.

God this sound system is good, the beats bouncing off the walls into your body another body. We just need a disco ball. Joey starts flashing the lights—oh, perfect, oh.

I go to the bathroom to look at my eyes. And then Polly's there beside me and we're pointing at one another. You. Yes, you, bitch, you.

Back into the living room and Joey's still flashing the lights, announcing all her favorite T stops—Maverick, Maverick Station. Next stop, Maverick.

What about Wonderland?

Wonderland, Joey says. Next stop, Wonderland.

"X, X, Xtrava ..." so I start giving high-heeled falling-over runway and the music's flashing with the lights, wait are the lights still flashing, and here's the build, here's the build and the bounce, here's the build and the bounce and the dribble and those drums oh those drums and then suddenly the song skips like there really is a record and that's when Sage comes out in her platforms, dressed to the nines in raver realness, complete with Day-Glo plastic watch chain all the way to the floor. And pacifier. And I realize she's been deejaying from the bedroom the whole time. Now we're all jumping up and down, even Sage, though I'm worried she's going to hit the ceiling.

We are the ceiling.

But where's Polly? I open the bathroom door, and Polly and Avery are leaning over the tub. Oh, vomit, gray and mushy on the left, orange and chunky on the right—should I run the water? Are you okay?

And then Avery starts to spasm, Polly's petting his back and saying it's okay, it's okay, and then when they stand up I look at their eyes and it's flying-saucer realness and I'm starting to feel nauseous too. Dammit, I didn't think there was heroin in this X.

Juniper comes in and says oh, it's okay, sometimes that happens with the good stuff, let me just turn on the shower.

Oh, the shower. Do you mind if I take a shower?

Are you sure? It's a little funky. Okay, let me get you a towel.

Juniper comes back with a big fluffy pink bath towel—oh, I love it. If anyone needs to use the bathroom, just tell them to come in.

Of course, Alexa, of course. Let me just make sure it's clean. All yours.

She leaves the room and I don't feel nauseous anymore, just my stomach gurgling and yes, another rush—this ecstasy is so fucking good. I take off my clothes and I can hear the music coming through the window and under the door and up through the drain. Yes, especially the drain. Listen. The water's so warm it's like it's pouring through my body is this all me I think it is but how do I know I mean I know these are my hands but what about the rest?

But then I need to shit—luckily that's the toilet right there, I step out dripping wet, sit down, and it all comes shooting out, that felt kind of good, flush, open the window, back in the shower. Yes, that's the Danny Tenaglia track where he eats ice cream and licks the floor and then oh my fucking God it's like the record is stuck there in the melted mess—strawberry, vanilla, chocolate, raspberry meringue, peppermint patty, cookie dough, mint chocolate chip, peanut butter toffee crunch, yes, lick that floor and is this Sage deejaying or Junior Fucking Vasquez?

Oh, this water in my beats—rattle ship battle skip tattle rip scattle drip—oh, wait, someone's knocking. Come in!

Is it okay to pee, Avery asks. I'm kind of pee-shy.

Oh, don't worry—the water is running. I'm having so much fun.

I'm having fun too.

Avery pisses—that didn't take long, but then he's standing there for a while and there's the shower curtain between us so I can't tell what's going on but Avery's moving around and maybe he took off his shirt and I'm trying to act like I'm not thinking about it and then wait, he's pulling the shower curtain back and when I look over I see he's totally naked so I pull the shower curtain all the way open and Avery squeezes in.

Then he's under the water and I'm rubbing his back with the soap, usually I don't like the smell of Irish Spring but Avery says oh, that feels so good, oh. So then I hold him from behind, breathing with his breath, I like the way his body feels so solid. Kissing his neck with my eyes closed, searching the way skin becomes little hairs and salt and moisture and breathing until Avery turns around and reaches for the back of my neck with his hands and I'm watching the way his eyelashes are so thick and long, those big brown eyes almost orange in this light he's staring right into my eyes and what does he see, I mean there's so much there between our eyes my hands on his neck too and then we just stand there like that staring at each other with the water spraying into our eyes until he pulls me toward him like we're in a movie, oh this movie is nice and wet and warm or maybe cold yes cold until I pull Avery toward me, and I turn off the water.

So we don't get too cold, I say, and then I kiss his lips just once and he kind of shudders, then again, and then we're kissing each other and laughing, I'm rubbing the sides of his head and he's holding my back, squeezing me squeezing him and I'm letting go, squeezing again, that feeling between my legs even though I know I'll never get hard still that feeling, his lips something to taste, tongue into his mouth how far does it go? And then someone pulls the shower curtain back, and there goes our movie. Now it's just coked-out Joey saying: Oh. That's what's going on. I'm. Leaving.

Joey slams the door and Avery looks embarrassed, reaches for the towel, hands it to me. You go ahead, I say. I'm glad you joined me in the shower. And Avery smiles. He's actually really cute with his curly hair all matted and those eyes oh those eyes, maybe if we were on ecstasy all the time we could be boyfriends. He hands me the towel. I don't know if I'm ready to leave the shower, but somehow Avery's already dressed. What time is it?

Avery looks at his watch, I guess it's waterproof: 3:25.

Oh, it's still early. Are you really leaving?

I guess so. If Joey's still here.

After Avery leaves I stare at the light bulbs on the vanity and let my eyes roll back. I'm drying myself off, and Polly comes in. Alexa, she says, it's so hot in here, Alexa, it's so hot, I can't stand it. Polly's splashing water on her face, and I open the window wider. She looks at me, but I can't really see her eyes because her face is shifting so fast and is that the light? Polly's staring in the mirror like she doesn't know what's on the other side, and then there's that knock on the door no it's in the door that becomes a laugh track, yes, Josh Wink, yes, Josh Wink, the laugh track, I love this track.

And Polly says don't laugh, and then the beat crawls up the wall and into the ceiling and back down into the floor yes the floor and Polly says it again, don't laugh, and yes, you're right, that's what it's called—I love this song, but wait, is that the child's piano from the Osheen song, climbing up the wall with a brigade of horn players and then Polly says it again, don't laugh, is that Polly or is that the music and then static in the mirror yes static I'm holding the sink shaking my head into this world of broken laugh-track static magic and there's the knock again, inside or outside a heartbeat a tin can a drum and then the build I'm shaking it out for the mirror I'm shaking it out for the lights I'm shaking it out for that chirping cricket crack it jack it racket attack it smack it, and right then the beats break open and everything goes right back to eating ice cream off the floor, I mean I'd lick the floor, I'd lick the floor right now because Sage is a fucking genius—I wish the Loft wasn't closed, maybe Joey was joking.

And Polly says Alexa, do you believe in hell?

What?

She turns toward me, her face all red: Do you believe in hell?

Of course not. Polly, are you okay?

Alexa. I just want to know. How you know. That we are not. Going to burn in hell.

And then Polly starts to shake, and I wrap the towel around myself so I can put my hand on her back. She's really sobbing. Polly, it's okay, I say, it's okay, that's just your parents, it's brainwashing, it's bullshit, there is no hell, you're not going to burn, and she looks at me and says Alexa, I don't want to go. And I'm not sure if she means she doesn't want to leave this house, or she doesn't want to go to her parents' house, or she doesn't want to go to hell.

Finally she says Alexa, I have to go. I bought a ticket.

You don't have to go.

Polly leaves the room and at first I think maybe I'm not high anymore, but then I close my eyes and oh, yes, this is where I want to stay, can't I just stay here with warm water on my hands, yes, little currents going up my arms and into my head and should I get back in the shower?

But I have to go out there for Polly so I better get dressed. Clothes are weird—too much fabric, I wonder why everyone wears clothes all the time. My hair, how am I going to fix my hair? Oh, gel.

Luckily when I get back in the living room Sage is taking a hit off a huge bong, she hands it to me while holding her breath and yes, just what I need. I look at Polly and she seems calmer, and then Lisa shows up in her platforms—those are the platforms I want, combat boots with six inches extra. But I don't want to look like I'm copying Lisa.

Lisa's carrying another pitcher of Kool-Aid. This one's lime green, and I wonder if there's acid in it, but mostly I'm thinking about these drums and chants rolling around in the background but is the music getting quieter? I look around to see if anyone else notices. Until it's so quiet that you can hear Juniper laughing from the other room, or maybe that's in the song, I'm looking around to see and then suddenly the volume goes way up and it's "get somebody you need somebody"—oh honey, oh honey, this is so good, we should come here every night.

Juniper comes out with the little glittery ecstasy box, waving it in her hand like celebrity is here, a round of applause for celebrity. Then she takes out a capsule, pulls it open and somehow Sage is there with a mirror to catch the powder, Lisa sweeps it into five small lines and I'm looking at Polly like is this really happening but she's got her eyes closed, nodding to the beat. Juniper hands me a purple straw and says ladies first and oh yes oh yes I didn't expect it to burn I mean I know it's a waste to snort ecstasy but what an amazing waste and Polly shakes her head no, I'm fine—that's a first—and then I can't help staring at the last line until Juniper hands the straw back to me.

Are you sure?

Oh. Honey. It's the least we could do. We invited you over. And then abandoned you.

So it's time for the left nostril—this might be the best moment of my life as Sage hands me the magical lime elixir and I drink the rest and then walk toward the bathroom and go right to the mirror—honey, my eyes are gone.

Back in the living room Juniper is waving around a sparkly jelly snake, where the hell did you get that, and Polly's twirling around with her eyes closed and yes, here it comes again, "X, X, X—trava—ganza."

Have you seen this, Sage says, and she starts bouncing a big silver ball that lights up every time it hits the ground and honey, this is too good, and there's the vocal slowing, slowing, slowing down until it stops, and now everyone's so tall. Suddenly we're heading downstairs in a hurry and out into the night air, oh the air, you didn't tell me about the air, and there's no one around. I take Polly's hand because she looks a little scared, are you okay?

The way the deepest part of the night is so blue your eyes in the sky and we're walking and walking and walking, turn, yes, Tremont has never seen anything like our sidewalk glidewalk— watch out for the cars, only a few, even that guy up ahead who's staring. Of course he's staring. What's not to stare at? I love the way someone arranged these buildings like little toys.

Somehow Juniper and Sage are way up ahead, how did they get so far ahead, and now they're running back from the Loft in excitement and Juniper says Joey was right, there's a padlock on the door—I just had to know, I just had to know if Joey was lying.

Polly's shivering and suddenly I realize I'm freezing too, and just like that a taxi arrives, we open the door and it smells like cinnamon, peppermint, chocolate chip cookies, vomit, Pine-Sol, oh, soft warm seats and then into the tunnel of love I love this tunnel and Polly says I'm sorry I got so dramatic earlier.

THE REST OF MY LIFE

All Polly's note says is "Have some coke and a smile," but I keep staring at it like it's going to tell me why she isn't back yet, I mean she's four days late and Joey and I keep calling her parents' house but no one answers. Joey thinks we should drive down there. To Bel Air, Maryland? We don't even know the address. Should we just look it up in the phone book under Christian fundamentalist cults?

Joey says we should get cocktails, we can talk about it over cocktails.

I don't want cocktails, I want to figure out what's going on. I want to figure out why the fuck she isn't back yet. This is ridiculous.

Well, you're not going to figure it out by not drinking.

Okay fine, fine, let's get cocktails. Do you want to call Avery?

I told him you're a whore, and now he's embarrassed.

Did you tell him you're a whore too?

Alexa, it's different.

What's the difference?

I'm just doing it for extra spending money.

Did you tell him you got arrested for extra spending money?

I didn't get arrested—they took me in for questioning.

Oh, that's interesting—because when you called Polly, you said you needed bail—and I'm the one who went down there to rescue your fucking ass. I didn't even know you had a thing for Avery.

Alexa, I don't do Asian.

Joey, that's disgusting.

I'm just being honest.

That's not honest, it's racist bullshit.

Why are we fighting?

We're not fighting—I'm just telling you that you're a fucking tired bitch.

Okay, I'm a fucking tired bitch. Let's get cocktails.

I must really be a mess, because somehow Joey convinces me to take the T to Back Bay just to go to Club Café—this has to be the worst gay bar in Boston, I mean there's so much competition but I can't believe these snotty bitches who won't even look at you in the bar but then you go to the bathroom and suddenly they're cruising your cock, probably because the bar is renovating so the bathroom is downstairs by the gym and these bitches think no one will notice. Everything in Boston is about no one noticing. I'm cruising the bathroom anyway but after my fourth cocktail all I can think about is coke, so Joey and I take a cab back to East Boston and Polly was right when she said have some coke and a smile, this is the best coke I've ever done. Except for that time when we did the government coke study, and everyone knows the government has the best coke. But you had to sit in a hospital room for two hours with electrodes attached to your head, filling out a multiple-choice questionnaire on the computer that said things like: A) I feel on top of the world. B) I'm feeling pretty good right now. C) I'm starting to get depressed. D) I feel like nothing in my life is going right. E) I'm feeling suicidal.

So you filled out those questions over and over, and guess what? Eventually you were marking D) I feel like nothing in my life is going right. And, yes, even E)—I just love scientific studies that tell you what you already know. At least they paid us $100, but it would've been much better if they'd given us a bump or two for the road.

Anyway, after this coke I feel on top of the world. It's almost like ecstasy it's so good—I'm ready to dance but Joey wants to look through Polly's stuff to see if we can find any clues. She's already in Polly's room, opening up the drawers of the desk and I figure she's looking for the address of the cult but when I get in the room she has six vials of coke lined up on top of the desk.

Where did she get all this, Joey keeps asking. Where did she get all this?

I've already told her Polly has a trick who pays her in coke, but now Joey says: I should be a chick with a dick.

You are a chick with a dick.

Joey goes in the other room, so I figure I better stash that coke somewhere safe, where should I keep it? Oh, in my multivitamins, Joey definitely won't look there.

Now Joey's at the makeup table, working Polly's black bob. She already looks like someone's messy eighties teenage daughter, I mean she could totally pass, and then the music's on, why wasn't the music on before? Oh, this song, I love this song—where did you find this?

Turns out Joey had one of Richie's mixes in her pocket, waiting for just the right moment, and luckily we are waiting no longer. Four hours later and we keep turning it over, yes there's the part where "Work me Goddammit" goes right into "Tyler Moore Mary," and I know everyone in Boston is getting tired of that song, but honey, every time I hear "She works up the block, she lives up a block" I can't help thinking yes, my life, that's the story. Even if Joey is saying she's Murphy Brown she's scary—well, that's true too. Another line, Candice?

Speaking of working, now Joey's trying on Polly's dresses—somehow they actually fit, even though Polly's at least a foot taller. Oh, Joey, yes, the pink one, yes, prom queen, bring it on.

The music is back to "Eternity, because you're ugly forever," and Joey is saying Winona Spider. Winona Desire. Winona Tried Her. Winona Revive Her.

Winona Revive Her—that's the one, Winona Revive Her.

Why-Own-It On Fire. Wino Ride Her. Why-No-No Mac-Gyver. Wyoming Mac-Jive-Her.

Joey's on a roll, but then she starts freaking out because the sun is coming up so she rushes into the shower to wash away any hint of Polly's makeup before getting on the T and just like that I'm crashing and where the hell is my pot, I can't find my pot anywhere. Forget it—I cut up a Xanax and a doxepin and snort it with a little bit of coke, yes, perfect. And just because I'm the sweetest girl in East Boston, I make a shiny little silver origami envelope—cocaine-to-go, just for Joey and her shift at Glad Day. Finally she's out of the shower and it's my turn—oh, the shower, the shower will solve everything.

Except sleep, yes, sleep, I'm trying to focus on sleep, but really who am I kidding I mean why do I even have a bed? Sure, I like getting under the covers, but every time I start to drift into dreamland my body does that thing where I shake from inside like there's a tiny earthquake and why does that keep happening?

Finally I give up and look at the clock, 1:30, too late to fall back asleep I mean I wasn't sleeping anyway so I go in the dining room and sit at the table in my robe, trying to figure out what to do. What to do about Boston, what to do about my life, what to do about this horrible world, what to do about those stupid fucking kids outside, what are they doing out there already, I need a fucking cigarette and Polly isn't even here smoking in my face, oh, where the hell is Polly? I mean she better get back here soon.

What to do about the weather, I can't tell if it's hot or cold out, what the fuck am I going to wear? What to do about religion, yes, what to do about all the horrible religious people in the world, and what about my acne, my body, I mean I hate this fucking body, or maybe I just need something to eat, but what? I'm not hungry, but should I eat something? What about music, I mean what should I play, I really can't decide, all my CDs are crap. I try Moby but that's too sad, Cajmere is too clanky, I can't deal with that tired Danny Tenaglia mix. Billie Holiday? No, no, no. Memphis Minnie?

Wait, did Joey leave Richie's mixtape? No, of course not, she would never forget something that gives her status. What is wrong with my head, oh, why does my head hurt so much? I'm not doing more coke.

And just like that, the phone rings—I grab it on the first ring, it must be Polly.

Oh, shit, my mother. I shouldn't have answered. Usually Polly answers, and tells her I'm not here—what am I going to do without Polly?

My mother sounds so excited. She's telling me I'm going to be so proud of her, I'm going to be so proud because she's finally learned how to drive on the highway. Yes, really. Your mother is driving on the highway. Can you believe it?

And the fucked-up thing is that I actually do feel proud of her.

And then she says she's been thinking about something I told her a long time ago, about how I was raped, and when she asked if it was someone in the family I said yes. She's been thinking about that, because there was never anyone around.

And here's the moment where my heart stops, I mean I can't tell you about that moment I can only tell you about the moment after. Because my father's on the phone, and he's saying: Karla thinks you believe something sexual happened between us.

And I don't know what to say.

And my father says it again.

I wanted to invite them to Boston, I wanted to spend a day together first, do something relaxing, appreciate anything of value that we might have together.

My mother says are you there?

Maybe I can just hang up, hang up and pretend we got disconnected. Instead I say hold on, and then I go in the bathroom and look in the mirror: Who are you? Who the fuck are you? I'm shaking. I don't know what to do. I have it all in my head, it's all there, I could confront him now.

I sit on the toilet because suddenly I have to shit. I think about leaving this apartment, and never coming back. I think about rushing into the other room and smashing the phone with a hammer. I think about doing a bump of coke.

A bump of coke—that's so completely wrong it's perfect.

Oh, yes, little tiny diamonds, bring me home: "I am ready. I am ready. I am ready" is speeding up in my head until it's just the drumroll and I'm six feet off the floor. But I'm on the phone. I'm on the phone again, telling my parents I decided to go to therapy in order to get ready to confront my father.

Confront—my father doesn't want me to use the word confront. He says it again, it's like a script they've agreed upon, no deviating from the script: Karla thinks you believe something sexual happened between us.

Confront—what was I saying about confront? I'm trying to stay focused. I say I never understood until my first relationship, my first relationship with another boy, in San Francisco, when there were places he would touch and I would completely shut off. Anywhere near my neck. Down my belly. I just thought oh, he's having fun, and I don't want to spoil it.

My mother says she's worried about my hustling. They're worried about my hustling.

I'm not talking about hustling, I'm talking about my life. I'm talking about when I was a kid and whenever you would invite your friends over they were impressed because I knew the capital of Madagascar, they liked it when I would name the different kinds of cheeses or when Dad told them I was reading the same books he was, like that biography of Stalin, remember that? They thought I was so smart—what do you want to be when you grow up, doctor or lawyer? And there was that time Dad was driving me home from school, and I was telling him about my day, and he just kept nodding his head and I knew he wasn't paying attention. So I said: I'm just going to open the door right here and lie down in the middle of traffic. And he said okay, that sounds good. That sounds good. He said: that sounds good.

And my father interrupts me again to say Karla thinks, and I say: You've never given a shit before what Karla thinks, so what has changed now.

And my mother says: We're worried about you. We're worried about your hustling.

And my father says: Are you on drugs?

And I say: Am I on drugs? Am I on drugs? I am on so many drugs that I finally figured out how to think.

My father says: Do you need help?

And I say: Do I need help? Do I need fucking help? Look who's asking me now.

My father says: You're psychotic.

And I say: Look—the psychiatrist is making a diagnosis. Maybe I'm on the wrong drugs. What would you like to prescribe for me, Doctor Freud?

This is when my father starts yelling, I knew he was going to start sometime so I'm studying the way the floor in the kitchen slants in the opposite direction from the floor in the dining room I guess because this building is so old but I'm not sure how old, maybe the late 1800s but when did they put this linoleum in, I guess the sixties or seventies, and my father's yelling something about how I'm psychotic, I need help, they're going to come up to Boston and make sure I get the right kind of assistance, obviously I'm not seeing the right therapist, this is my therapist's fault, something needs to change, I'm in danger, it's about my lifestyle, they're worried about my lifestyle and something needs to change.

And just then he pauses, and that's when I say it. That's when I say I know you sexually abused me, you raped me, you molested me, and I don't want to talk to you ever again unless you can come to terms with it. And then he starts screaming again so I hang up the phone. I hang up the phone, and unplug it, and then I take a deep breath. I go in the bathroom, and I do another bump. I feel like a different person. I feel totally calm. I feel fine. I feel like I can go on with the rest of my life.

I want to do something relaxing, maybe a movie, what's playing? Oh, *Kids*—the one that got the NC-17 rating, that's at the Sony Nickelodeon. I need to eat something, but first I'll take a shower, yes, a shower, my favorite place.

I forgot this theater was literally on the BU campus. All the most horrible people in the world, really, all of them, right here. And can you believe they card me when I buy a ticket, I mean do I really look like I'm sixteen? And then, what the fuck is this movie? It starts with a het preteen make-out scene, you can see the sweat on their skin, little zits on her face. I thought Larry Clark was gay. I've seen some of his photos, and it's all shirtless boys. Like this boy, I guess—his skinny body fondled by the camera while he says: "I'll be gentle."

Teenage boys talking about virgins and pussy and how AIDS is a make-believe story to get them to stop fucking. And what is up with the fake New York accents? Especially this boy Tully, who looks like he's about twelve, slurring all his words in the voice-over, talking about how he really likes virgins, and then you see the girl from the opening scene, Jenny, going with her friend to get her HIV test, they're both getting tested but Jenny's only had sex with one guy, Tully. So we know what's going to happen.

And here she is after her results, stunned, this can't be possible, driving around New York with shorter hair, right, wasn't her hair longer before? Here she is, telling the taxi driver that everything's wrong. And yes, this is cheesy, it's obvious, but still I'm thinking dammit, she's right—everything is wrong.

And then there's a scene in Central Park, this group of kids smoking pot and two guys walk by holding hands and all these boys are yelling faggots, you fucking faggots, and one of the faggots, who's kind of cute and a little bit industrial or something, he starts to yell back and oh how I know that feeling.

Then Casper, a white guy who's best friends with Tully, who's also white, he gets in a fight with a black guy who's a few years older, and then suddenly his whole group of friends, mostly white guys, a few girls too, all of them are kicking and punching the guy until Casper slams him in the face with his skateboard and the guy passes out, blood all over his face and everyone is laughing.

He might be dead, that's what some of them think. They leave him there. I don't know if I've ever seen the violence of teenage boys depicted so accurately.

Jenny walks right past the line at the club, where no one's dressed up at all, tank tops and cutoff shorts, do people really go out like that in New York, guest list for Jenny and she does look better than the rest. Some guy hands her a pill, no actually he pushes it into her mouth, says it's better than K or ecstasy. Jenny's trying to find Tully to stop him from fucking another girl, she keeps missing him until the end of the movie when she walks in on him with a thirteen-year-old, saying: I'll be gentle—of course I care about you.

And then Jenny starts crying, stumbles over to a sofa in the other room, and passes out. Casper the friendly ghost rapes her while she's sleeping. We see his ass, muscular, pumping away while he's telling her it's okay.

And I'm crying because I know these teenage boys. These were the boys I went to school with—everyone went to school with them. I'm in the bathroom stall hugging myself and saying it's okay, Alexa, it's okay.

I call Joey. She says we should get cocktails.

I can't get cocktails.

I need to talk to Joanna, I really need to call her before it's too late—it's almost 10:30 on the West Coast, and now Joanna goes to bed early. I could go to the phones on Newbury but what if they don't work so I hail a cab and then when I get home it's almost eleven, I mean eight, and Joanna's mother answers and says she's already asleep.

I call Melissa, and I'm so excited when she answers. Melissa, I say, I just went to this movie, *Kids*, have you seen it? Oh, it's horrible, it's so horrible, I mean it ends with some het guy raping this girl while she's asleep, all these kids beating up this one black guy in the park, two girls kissing each other for Truth or Dare in a swimming pool while these guys watch, the only fags in the movie are just walking by while the straight boys yell faggot at them, and the movie is about AIDS, do you see what I mean?

And Melissa says Alexa, you're speaking too fast.

And then I start sobbing and saying Melissa, it was awful, I mean it was about AIDS but it wasn't about AIDS, he doesn't care about AIDS. No one cares about AIDS. I'm sick of AIDS. I don't even know if he's queer.

And Melissa says Alexa, are you high? And I say no I'm not high, I'm not high at all, I mean I did some coke earlier but that was hours ago. And Melissa says Alexa, I need you to call me back when you're not on drugs.

So I get off the phone without even telling her what really happened. And then suddenly I'm angry, really angry—Melissa hasn't ever done drugs, any drugs, not even pot. I'm not high just because I did a few bumps of coke four fucking hours ago and dammit I need to eat something, what is there to eat?

Oh, I can't wait for this water to boil for pasta, I'm so fucking hungry. Maybe a spinach salad—oh, there's no spinach. What the fuck am I going to do? Everything was fine, everything was fine before I went to that movie. I mean I confronted my father, and then I felt great, I felt amazing, I felt incredible, remember?

But why am I thinking about calling Michael in Arlington, just because he said he used to hire that hustler who was a crack addict, and then the hustler would show up in the middle of the night, and I remember thinking it was kind of touching when Michael said he understood. Maybe he'll understand me.

But that's ridiculous. And I have coke right here. I'll just do the rest of this vial, two big lines, oh my, yes, just what I needed.

But what am I going to do now? Oh, a page, I have a page, yes, a page. He wants to know where I'm from. What an original question. I tell him I'm just waiting for my dinner, is an hour okay, and he thinks that's funny, I'm not sure which part but he says take your time.

He lives on the fancy part of Comm. Ave. but I don't realize how fancy until I get there and pretty much everything on the block is posh, but his place is one of the white stone ones that I've always thought were the most impressive, and when he opens the door there's a marble entryway with a huge chandelier. And then we walk through another set of doors and enter a living room with ridiculously high ceilings, long white sofas and armchairs arranged in different seating areas around Oriental carpets—antique tables, huge paintings in gilded frames, nudes and crosses and God.

I wonder why someone this rich would have such bad hair, almost like a bowl cut from a barbershop but he's already asking if I want something to drink, sure, and then we sit down on one of the sofas so white it's kind of iridescent, or maybe that's just the effect of the chandeliers and recessed lighting from way up like we're in a museum and a ballroom at the same time. And when he puts my cocktail down I notice there's $200 on the end table, just the way I like it. He says: You don't mind if I sit with you, do you?

It's funny how he's so formal even though he's wearing just a silk robe with leather slippers, gray and blond chest hairs on his pockmarked skin. He crosses his legs, and I focus on his droopy eyelids, I can't tell if he's tired or if that's just his expression. Of course he wants to hear about how I'm paying my way through college, and yes, it's hard, but it's worth it, right, because I want to get an education, I'm thinking about my future. And, hey, I really like sex with older guys, so why not mix business with pleasure?

And he laughs like I just told the best joke in the world and says do you want to go in the bedroom so we head upstairs. I can't believe this bedroom—it's like a hotel except everything is white instead of beige. Calla lilies on the dresser. Photos of naked men on the walls. Gilded mirrors. Is that his wife and kids? A huge four-poster bed that looks like something right out of some British colonial fantasy. Wallpaper with flowers in raised velvet. Little chandeliers on the ceiling, the ones where the crystals drape across, I've always loved those, whatever they're called.

He pulls the covers down so I finish my drink and then lie back and look at the ceiling and think about coke and cocktails and how chandeliers really make the light so much more beautiful, and he starts to unbutton my sweater, my shirt, then he's sucking my dick and when I grab his head I realize oh, the hair, it's a wig, but why this wig?

He's moaning so I pull him up to me like I need to kiss him right now yes now I'm so present in his fantasy that I actually feel possessed by this power that isn't really power as he slides the condom on my dick and yes, he already told me he wanted me to fuck him. Of course I said that sounded great, and I'll admit that now that he's face down it actually does feel pretty good. Because I don't care, I don't care about anything except whatever it is that's keeping me hard, whatever it is I'll just go with it, pretend to come in the condom and then pull out so I don't crash afterward but this time dammit I'm so in the role that I'm actually thinking of giving him the real thing until he comes on those white sheets that someone will bleach in the morning and yes, that's the place to stop so I pull out and he says do you want to wash up.

Sparkling glass doors to a shower three times the normal size with floor-to-ceiling blue tiles, and he goes in another bathroom so I have three shower heads all to myself—one for front, one for back, and I guess the other one is for my asshole, right? Black marble counter with two sinks, plush white towels but for some reason all the toiletries are sample sizes from hotels, I can't decide if that means he's cheap or boasting. I do like this mirror, that's for sure, front and back, and when I meet him downstairs he has another cocktail waiting.

THE PROGRAM

Now that Joanna has replaced Polly, the kids in East Boston are confused. They don't carry sticks anymore, but they still stare and point and try to make fun of us and we just laugh. Where's your friend, they keep asking.

Finally I say: This is my friend. Then they look more confused. At least they're just kids. Sometimes on the T people act like we're some punk-rock couple—oh, look, it's Sid and Nancy.

How could anyone be so stupid?

It's still warm out so we go to the park on the piers every day to watch the sunset. Sometimes we even bring food in two big straw purses and set everything out on a plaid blanket for a picnic. It's kind of like we're on vacation except this is our life, our life together. Sometimes I can't believe this is really happening, I mean I keep thinking back to that conversation on the phone when Joanna was still in Issaquah and she told me she wanted to move to Boston, but her mother wouldn't pay for it—she was still upset from the last time, when she gave Joanna a thousand dollars and she spent it all on heroin.

I told Joanna I'd pay for the ticket, it wouldn't be a problem now that I have this trick who pays me monthly. I said I'd pay her rent for a few months too so then she wouldn't have to worry about looking for a job right away, and at first she said no, she didn't want to owe me anything, but I told her it would be for me just as much as her, I mean now that Polly's gone I have this apartment all to myself anyway, and what am I going to do with all this space?

And then Joanna said okay. I got all excited and said I'd stop doing drugs too, so Joanna wouldn't be tempted, and she said you don't need to do that but I said don't worry, it's done, I'm stopping right now. I'll even stop drinking if you want. But Joanna said you better not stop drinking—the first thing I'm doing when I get on that plane is ordering a shot of Jack Daniel's. And I said are you sure that's okay? And she said I've never been drunk when I shot dope, what would be the point? Drinking and pot are totally safe. And I said I don't know about pot—remember when you first started shooting up? And she said oh, good thing you're here to watch out for me.

So we made an agreement that neither of us would do any drugs, but we could drink. And I said wait, how about if we only drink when we're having a meal, so that it's part of a ritual that doesn't involve drugs? Maybe that was more for me than her since I'm the one who always wants drugs when I have cocktails. But the ritual, that was for Joanna, she's the one who likes rituals.

One of our favorite rituals is to go to Bread & Circus and choose all the most expensive things from the salad bar, like artichokes and smoked tofu and grape leaves and quinoa, and then we walk right past the registers and sit down in front and eat everything. Once our blood sugar has leveled out we buy broccoli and tofu and pasta, scallions and carrots and tomato sauce, rolled oats and brown rice and fresh dill, basil and mushrooms and sweet potatoes, and then we stuff all the expensive things into our bags.

We dream a lot. I dream about my parents in dark rooms. I

dream about hanging from the ceiling like a piñata. I dream about the ocean pulling me out while I'm fighting the tide. I dream about fleeing from my father's hands, he's choking me with shit smothering my nostrils, I'm flying off a cliff in a car I don't know how to drive.

I dream about my father banging on the door, and when I wake up I can't tell if that's now. He called once, and left a message saying only a monster could do what I accused him of. He said he was in analysis at the time—nothing like this ever came up in analysis so it couldn't be real. And then I left him a message telling him not to call me again unless he was ready to acknowledge the abuse. So now it's always my mother who calls, and I don't answer.

Joanna dreams about her father smoking in the bedroom, dropping the cigarette into the carpet and then everything is on fire and she wakes up drenched in sweat. She dreams about getting stuck in her mother's refrigerator, pounding on the door but no one can hear. She dreams about feeling my heartbeat in her chest and is this okay?

We both get up late, and then we paint each other's nails and plot out our hair. We go to Bertucci's and ponder the rolls made out of pizza dough—how can they always be this fresh? We talk about drugs, and whether they're really in the past. Whether they ever will be. Joanna says she can never go back to San Francisco so I'm starting to wonder if I ever can either. We chop vegetables and make carrot juice with ginger and put lemon juice on our faces—oh, how it burns.

Joanna says Boston is what she always thought San Francisco would be like.

But what do you mean?

She says I'm living in a house with you, it's us against the world.

And then I kind of don't hate Boston anymore.

Joanna says she's been in love with Boston ever since I met her at the airport, even though I didn't recognize her because she was so skinny. And then, when we got back to the apartment, and she saw the new living room, purple walls with magenta trim and that big gold sofa set I bought at a yard sale down the street, and then all my lists taped together on the wall behind a gold frame, it was like a dream if dreams weren't just nightmares. And I didn't even tell her I created this room just for her.

One night Joey wants to get ready at our house—it's her first time out in full drag so she wants to borrow one of Polly's wigs. Joanna and I make a stir-fry with peanut sauce, cashews, dill and liquid amino acids. That's Joanna's special. We already know that Joey isn't going to eat, but we make food for her anyway.

Joey arrives with Avery, who won't even look at me so I keep saying oh, Joanna, this is Avery—he thinks I'm going to give him AIDS. And Joanna thinks that's the funniest thing on earth. Do you want some AIDS in your cocktail? Vodka, cranberry juice and AIDS. Don't worry—no extra calories.

We've moved all Polly's stuff into the extra room, and when Joey comes out her face is candied up and she's wearing some blonde wig I've never seen before, all curled like it's fresh from the store. She holds out her hand and says Anita, Anita Bump.

Speak the truth, honey. Speak the truth.

Once Anita and Avery leave, Joanna and I go on a walk to clear our heads. I always forget about this cute square and all the grand old houses up here at the top of the hill but next time we should walk in the other direction because it's not looking that cute once we get to the airport.

Joanna loves my list project, especially now that the lists are expanding beyond the frame in the living room, spreading across the whole wall—she keep saying Alexa, you're so inspiring. At first I think she's joking, but then one day she takes the cardboard from one of my underwear packages and paints it gold, sticks her fingers on the sides, fingerprints forming a frame. After it's dry, she glues a smaller piece of cardboard to the center of the first one, then draws two figures with oil pastels and markers, one with purple hair and the other pink, facing in opposite directions in the corners like on a playing card. I'm the one in pink, and she cuts out the word TREASURE from the newspaper to go over my lips, TRUTH to go over hers. And then, at the bottom corner, in small letters, also cut out from the newspaper: SMOKESCREEN?

And then we're on a roll. I find one of those gaudy jewelry boxes with a soft red velvet interior and a ballerina on top with a big mirror. I'm spelling out the word HELP on the mirror with contact lenses, I've been saving them for a while but I still don't have enough so I'm trying to decide whether I should ask other people for theirs. I guess I can take my time—what's the rush, we have time.

Then I do the same thing with used razor cartridges on a plain wall mirror. I have plenty of used razors. Now I'm working on a bigger project about rape, using playing cards and an old table and chairs, and Joanna's started a series of faces that she tapes to the wall. So, yes, our apartment is now officially an art gallery: old school meets new school meets no school.

Over the river and through the woods—or under the harbor and through the tunnel—there's Nate in his own art gallery, Nate who pays me monthly, now that we have an arrangement— he deposits the money directly into an account for me, it's in his name but that's better for me anyway. Nate didn't come out until he was fifty, married with kids and everything. He says he's fifty-two now, so even though he's at least thirty years older than me, I have way more experience as a fag. I think that's one of the things that makes him listen so carefully. At first I just talked about bullshit anyway, like the college I don't really go to, the former sugar daddy who never really existed, my day that didn't really happen, but Nate kept asking questions so eventually I got bored of telling stories and started telling him some things that are actually true.

I tell Nate how Joanna moved in with me to get off heroin, or to stay off heroin, and how it's so exciting having her here—it's like I finally have a home. But I don't tell him I'm supporting her—I don't want him to think he's giving me too much money. Nate asks me if I've ever done drugs, and I say yes, but not heroin. Nate says he's never been around drugs—but he sure does like his liquor.

When I first started coming to Nate's I only glanced at the art because it looked like pompous old European garbage—but then I realized that's not exactly the case, like the one that looks like Adam and Eve from a distance, but then you get closer and they both have two heads, Picasso style, one male and one female, and then coming out of their mouths are snakes instead of tongues.

And it turns out that Adam-Eve and Eve-Adam are standing in supermarket bins of apples and oranges and grapefruits and pomegranates and pears, with labels from all different countries. The piece is called *Bruised*. Nate says it was the first one he bought, because of the global outlook—he travels a lot. And then after that he started going to this artist's shows in New York and buying a new piece each time. Somehow I can't picture this pasty old guy with a ratty gray wig at some fancy New York opening, but he sounds so excited that I tell him sure, I'll go to the next one.

And then upstairs, the first time I just assumed all those photos of naked men on the walls were tacky gay garbage, and yes, some of them are definitely cheesy, but one day I find myself looking at the one of two naked dancers or gymnasts and the way their combined shadow plays out behind them on the wall, and I realize I'm wondering how the photographer managed to get those in-between facial expressions, like the moments you're not supposed to see.

Then there's the photo of some guy bending down to grab onto his ankles, his ass and legs forming a giant upside-down V against the sky. Even though these photos are black and white, there's so much variety in tone and texture. Like the way the clouds are not exactly the same color as the guy's inner thighs, which somehow shine in the light, and the part that's shining isn't exactly the same color as the bright white sky underneath the guy's head, and even that white isn't the same in the center as it is on the edges.

How is it that he bends that far over, but we don't see any of the details of his face? And what is that bone that sticks out at the base of his back—I guess I've never stared at a guy in this position for so long, but the composition is so formal that it almost becomes abstract. This is the photo that's in my field of vision while I'm fucking Nate, this one or the one on the wall to my right of some guy bent over on his hands and knees, pulling his stomach in, and that one's hotter, more details, like the hair on his legs, and maybe the sneakers he's wearing add a kind of excitement too. I can't tell if these photos are old or new. I keep meaning to ask Nate about them but every time we head to the bedroom I'm busy thinking how on earth am I going to get hard? Because all he wants to do now is lie on his stomach while I fuck him. Usually once I'm actually fucking him it's okay, I can just keep pumping away and grunting and moaning while I study the little rainbows making their way across the wallpaper because of the chandeliers.

When Joanna was staying with her mother in Issaquah, her mother made her go to AA meetings several times a week. Joanna said half the guys in the room were just like her father. Some of them actually knew her father, they'd been drinking buddies, and Joanna said it was so embarrassing, she couldn't believe she'd put herself in a position to be stuck in a room with all these assholes talking about God and how they were going to turn their lives around.

Joanna isn't even an atheist, I mean she doesn't think that religion is the stupidest thing in the world like I do. So these guys at the meeting would say God or Higher Power or whatever, and Joanna would think Goddess and her own power. She says I know that's not enough, I know there's so much more filtering and figuring out that I need to do, but I got used to the meetings. At least they got me out of the house, they became familiar, something to do, a ritual.

So one of the first things Joanna did after she moved in with me was go to an AA meeting in East Boston. She said it was kind of like the meetings in Issaquah except everyone was poorer, but then as soon as the meeting ended all these guys wanted to walk her home and that creeped her out so she decided to find the lesbian meeting. Even though before she got to Boston she said she didn't want to see any lesbians for a long time, lesbians just made her want to shoot up.

So I suggested she go to a meeting in JP, and I guess she started to like it because now she goes every week, and to a few other meetings too. She says the meetings make her feel more confident that she's not going to do anything stupid. So whenever I spend the night at Nate's, she stays at her sponsor's house. Her sponsor is this older dyke who wears overalls and smokes cigars and lives in a big old house she renovated herself. Sounds kind of like Joanna's daddy in San Francisco, but without the drugs, except when I say that, Joanna starts laughing hysterically.

A week later, she comes home and says she slept with Tina. But isn't that against the whole program? Alexa, Joanna says, I go to AA, and I drink almost every day. That's definitely against the program. But it's part of my healing process—even if no one in AA would agree with me on that. And I haven't done heroin in four months. Four months, can you believe it?

Four months is a long time. And I really don't know anything about AA, except for the flyers Joanna brings home sometimes, and we can thank those flyers for inspiring the curatorial statement for our glamorous art show:

DON'T GET BLOOD ON THE CARPET

1. We admitted we needed a power vacuum.

2. Came to believe that a power vacuum could restore us to sanity.

3. Made a decision to turn our will and our lives over to the care of Vacuum *as we understood Vacuum.*

4. Made a searching and fearless moral inventory of every brand of power vacuum, including ourselves.

5. Admitted to Vacuum, to our own vacuum, and to another vacuum the exact nature of our wrongs.

6. Were entirely ready to have Vacuum remove all manufacturing defects, including character.

7. Humbly asked Vacuum to remove our shortcomings.

8. Made a list of all vacuums we had harmed, and became willing to vacuum amends.

9. Made direct amends to such vacuums wherever possible, except when to do so would injure them or other brands.

10. Continued to take personal inventory of the vacuum industry, and when we were wrong, promptly admitted it.

11. Sought through prayer and meditation to improve our conscious contact with Vacuum *as we understood Vacuum,* praying only for knowledge of Vacuum's will for us and the power to vacuum that out.

12. Having had a spiritual awakening as the result of these steps, we tried to vacuum all our affairs, including anyone who doesn't believe in vacuuming.

Don't worry, you don't have to remember those twelve steps. Yet. Just enter our apartment and there's seven feet of pure white runway now, featuring big black letters on the sides saying DON'T GET BLOOD ON THE CARPET.

And that leads you right over to the table and chairs, covered in cards. This is the project I've been thinking about for years, ever since I remembered about my father. Now it's finally out of my head and into the world.

WHAT TO DO WHEN YOU'VE JUST BEEN RAPED: Fix your hair. Brush your teeth. Smile. Make dinner. Fix your lipstick. Shave. Make coffee. Get ready for work. Tie your shoes. Find new buttons. Wash your face. Get groceries. Trim your nails. Take a Xanax. Do the dishes. Push-ups. Sit-ups. Deodorant. Shopping. Watch a movie. Vacuum. Cocktails. Read the newspaper. Take out the garbage. Wash the sheets. Rearrange furniture. Buy flowers. Drink juice. Read a magazine. Get the mail. Turn on music. Make tea. Clean the toilet. Organize your room. Weed the garden. Air freshener. Take a Valium. Go to work. Go to school. Go to bed. Go dancing. Smile. Do laundry. Get a tan. Go to the gym. Pour wine. Drink a beer. Cocktails. Make a salad. Get a haircut. Take a shower. Remember to floss.

All these things we do in order to keep going, right? And rape, it keeps going too—your heart, maybe it's broken. And then you look up at the wall and oh, honey, Joanna's snakes—slithering in every direction, layered in paint and oil pastel and marker and scratches and spit and blood and cigarette ash and glue. Snakes of every messy gooey oozy cracked and exploding color, but all the faces are blank, some with smears and smudges but otherwise pristine white with words in the middle made from newspaper cutouts: Medusa Oblongata, Medusa Fermata, Medusa Desiderata, Medusa Stigmata, Medusa Tomato Insalata, Medusa Carne Asada, Medusa Yada Yada, Medusa Piñata, Medusa Regatta, Medusa Dada, Medusa Messiah—and, of course, Medusa Matzo.

But which Medusa represents which step? Darling, choose your own adventure.

DREAMING BIG

The worst part about flying is always the landing, that's what rips my ears apart and then it feels like my head is filled with steel wool and we're driving through the Everglades, is this really the Everglades? I can't believe how ugly everything looks. But then we get to the hotel and it's a gorgeous renovated art deco building—Nate says it's from the 1920s, I didn't realize Florida was already a tourist destination then.

Should we go to the beach? I guess that's why we're here, but first we stop at some weird health food store where I get fresh carrot juice and a bunch of premade wraps to put in the refrigerator. I can't believe how hot it is, but I guess that's why Nate wanted to come here—it's barely even fall, but it's already getting cold in Boston, which is fine with me but Nate realized he hadn't been out in the sun all summer because he was working so much. He asked me to go on this trip so many times that I finally said yes—I hate the heat but I do like the beach, and I never made it to P-town.

I need to get a bathing suit so we stop somewhere and Nate keeps pulling out the Speedos so I decide I'll humor him and try on a pair, the square-cut kind that aren't so ridiculous, and Nate's got that skeezy old guy look in his eyes. The rest of the bathing suits are either tiny thongs or huge baggy surfer shorts so I go with the Speedos. I'm pretty sure I'm not going to run into anyone I know. I ask Nate to buy me some wacky Astroturf sandals because I need something other than combat boots in this heat—why didn't I think of that before? At first he tells me these sandals are too expensive—I should just get regular flip-flops because will I ever wear them again, and I feel like I'm arguing with my father. But then Nate takes the sandals to the register and we go back to the hotel to change.

The beach is so large it looks fake, but as soon as I pull off my sandals to walk in the sand I feel like a little kid—maybe Nate was right, and I do need a vacation. He reaches over for my hand and I make sure no one's looking. We go to a restaurant on some pedestrian-only street that I guess is trying to look like Europe, angel hair pasta and a salad is all I can eat though the pasta with broccoli and pesto is delicious, and of course the cocktails help. Cocktails help with everything. Nate reaches over for my hand again, and I'm trying not to pull back.

When we get back to the hotel, Nate lies down on the carpet because he says that helps with his back pain, but I guess not enough because then he takes some pills and gets in bed. Four nights left.

I go on a walk, and I can't figure out why anyone would actually think this place is glamorous. Screaming drunk suburbanites driving down the main streets in convertibles, and then at every hotel bar near the beach there are Eurotrash in designer suits and stilettos. One woman is even wearing a fur coat, though it still feels like it's ninety degrees out. People look at me like I'm trash because I'm wearing a T-shirt. There are supposed to be gay people here, but I have no idea where. The waiters at the restaurant were gay, but that's true everywhere.

The next day it's even hotter, especially once we get to the beach. There's almost no one around, and I'm trying to remember if I've ever seen this much sun—you have to squint even with sunglasses. Nate snaps pictures of me in my embarrassing bathing suit, and I hope the sun doesn't bleach out my hair. Nate's chest is already bright pink so we better get inside to rest—who knew that lying in the sun would be so tiring.

We go to the same restaurant for dinner, and it turns out there's a gay bar nearby so we walk over and it's a suburban nightmare—people are yelling ooh ooh with their hands in the air like they're on *MTV Spring Break,* and there's so much CK One you could open an outlet store. But then the DJ puts on "Divas to the Dancefloor," and yes that song has been tired for at least a year now but honey I still can't resist, especially once Nate hands me another cocktail and I realize there are some cute boys around, I mean once you get past all the Lycra and frosted eyebrows.

Nate joins me on the dance floor and at first that's fine, right, whatever, just some old guy I happen to know and I can shake a few moves in his direction, but then he gets really close and pulls me to him from behind and I can smell that stale liquor breath and his baby oil sweat. I don't like grinding with anyone, but especially not with Nate. I try it for a moment anyway but then I pull away and try to make it seem like I just want to twirl around, I mean I do just want to twirl around but also I'm watching people to see if they're watching me with Nate.

I get water, and then I look at Nate and he's starting to sway. He doesn't usually get this drunk, maybe it's because it's past his bedtime so I ask if he wants to go. In the cab he reaches over for my hand and I close my eyes and think breathe, Alexa, breathe. We get back to the hotel and Nate starts pulling off my clothes, and I guess he notices I'm annoyed because then he says what, you don't like being seen with the old guy on the dance floor?

I look him in the eyes and start kissing his liquor breath, and then I remember the big tub in the bathroom so I say let's sit in the Jacuzzi. Nate keeps grabbing my dick, but I can't get hard. What's the matter, he keeps whining, and I really want to smack him. In the hot tub he starts to look like a lobster, says oh I'm getting overheated.

Better take a cold shower, I say, but then he looks at the clock and notices it's one a.m., says I'll see you in the morning, kisses me goodnight so then I stay in the tub until it gets cold, let it drain and then fill it up again, three more times until all my skin gets crinkled up and I guess I'm ready for bed. Except I don't want to get in bed with Nate so I pass out on the sofa until Nate wakes me up in the morning and then I stumble into bed and sleep until it's time to go back to the beach.

Yes, the same restaurant three nights in a row because Nate likes routine but this time he gets tired right away, says he's ready for bed. When we get back to the hotel I can tell he wants me to seduce him, but the problem with doing something so boring so many times is that it gets harder and harder. I knew this would happen if we spent this much time together. I told Nate this would happen. He didn't believe me.

When Nate first suggested a two-week vacation, I just smiled and said I would be too busy with school. Europe, that was his original idea. What the hell would I do with Nate in Europe?

When he first suggested Florida, I just laughed. But I could tell I was going to have to agree to something, right? So I got him to cut down the time by suggesting a long weekend so then I'd only miss a few days of school, but we could go earlier. He liked that idea, I could tell, he thought I was excited.

Tonight's the night for the big gay club—Sunday, just like in Boston except it's open later. I go over around two a.m. after Nate passes out—the music's pretty good but the crowd is wall to wall muscle boys, it's like a whole club filled with the strippers at Avalon. I'm not even dressed up, but I feel like an alien. I'm trying to dance, and some guy flying on X comes over to me and says: You look different. No kidding.

I'm not attracted to him, but we start to make out. Then he says he needs to piss, will I wait for him, sure. But then he doesn't come back, and when I go to the bathroom I notice the handicapped stall is shaking so I look inside and sure enough it's some guy getting fucked but when I see his face it doesn't look like pleasure it looks like he's not even sure why he's there. I realize I'm not sure why I'm there either.

The next day Nate and I drive to the place we're staying in St. Petersburg, which looks like a big pink castle. But it turns out our room is in a different building, and that building just looks like your average tacky motel. Nate says he chose this building because it's right on the beach and that's what I wanted. I guess he's right—I wanted to hear the ocean when I went to bed. We're on the Gulf now, so the water is quieter but the sand is so soft. You can even find the kinds of shells that I've only seen before in stores, tiny and delicate and unbroken.

This was supposed to be a spa, but it turns out that really it's just a resort with spa services, which I guess means you pay to be healthy for a few minutes instead of the whole time. I decide to try a seaweed wrap—I figure that means I'll sit in a tub and someone will wrap me in seaweed, but it turns out that I lie on a hard table and some blonde woman with a squeaky voice scrubs my body with some orangey apricot oatmeal stuff that happens to contain a little bit of seaweed, and then she wraps me in sheets of Mylar and turns on a heat lamp. I'm probably getting cancer already.

Monday night and we're on our way to a gay bar that looks like a converted Holiday Inn on the side of the freeway and when we get inside there's a courtyard with a tiki bar, a leather bar, an antique store, even a lawyer's office. There's a little store selling postcards and a bunch of other crap, including a big road sign that says MANATEE CROSSING. I think that's hilarious, but for some reason it's $39.99, and Nate doesn't want to buy it for me. Something in my body needs me to win, but nothing's working until I say I'd really like to have a souvenir from our trip, and Nate says okay.

The main bar is like every terrible gay club in the world—disco ball, TV screens, dance floor, stage, cologne, mirrors—I'm taking in all the hideousness and some guy wants to know if I'm wearing a wig, that must be a wig, that is a wig, isn't it, where'd you get that wig? Hey, he says, hey—are you in the circus?

I thought this place would be deserted, but it's packed and someone's walking around pouring fake champagne for someone's birthday—Nate's actually drinking it. We toast to our relationship and he kisses me on the lips, I try not to pull away too fast.

The next day's our last day at the beach with all these horrible straight Europeans, what are all these Europeans doing in Florida? These aren't even the Europeans that were in South Beach, partying in designer clothes—these Europeans walk around in straw hats and khakis, with stars-and-stripes beach towels, holding their kids close when Nate and I walk by. And the restaurant—oh, the restaurant—did I tell you about the restaurant? They serve iceberg lettuce: that's all you need to know.

We go for a walk on the beach after dark and I get excited about the way the sky spreads out in the distance. But then Nate says I feel like every time I touch you, you cringe. And I can't think of what to say. We keep walking, and eventually I say something about how pretty the stars are, that I really do love the beach, that it was nice to get away, thank you.

And then I'm thinking shit, what the fuck am I going to do? This is my financial stability, this is how I'm supporting Joanna. We get back to our room, and Nate asks if I want a drink. He takes out the mini liquor bottles and pours me one. And then another. We're not saying much, just staring outside at the water and he reaches over for my leg. I move closer. I kiss him on the lips. I lick his lips while I look him in the eyes. He moans. I start to unbutton his shirt, move down to lick his nipples, biting just so slightly on the tip of one and then the other. I pull off his pants, his boxers, start kissing his inner thighs, even where the rash is, lick his balls and then up his chest to his nipples, one by one, just the way he likes it.

The whole time I'm thinking: I hate you. I hate you I hate you I hate you. Somehow I'm hard, finally, so I move Nate's hand over to my balls and he squeezes like this is his toy, he's testing it out, and I'm thinking I hate you. I hate you. And then I say let me get a condom. And the expression on his face is like a little boy dreaming big.

When I get back in the living room I kiss Nate like I'm carried away by passion yes passion. Then I lean on the sofa and I push his face to my crotch. He still doesn't know how to suck cock. Now he's on his knees in front of me, and I wonder what one of those Europeans would see if they looked up from the beach. I stand up and smack Nate's mouth with my dick, back and forth, and he's moaning yes, Tyler, yes, and then I put the condom on. He says do you want to go in the bedroom?

No, I say, let's do it here, and he gets on his hands and knees on the carpet, facing the balcony so I can see something beyond this room.

THE CURE FOR CRYING

I get so excited when I open the front door, step inside our purple gallery and look at all the art. Time for a shower yes a shower to wash Florida away. Sure, this shower doesn't have the same water pressure, but at least I don't have to share it with Nate. I'm all excited about Bertucci's, checking the machine to see when Joanna will be back.

But then this message.

She's saying she can't keep depending on me. She's saying she's moving in with Tina. She's saying she'll call me when she's ready.

Is this a joke? This must be a joke. I go in her room—it's empty, except for the furniture. Polly's furniture. This isn't happening, this isn't happening, this isn't happening. Not again.

Breathe, Alexa, breathe.

But what if I don't want to breathe?

There's something wrong with my body, because it's making the shape of crying but nothing is coming out. I thought everything was finally going right. I really did. I really did, this time.

Another message. It's Joey, she wants to go out for cocktails. She wants to hear all about Florida. I meet her at Bertucci's because what else is there to do? Heavy-Handed Wendy is working. Joey is actually eating. Alexa, she says, you're taking this too hard—it was obvious Joanna was using you.

I don't think you understand.

I don't think you were paying attention. You were right—this

145

pizza is good. Eating isn't as bad as I thought it would be. You always said I should smoke more pot, but that shit stinks—and now, thanks to Marinol, pot-in-a-pill, I'm getting my rosy cheeks back. Want a bump?

You know I'm not doing drugs.

I thought that was because of Joanna.

You are such a piece of shit. Let's go to Luxor.

Now you're talking.

Speaking of talking, Joey's right, this coke is good. I don't know if it's because it's been so long, or if she finally got the right connection. Turns out she's the connection now and I really have been missing out, then we're in a cab on our way to Paradise, where that snotty bitch at the door acts like she hasn't seen me a hundred times, asks me for ID. But then Joey says Kelly, it's Winona, and Kelly looks up at Joey and says Wi-no-no-NO—you're actually cute as a boy. And then she waves us both in.

We walk downstairs, and there's Lady Dionne in front, fanning herself while the other black queens do their runway around her, and everyone's saying uh-huh, that's right, uh-huh, because that's the song—and just then Lady Dionne actually starts wailing big deep high notes, and the queen who's always there with her handkerchief just keeps walking like there's no one else in the world, honey, there's no one else, and I realize I'm staring because I love her so much, but I wonder if she knows that's why.

I drop off my coat in the DJ booth and then I'm in the back corner like I never left, flying in the air with all my old friends and yes, friends is an overstatement, but friends right now while I'm shaking jump rope to some mix of "Tyler Moore Mary" that just goes Mary Mary Mary Mary like the record's skipping we are all skipping Mary Mary Mary Mary until "Get Your Hands Off My Man" comes on, get your hands off Mary, with Jon B. giving me the usual glare but that's friendly for her, and there's Billy without her platforms, shrieking and saying fierce, and even Elana, she's back, a kiss on both cheeks and oh, honey, how are you, and then my favorite, Marc of the flying feet, and I do a quick spin on the floor right under him, I can't believe that actually worked. He gives me a high-five—really, high-five, can't you do better than that? So I lick his hand and then we're twirling around and he actually gives me all his weight so I lift him onto my back like contact improv, I mean we're flying and melting our bodies so graceful and tough. And that's when I realize yes, the coke cure, this is what I need.

Now Joey's the dealer, I've got concealer. Any time something gets a tad too dreary—honey, time for the bathroom. The problem with drugs is that you have to go back to what you were feeling before. But why?

After-hours at the MIT Café—yes, I'm serious. Joey found out it's twenty-four hours, and what more do we need than chamomile tea with the math maniacs? Talk about institution runway—restitution, constitution, pollution, ablution, Confucian, evolution. Turn.

Not to mention more of that pure white in the white bathroom, heavenly, and I tell Joey my new plan. Fabulous, she says, that sounds just like me.

Eventually I'm back in East Boston, cushioning my demise with a little bit of Xanax, Valium, Ativan, taking it all slowly, a little at a time, savoring it, evening it out. Yes, I've decided to make everything into that moment when you walk into the club and you first hear the music—yes, this East Boston runway to the T, yes, this ride with the paparazzi, yes, this walk down Newbury, Boylston, Arlington, Tremont, Mass. Ave., yes, the line at Bread & Circus, yes, this conversation with who, who am I talking to, wait, the bathroom, oh so much better. The weather? I didn't even notice.

And Nate—now that I've realized how to channel hate into a hard-on, the sex is almost hot. Just a quick bump to mix with the cocktails and small talk on big topics or big talk on small topics and then I'm a pounding porn machine and Nate thinks he's in love. Soon enough he'll fall asleep and then I can do runway all over the rugs downstairs, adjust the lights, oh, that's the way I love it, look in the mirror at that gorgeous glossy glassiness, eyelids fluttering until they roll back again, yes, I love rolling back and look, honey, my acne has even gone away—obviously what I needed was more drugs, a regular allotment, no need to take a break, just keep it balanced, yes, darling, balanced—oh, I love this balance.

And, yes, Joey was finally right about something: Marinol is the answer. I take one of those pills and boom, I'm out. Or, no, don't exaggerate—the first time it doesn't happen right away— actually it takes so long that I think it's never going to happen, but then it's already ten hours later and I can't even remember how I got into bed. Nate's bed. I didn't even wake up when he was getting ready for work. How much pot do they squeeze into one of those pills? New day, new promise.

Do I need to powder my nose? Luckily Nate has Puffs Plus. Yes, a little coke can go a long way. And a lot of coke can go even further. Oh, brown glass vial! Can you see my reflection in your curved surface, maybe just a hint of my eye checking the level? Oh, black cap, such a comfortable place for my nose to rest. Oh, white powder in my head, my head in this house of shimmering white, yes, even the carpet on the stairs.

Oh, Nate, who started to worry about me, started to worry because I was getting a little edgy, he didn't want his fuck machine to get edgy so he sent me to the pill doctor. Oh, dear pill doctor, provider for every need!

Oh, Marinol, blackout on white sheets.

Oh, Valium, a toast to all the fifties housewives—you were onto something, you were definitely onto something.

Oh, Xanax, a walk through pillows.

Oh, Ativan, so the lights get softer.

But stay away from Klonopin—I prefer my incest flashbacks without drugs, okay? And Dalmane, what a disaster—asbestos behind my eyes.

Back to Marinol, blackout in black and white, study the light and shadow, shadow. It's a miracle drug. I mean it even helps with Joey's appetite, and if you can help that cokehead eat then you're seriously onto something. And the other thing it helps with is getting hard for Nate's flabby ass, I swear, because when I wake up I'm laughing I mean I'm laughing once I remember where the hell I am, oh this comfortable bed. They should put

Nate's flabby ass on the Marinol label, right next to the part where it says WARNING: DO NOT MIX WITH ALCOHOL. Unless you've had a few bumps, right? I swear it says that in the fine print.

And who needs to remember the bed, when you can just enter, and exit. Speaking of entering, and exiting, Nate keeps asking me to move in with him. And even if we ignore the obvious reasons I've said no, no, and no, the truth is that, yes, his house is palatial, but there aren't many rooms. The entire downstairs is open except the bathroom. Upstairs, there's the bedroom in back, with two huge bathrooms and two enormous closets, and then a huge sitting room in front overlooking Comm. Ave., but there's no extra bedroom.

I can't believe I'm actually thinking about this, but here's the thing: now I hate East Boston. It feels like I'm stuck there, like I have this apartment to myself but it's supposed to be for me and Joanna—even with the coke cure, I can't stop thinking about Joanna. I look at those purple walls and think: that was for Joanna. I look at the sofas, the table, our art, and I can't stop thinking about how I thought everything was coming together. And then I look in Joanna's room, and there's nothing of hers except some dyed hair in the carpet.

Then there are the nights when I wake up thinking my father's in the other room, he and my mother are here to take me away. With Joanna I could laugh about the panic, but now there's just the panic. If I leave this place they'll have no way of tracking me, right? I won't even have the same phone number.

Nate keeps reminding me that we don't have the same hours,

we wouldn't even see each other that much, he travels so often for work and then I would have the place to myself. I keep saying there's no way I could live here without my own room, and that's where the conversation generally ends. But this time he acts like he just thought of a new idea: What about one of the rooms on the third floor?

The third floor. I tried the door once, but it was locked. I figured it was just storage. Apparently I was wrong—Nate says he just hasn't gotten around to renovating, and when he unlocks the door it does smell musty. But then he flicks the light switch and there's a gorgeous chandelier in the hallway, but a different kind, more old-fashioned, with copper flowers intertwined among the crystals. My office is in back, Nate says, but I don't use it much. Take a look at the rooms in the front.

Oh my God one of these rooms is perfect, with a chandelier like the one in the hallway but bigger, and a window alcove looking out over Comm. Ave. and the trees. Nate's saying he can have the floors redone—no, the floors are gorgeous. I'll get you a mattress like the one downstairs, he says, a king, I know you like that mattress. We can replace the wallpaper, what color would you like? The bathroom up here isn't much, of course you can keep yours downstairs. What do you think of that dresser?

Two weeks go by, and then the next time we go upstairs the door to the third floor has been removed, which is kind of disappointing because I was looking forward to having my own front door but oh well. When we get to my new room I feel like I'm in an advertisement for cosmopolitan living—the windows are open and the musty smell is gone, the wood floors are shining. The new wallpaper is just like the wallpaper downstairs, but the mustard color I picked out. Huge burgundy velvet curtains matching the burgundy comforter. So many pillows. Two velvet chairs in the window alcove that somehow match the color of the wall exactly, with the most gorgeous oval coffee table in between them. The dresser has been moved over to the other wall, beneath a mirror with a frame of copper flowers that must have been made at the same time as the chandelier. I open the closet door, and there's a little chair inside, a full-length mirror, clothes bars on both sides, filled with wooden hangers. I thought you'd like it, Nate is saying—I'd been meaning to freshen things up in here anyway.

As soon as Nate leaves the room, I step into the closet and close the door. Even the lighting in here is amazing—oh my God there's a tiny chandelier, like the ones in Nate's bedroom. I sit down on the chair and realize it's facing a little vanity—I've never had a vanity before, I open it up and stare in the mirror. And then I do another line.

ETERNITY

Joey says she wants this to be the best day of her life, which sounds like a lot of pressure but she says listen, I only turn twenty-one once. It better be fabulous.

Of course we're starting by doing a bunch of coke, Joey's treat, and then we're going to drive out to the Burlington Mall with Avery so we can check out the scene in men's underwear at Filene's. I still don't believe Polly works there, but Joey called the store right after she heard the gossip from Elana so I guess we'll see. The original plan was to do ecstasy first, but then Joey said ecstasy would have to wait until later, I'm not sure why but it's her birthday so I'm not complaining.

Speaking of Avery, ever since she apologized when Joey and I ran into her at Moka, it's like we're best friends or something. At first she just said I'm sorry, but I said sorry for what? She said I'm sorry for judging you. And I said judging me for what? And she said you know. And I said no, I don't know. And she said I'm sorry for judging you for being an escort. Everyone has to make a living.

Okay, and what made you realize that?

I don't know what I'm doing next semester—I'm failing out of school. Maybe I'll be doing the same thing as you. Or Joey.

Or Joey?

You know, selling drugs.

Oh, right—selling drugs.

I know sometimes I act like a rich bitch, but my parents don't really have any money.

What about the Mercedes?

My father runs an auto repair shop—he got it when someone couldn't afford to pay. Don't tell Joey this, but all my clothes— I'm a klepto.

Well, don't tell Joey this, but that bitch wears the same raincoat all year 'round.

You mean the trench? It's Burberry.

Anyway, after the Burlington Coat Factory, our next destination is Bertucci's—yes, Joey might be losing it, because she said she wanted to pick a restaurant where we both could eat. Then she asked if I wanted to look for Joanna after we find Polly. She said she wanted to do something for me. But what about Avery?

Avery wants to do ecstasy. Well, that's easy. We'll do ecstasy at the palace—Nate's out of town for the weekend. So here's the plan: Filene's in Burlington, Joanna in JP, Heavy-Handed Wendy at Bertucci's, ecstasy at the palace, the Loft, the Jacuzzi, sunrise on the Esplanade. Yes, this certainly is Joey's magical twenty-one, but is she ready for her first drink?

By the time we get to Filene's, we're already flying off our asses. Maternity, eternity—'cause you're ugly forever. Finally we get to men's underwear. But where can I find a bedazzled zebra-print metallic thong? Joey says this place isn't that sophisticated, but then Avery spots Polly over by the pajamas, and we step behind Calvin Klein.

We had all these plans. Joey wanted to go up and ask if there was a sale on shit-stained panties. But now we're all standing still like mannequins. Coked-out underwear mannequins.

Finally Joey pulls my hand, and then I reach for Avery's, and we head in Polly's direction—so now we're the Three Musketeers. Or Charlie's Angels. Polly doesn't see us until we get to the register, and even then it's like we're miles away.

Joey says Paul, what are you doing here?

Polly's ears get all red, and I can't tell if she's angry or scared. The suit she's wearing is like seven sizes too big. I'm so high I'm not even sure it's her. She says you have to leave, or I'm calling security.

Security for what, I say. I'm just looking for shit-stained panties.

I can't believe I just said that. It's not even my line.

Polly picks up the phone, and I say Ghostbusters, Ghostbusters on line two. Miami Vice, it's the Golden Girls. And then I'm laughing my ass off, damn this coke is good but Joey is in a different world, yelling are we dead to you? Are we fucking dead to you? Her jaw is so tense you can see the veins on the side of her face, dark circles under her eyes in spite of all the Dermablend. I've never seen her get this dramatic about something that matters.

Polly puts the phone down. She walks to the back of the store like she's heading to the dressing room but switches directions and goes through a different door. There's some big guy in an even bigger suit coming toward us saying can I help you gentlemen? And Avery says I'm sorry sir, but can you show us the way to men's underwear?

She's brilliant under pressure. Thank you, sir, she's saying, like she's British royalty. And the guy smiles like he actually believes her.

What should we do now? Yes, the bathroom for another bump, this is a nice bathroom, how do you tell the difference between granite and marble? Back outside into the largest parking lot on earth, and Avery starts pulling things out of her pockets. Polo ties, five or six of them. Oh, she really is a klepto—that's cute. Which one do you want, birthday girl, she says, and Joey says I'll take the one with the enema pattern.

Back to normal, I guess. We smoke some pot in the car and then we're on our way to JP and we get there way before Joanna's meeting's done so should we go to Five Seasons for a snack? I know you don't like vegan food, but it's right there. Look, Joey, it's snowing—it's snowing for your birthday. See, there's a reason it's been so cold lately. The first snow of the season, for your magical twenty-one. But Joey doesn't like snow—how could anyone not like snow?

Anyway, we get back outside after splitting a tempeh appetizer that's so good it tastes like caramel, and the snow's actually starting to stick so I'm jumping up and down, I'm jumping up and down for the snow. Joey, are you having fun on your birthday?

Yes, I just love freezing to death.

We get to the place where all the smokers are standing outside and this must be the right meeting, but I don't see Joanna—let's just keep walking. Joey stops to stare, I wonder why she's so invested.

That's when I recognize Joanna's coat—the army green parka we got at Dollar-A-Pound, or not Dollar-A-Pound but the store upstairs, what the hell is that store called? I recognize Joanna's jacket because of the bleach stain on the back, and for a second I get excited, like maybe we can rescue her. But then she turns around, and Joanna, this is horrible—she's wearing gold hoop earrings and a baseball cap. Red lipstick that matches the red in the cap. She's right here, and she's gone. I hope Joey doesn't notice anything.

Let's go, I say, and we start walking again in the snow, yes the snow, just pay attention to the snow, oh how I love the snow. When we get to the car, I can do another bump.

Except there's someone coming toward us, smiling in that way that's so fake it must hurt her face. Alex, she says, Alexander?

Excuse me?

Tina, she says, and she holds out her hand like I'm going to shake it. I didn't expect her to be wearing makeup.

I look over at the meeting, or what's left of it—I don't see Joanna anymore. Joey and Avery are already in the car with the motor running.

I wanted to introduce myself, Tina says, because I know you've meant a lot to Joanna. I wanted to let you know that it's not healthy for her to see you right now. It's not good for her recovery.

Joey's out of the car now. Front or back seat, she says, as Tina holds out her hand again and I turn away.

I told you she was using you, Joey says. She was using you, and now she's using that bull dyke. Why don't you get in the back seat?

Joey passes back the vial, but now I'm too wired. All I can think about is Joanna's art, I have to get rid of Joanna's art.

Can we stop by my place, I say.

Whatever you want, Joey says. She's never said that before.

Are you okay, Avery asks. He's never asked me that.

We get to the palace, and Joey and Avery wait in the car. It's still weird to walk right in like I live here. I mean I live here, and it's weird. When I get to my room, I grab a bottle of Valium and the portfolio of Joanna's art. All of it arranged so carefully, sheets of paper in between each piece so that nothing smudges. Then I look outside at the snow coming down on Comm. Ave., and it's a movie just waiting to happen.

That was fast, Joey says—we didn't even have time to do another bump. What's up with the portfolio?

It's Joanna's art.

Oh, this is getting good.

Let's go to the Fens.

Even better.

Do you think we can start a fire in the snow?

If we get lighter fluid.

Avery, can we stop for lighter fluid? And water. A couple gallons, so we can put out the fire.

We get to the Fens, and I don't know what I was thinking— the snow is coming down way too fast to start a fire. But I have a new idea: a ritual. Joanna always loved rituals.

Joey hands me the vial, and I do two huge bumps, white on white. We get out of the car and slide down the hill—everything is glowing, this is our own sparkling world. You can see right through the reeds—there's so much light, even though it's dark.

We walk to the clearing where usually you can look out at

the water, but now it's snow over ice. This is a ritual, I say. A coked-out ritual. Let's just see if Medusa doesn't turn to stone.

Or freeze to death, Joey says.

Medusa Oblongata. That's the first one. I read the title, and look at all the layers of color and pain, then I hold it out in the falling snow to get it wet, crumple it into a ball, pack it dense-ly with snow. Take the snowball art and throw it out onto the frozen water. Avery takes Medusa Fermata. Joey, Medusa Desiderata. And then I make Medusa Stigmata, Medusa Tomato Insalata, and Medusa Carne Asada into one big mess. I haven't thrown snowballs since childhood. Medusa Yada Yada, Medusa Piñata, Medusa Regatta.

I'm getting cold, Joey says. Really cold. Medusa Dada, Medusa Messiah. Medusa Matzo—and this is Medusa in reverse: when the ice melts, everything will be gone.

Someone's watching from the bridge so I wave. No one ever waves back. It's harder to get up the hill than it was to get down, and when we finally reach the car I realize I'm thirsty, really thirsty, good thing we have all this water—Joey is warming his hands under the heater vents, I can't believe she wasn't wearing gloves. We smoke more pot, and when we get to Bertucci's it feels so festive—something about the snow, and all this brick, and these windows. There's a full band playing jazz standards, no Heavy-Handed Wendy in sight but these cocktails are still the answer. Whoever invented cocktails should get the lifetime achievement award.

Spinach, Joey says, I know you like spinach. Artichokes, I say—Polly's favorite. Avery says extra cheese—oops. Joey says broccoli, to fight cancer. I say sun-dried tomatoes—Joanna's favorite. Joey says stop it with Joanna and Polly. And I say no, it's a ritual. When we eat those sun-dried tomatoes, and those artichokes, it'll all go right into our shit.

Now the band is playing "Will You Still Love Me Tomorrow" and Joey starts singing along. Everyone looks over. We look back.

After dinner, it's a winter wonderland outside—there must be six inches of snow already. Good thing Avery's Mercedes has four-wheel drive. We get to Ecstasy Unlimited, and Joey says it's her treat, she'll just go upstairs, Juniper and Sage are out of town.

But it's your birthday, Avery says, and I nod my head.

Joey says don't worry, I made $15,000 last month. So she gets out, and while we're waiting Avery asks me if I think Joey's lying.

I don't know. Fifteen thousand sounds a bit over the top. I only make two thousand. But I guess I do get free housing. And groceries. Not to mention that bottomless liquor cabinet.

Avery wants to know if I like my sugar daddy—I don't think I've ever called him that. She says is he attractive—are you kidding?

We get to the palace, and it's fun having guests here. I open the liquor cabinet and the girls look around while I go upstairs to take a shower. I'm kind of drunk, how did I get this drunk? It must be the Valium. After the shower, I go downstairs in my robe, and Joey says that's what you're wearing to the Loft? She and Avery are watching something on TV.

Joey says Alexa, it's better than *Cats*.

And Avery says no, bitches, it is *Cats*.

There's Joey's mirror on the table, covered in white powder. This is going to be a messy night. It already is a messy night, and we've barely started. I do a line and sit down to watch—blue light Jazzercise whisker fetish gymnastics playoffs.

Joey says let's do the ecstasy as soon as this is over, okay? Ecstasy for *Cats*, meow. I go upstairs to get dressed, can't decide what to wear—the skirt that looks like a carpet, with the tulip tights? Okay, with the blue sheer shirt, silver phone cords wrapped around my arms and then the pipe-clamp bracelets. What should I do with my hair? Something different. Maybe I'll spike up the back—yes, yes, a halo of yellow behind the purple and green—perfect. I go downstairs, and Joey says look, snatch attack.

She's just trying to annoy me, but I'm going to ignore her, because it's her birthday.

Avery's wearing a shirt I haven't seen before, some pink silk thing with puffy sleeves like a troubadour, and she says girl, we match.

At least the TV's off. Joey hands us our magic capsules, and we toast with Nate's crystal glasses. To the birthday girl, for bringing so much ecstasy into our lives!

And snatch, Avery says. I guess I shouldn't leave the two of them alone.

But it's already 1:30, how did that happen? Two o'clock and we're supposed to be on our way, we're going to make it to the Loft on time for once. We open the door and wow, so much snow, and then there's that wind. We go back inside, so I can get another scarf. Good thing Joey isn't wearing heels. I'll never wear heels again, she keeps saying.

We manage to get a cab on Boylston, and when we get to the Loft we tell them it's Joey's birthday but they're not impressed. Avery pays—she says it's the least I can do for you two snatches. We shake off our coats at the bottom of the stairs before heading up to say hi to Michael Sheehan in the DJ booth, I think he says he likes my outfit.

Oh, these lights, I never noticed these lights before. I look at Joey and her eyes are huge. The beat is pounding, a big drumroll, and then wait, "She works up the block, she lives up the block."

It's your song.

It is my song.

Avery's actually a pretty good dancer—she stays in the same place but really shakes out her head and she knows how to turn at just the right time like we're magnetic sensors and the song is going double-speed until it's stuck on "Eternity, Eternity, Eternity, Eternity ..."—oh my God it is eternity and everyone is shrieking because we all know what's next except it doesn't happen because Michael Fucking Sheehan goes right into the whistling song, oh that bitch is cunt, I can't believe I just said that but I'll say it again, okay? Listen. "Just whistle just whistle just whistle," I don't think I've heard that whistle on so many levels before, like it's a whole room full of whistles and then, wait, there it is, just when we're least expecting it: "Because you're ugly forever."

And just when I fling it to the floor I'm thinking how does Michael Fucking Sheehan make everything shake like a heavenly heart I mean heart attack because now there's nowhere to move, where did all these people come from but I can't take a break while the music is this good so I step to the side and shake it out with the lights all over my face while I ask everyone's favorite twenty-one-year-old coke dealer what's going on? Yes, she says, yes, Alexa, yes.

Now I have to push to get back on the dance floor, and when I get to Avery she pulls me close, that look in her eyes into my eyes and I know it's the drugs and it's worth it, honey, anything is worth these drugs, I mean anything. Now the music is back to bitch queen madness and I'm trying to clear some space, all these sweaty shirtless muscle boys with their shiny chests and I can't decide if it's the grossest or the hottest thing I've ever seen, and Joey's trying to part the crowd just as the drums really start to pound the floor I mean the floor was shaking before but now it's all these feet and my head in the lights yes the lights oh the lights and Avery grabs me from behind to try and grind until I twirl right around her, into someone else's arms, someone who says ooh girl and then the beats get so layered that the only thing I can do is jump in the air with my special kick, fling myself to the ground and around, good thing I didn't hit anyone, and when I stand back up I know I did it right because there's even some muscle queen shaking her finger like bitch better work, work and work and work, and then Joey is pulling me and Avery through the crowd and into the hallway where there's a flood of people trying to get up the stairs, but where are we going, I didn't realize there was a third floor. Wait, it's slippery, watch out, and there's Jon B. up top, sticking out her tongue, and, okay, yes, these are our stairs, take them.

I don't remember it ever being this crowded before, I guess that's what happens after they get shut down. Someone's pushing to get to Joey—bleached hair, Versace T-shirt, arched eyebrows—of course, Joey says, holds out her hand, the exchange, and then we're finally there, up at the top, walking right out into the snowy sky where Jeannine rises up above, and if we could keep walking we would walk right into that window, look, the one that's orange, look. And someone's yelling shit, shit I just broke my ankle, laughing really laughing it's like some strange snowy village up here and I can't help it, I'm twirling around and then I slip and someone catches me, we're all slipping and Joey says do you need anything? Oh honey, no, no, I don't need anything, I don't need anything, I don't need anything at all.

And someone's saying happy birthday, Mama snatch. Happy snatchy birthday. Avery, of course, and I'm leaning against the wall so I can get a closer look at all the lights in the sky with the snow in my face and when I turn back around there's some woman wearing fur, is that really fur, and she's saying whose birthday? And Avery says hers, and the woman looks at me and says it's my birthday too, how old are you? And Joey says do you need anything?

But it's getting cold out here so I head back downstairs and into the heat, pushing through the crowd and into "gonna drop a house, drop a house, drop a house—gonna drop a house" right into the laser light stream as the song says "on that bitch." And are those lights new, I don't remember that pattern before, like a tunnel into your head, and some queen is yelling work, and Sage and Juniper are on the sides in their platforms with silver fans and oh I love these messes and then Joey's waving to me from the side so I go over and she says they're about to close.

What do you mean they're about to close?

I mean they're about to close.

What time is it?

Four thirty. They're closing early. The fire department. Trust me.

Wait—listen.

And everybody's screaming as the horns go into air-raid sirens go into nothing but a clack clack racquet attack-it and "10,000 screaming, 10,000 screaming, 10,000 screaming" and I don't know what Michael is mixing this with but it's the best it's ever been and we all know it, we all know it's the best it's ever been. Until the music stops. And Joey already has my coat, how did she get my coat? And Avery, when did they sneak off? We wave goodbye to Michael and the world and then head downstairs—oh, we forgot to say hi to Richie, who's already packing up her equipment, and she says are you girls leaving so early?

Outside—oh, right, the snow the snow the snow and the snow, can you believe it, the snow. Joey's already up ahead so we have to run to catch up except oh no, Avery, oh no, are you okay?

She slipped, but the snow caught her. And Joey says sorry, I needed to get away, there was someone, there was someone.

But are you having a good birthday?

Oh, it's fabulous, Alexa, it's fabulous—I can't wait. For the Jacuzzi.

Somehow it helps us stay warm just to think about it. I've got one scarf around my neck and the other wrapped around my head, but the snow is still coming in and eventually it gets too hard to walk on the sidewalk so we step into the street, no cabs around. Don't fall, don't fall. Okay. Walk. And walk. Turn. Slide. Glide. And walk. And fall. Close your eyes, it's a big surprise.

Finally we get to the house, shaking off our coats and, wait, did you see that? Did you see that chandelier? Oh, the lights here are amazing. I don't ever want to leave. Except maybe to go to the Loft. Wait, let me take your coats—let me take your coats. Do you need anything?

Joey says do you have any porn?

Porn?

Yes, porn.

Do I have any porn? I don't know. What about *Cats*?

Cats, Joey says—let's watch *Cats.*

I'll go upstairs and run the water.

Yes, I think, as I throw my clothes into the laundry, just enough time to take a shower, oh, a shower, yes, the cold tiles warming under my feet and the way the light sparkles on the glass door, look, little rainbows. And oh my body, this body, the smell of my sweat, I love the smell of my sweat, don't tell anyone, they're right when they say soft skin. Water in my nose, chlorine, this peppermint soap, oh, I love this peppermint soap, I wish I could eat it.

But, wait, I'm supposed to be running the water for a bath, right, a bath. Let me adjust the lights—up, or down? Or up?

Downstairs I sit on the sofa with the girls. Avery says oh, your robe. So soft. I touch her hand: Oh.

Joey says wait, it's almost the ending.

I go in the kitchen—I love this kitchen. Does anyone want orange juice? Vitamin C. Yes, vitamin C. Wait, did they hear me? Orange juice, does anyone want orange juice?

Oh, the bath—I rush upstairs and the bubbles are spilling over the edge—it's fun to watch them on their journey, pop. Pop. I guess the drain prevents the rest of the water from escaping and it smells so good in here, strawberry. I get back downstairs just as Joey is pressing off on the remote control. What music? What music should we play? Moby, *Everything Is Wrong*? No, that doesn't sound right. Moby, *Ambient*? That might be too quiet. Pussy Tourette. You love Pussy Tourette.

Pussy Tourette. *In Hi-Fi.*

Let's bring the orange juice upstairs. Towels—let me get more towels.

I'm first in the tub because all I need to do is throw my robe on the hook, good planning. I didn't notice the flowers on Avery's shirt before, where were they hiding? She's looking at me in that way again, like that time she came in the shower, I remember that, it was fun. Maybe I'm looking at her in that way too.

When Joey takes off her clothes, it's scary—I can't believe how skinny she is, you can see all of her ribs, all of them. I guess I'm staring, because Joey says what, my dick isn't big enough? And then she jumps in the tub and I turn the jets on—oh, the jets.

I lean back and close my eyes. Of course Avery's saying twat twat twat twat twat, but at least it's in the music and she's rubbing my foot, which kind of tickles but feels good too and whoever thought of putting a big circular tub in here must've been on ecstasy. Joey says French bitch French bitch French bitch—she knows all the words, but those are her favorites. And then my other foot, and it's amazing how each toe leads directly to a different part of my head and then up, up, up into the sky and when I open my eyes I realize Avery's rubbing one foot and Joey the other and I close my eyes again and say let's sit together. So then I'm in the middle and there's all this skin and even when we're all still there's some part moving. And maybe it's too much the way I can feel Avery's eyes through his skin so I say let's switch places, birthday girl in the middle.

Joey is so tiny between me and Avery and I can still feel Avery's breath like it goes through Joey's body. And the song is all about seventy dollars, "ain't gonna get you diamond rings," seventy dollars, but Joey isn't singing anymore she's just breathing really deep.

Seventy dollars, right, and the punch line is that it'll buy you a man, seventy dollars, a man, but we're all a little more expensive than that. Maybe not all the time. And Joey says oh, this is what I've always wanted. Oh my God she's crying, Joey Severe is crying, and I look at Avery. He starts rubbing Joey's back so that's what I do too, our hands meeting in the middle and then I kiss Joey on the cheek, and then Avery kisses her on the other cheek, and then I start licking Joey's face like a puppy and she's giggling, saying what, what are you doing, and now I'm making a slurping sound and Joey's still giggling and then Avery kisses my cheek so I kiss his cheek, and then Joey's, and Joey says: I think I'm starting to crash.

So then we sit up on the side of the tub, with our feet still in the water, and Joey says oh, wait a minute, oh, and she stands up to reach for something. She has so many different tool belts it's like she's in the military but it's drugs not bombs. That would be a good chant. Joey dries her hands with a towel, and then turns back to face us with a glass of orange juice in one hand and, no way, three more capsules in the other. I look at Avery. Avery's looking at the drugs.

I don't know if I want any more.

Joey says you have to, it's my birthday. So I open my mouth and she puts the capsule inside, I take the orange juice and swallow, here we go, Pussy Tourette. *In Hi-Fi.* I sit back in the tub. Avery grabs me from behind and Joey says you're right, I was jealous. I never admitted it, but I was jealous.

And I say birthday girl in the middle again, and then we sit there like that until the water gets cold. Then Joey goes into Nate's room to press play again on the music, she wants to hear the last song another time and I tell her there's a repeat button, we can just play it over and over. It's not Pussy Tourette who sings this one it's some woman who must be an opera singer saying "I hope he's not a fag, I hope he's not a drag queen. I hope he's not a queer, I hope he's not a Miss Thing," and when she says Miss Thing she rolls it into her throat and we're all saying Miss Thing, Miss Thing—Miss Thing, Miss Thing. That's the story of our lives, right? Until suddenly it's like the whole room is pulsating and is that my heart or my head or my stomach and oh, I need to shit, good thing my bathroom is right across the hall and when I open my eyes I realize I'm covered in sweat, no it's not sweat it's just the water from the tub, we filled it up again. And when I get back from shitting Joey and Avery are drying off and Joey says: Act Two, the Esplanade.

Now we're in my room. So soft, Avery says, petting the comforter and we need sunrise music, something with a drumroll. Oh, Armand is in the boom box, perfect. Avery's rolling naked on my bed so I lie down too, and then Joey—we're all still naked, but somehow it doesn't feel like we're naked it just feels like what's the point of clothes when you can feel this way? But put your hand on my chest, can you feel it? Can you feel it, Joey says, can you feel it can you feel it can you feel it. Should we get dressed, I say. Should we get dressed should we get dressed should we get dressed, Joey says, and I'm thinking about how we all take little parts of one another and is this what it means to love.

Oh, this closet—I love this closet. But I can't decide what to wear. Something soft. Joey wants a hat, so I hand her the one with blue and yellow and white flowers. Something warmer. Avery wants a scarf, maybe the red one with pompoms? Yes, pompoms.

Oh that horn that horn that horn on a boat in the distance and what is that sound between a yell and a clap and a monkey in a tree on the beach and someone breathing and then that horn again, no it's not a horn and not a siren except the way I need to shake out the shoulders into hips down to feet into ground flip around down to floor how did they make the floor so soft and witch, doctor, which doctor, witch doctor, doctor, Doctor Armand Van Helden.

Okay, shake, shake, shake your hips downstairs, back up, down, down back up and down, down, down, back up and down and I didn't like this song before, the second one, but honey this was made for stairs, oh, the stairs, the rattle, repeat, beat, repeat, what are they saying, do you know what they're saying, maybe they're saying it's all about the stairs, this song was made for the stairs, but do they call it tribal because of those African-sounding drums and isn't that fucked up but wait, the drums, oh, the drums, please more drums and oh, orange juice, that's what we need, orange juice.

Sunglasses? Do we need sunglasses? Let me get my sunglasses purse. But do you need gloves? It's cold out, remember, it's cold.

Oh my God it's so bright—are you sure we're ready? Comm. Ave. in the snow and it takes a while to get to the Esplanade even though it's right here, I mean it's usually right here but it's taking a while in the snow. But then we're walking up onto the bridge over Storrow Drive, up, up, up into the trees, don't slip, and then we turn and there isn't any water it's white all the way to Cambridge. Cross the drawbridge over the moat and look, look at those willows made of gold, are those branches or leaves? Then those old trees so worn out they're growing sideways, over-turned roots stretching out to sky, bark coated in white, irides-cent white, pure white, and we're ducking underneath to reach the other side. No, don't walk too far, that's the water, it's frozen, you'll fall in.

Your hair, Avery says.

I'm dying, Joey says. Do you want any orange juice? I'm dying. I'm dying for orange juice, thank you. Avery?

Yes, please. Pretty please. Pretty please with sugar on top. Pretty please with sugar on top and a hot fudge sundae. Pretty please with sugar on top and—oh, it's so good. Look at the colors.

Your eyes aren't open.

Yes they are. There's a head inside my head.

Oh my God that's brilliant. Joey, close your eyes, close your eyes. And then look, look at the snow, it's turning pink, we could ski to MIT. I don't know how to ski. That building, I've never seen that building before, is that the Jefferson Memorial? We could ski to the Jefferson Memorial. Wait, did you hear that? Birds, I hear birds. Look, tiny birds, chirping, what are those tiny birds doing here in the snow, chirping? I love those birds—look how cute they are. Oh, look how cute those birds are. Joey, are you cold? You look cold. You're shivering. I told you it was cold out, it's winter. Avery and I can warm you up. You want to go back already? Okay, it's your birthday, whatever you want. Let's turn around, back over the moat, onto the next bridge, what do they call this bridge, the bridge to the bridge? I think it needs a name. Look down there, cars. Cars are so loud. Oh, brick, look at all that brick, there's a lot of brick in Boston. I like the white one, with the green windows—who do you think lives there? I live in a white one. Where are we going? Store 24? I love Store 24.

This is a long walk, but eventually we get there and oh, it's so warm, yes, my head, we should start a club here, Club 24. Do you think we could get Michael Sheehan to DJ? Or Richie Rich. Look at that, that blueberry, strawberry, orange berry. How does it work? Joey, are you getting that microwave pizza? I don't think you should chew on the box, you have to warm it up first.

Oh.

Avery has Life Savers. See, she says, see. Life. Savers.

Should I eat something? What should I eat? Maybe a hot pretzel. Too dry. Oh, tea. Let's go home and have tea. Sunglasses, don't forget your sunglasses.

When we get back to the house, it's like there's someone there waiting for us. But it's us. Joey's eating the pizza with his hands, and Avery and I are staring. It's fun to watch like this is the zoo. But we treat our animals as good as humans. See— microwave pizza. We're at the dining room table. I'm making sure we use placemats. Place. Mats. I open the curtains, I thought they were already open but I guess someone closed them. Joey, do you need a napkin? This orange juice is even better than the other orange juice.

Avery's eating candy, and I can hear a soft whistle in the distance, way in the distance but it gets closer and closer until it's some kind of shrieking late-night DJ magic and I close my eyes, this is good.

Alexa, the teakettle.

Oh, the teakettle.

I'm dying, Joey says.

Do you want more tea?

Yes. The fruity kind.

We sit down together with our white mugs and liquid rubies

and I'm trying not to breathe so fast. Do you like Xanax better or Valium? I wish we could go dancing. Avery?

Do you have more pot?

Oh, pot—I knew I could make you into a pothead. But we have to go outside for that. I guess we could go in my bedroom and open the window all the way. No, that's too obvious. Okay, just this once. Oh, the bath—let's get back in the bath.

Avery's laughing again, and I can feel my head leaning back. Joey doesn't want any pot. Are you sure? It really brings back the X.

I already drank the orange juice.

What's next, birthday girl? A bath, do you want to take a bath? Or a nap? I wish we could go dancing. Should I put music on? What time is it? Let's take a shower, and then go somewhere. Yes, let's take a shower together, in my bathroom, upstairs. There are three separate showerheads.

You two go ahead, I think I'm going to walk home.

No, no—it's your birthday. We'll come with you.

No, I'll walk home, and meet you there.

Are you okay?

Maybe I'll take a cab. Do you need anything?

I don't need anything—I'm so high I can't believe it. Avery?

I don't know. I don't know. I'm so high I don't know.

Joey leaves, and Avery and I look at one another. I'm chewing on my tongue—Avery, do you have any gum? I forgot to get gum. Avery's giving me that look and then he leans forward and sticks his tongue in my mouth and I start chewing on it like gum, this is kind of good, I like the flavor. And then Avery grabs my head, and my tongue pushes into his throat and I can feel him breathing so I'm trying to get the rhythm right—inhale, exhale, inhale, exhale exhale, inhale, exhale, inhale inhale and I'm grabbing his head, sucking his tongue into my throat and Life Savers, yum, lime, I almost forgot about lime but then I have to pull back because I'm choking. And Avery takes my hand and says are you okay? She looks so worried.

Am I okay? I don't know—I don't know I don't know I don't know. And this time Avery sticks out his tongue before it gets to my mouth so I grab his cheeks and hold him right in front of my face, licking his tongue in a circle and then down to chin, stubble, neck, ear, the other ear, let's go upstairs.

In the bathroom I'm unbuttoning his shirt and he's pulling off my sweater, but wait, one at a time. Who goes first? Should we flip a coin? I don't have a coin. Kiss me again.

I love your eyes, Avery says. I always wanted blue eyes. I tried blue contacts in high school but everyone said I was trying to be white. I wasn't trying to be white, I am white. I'm white, and I'm black, and I can't think of the punch line. Why is everyone so stupid and racist? I've never said that before.

Never?

No, but I've thought it.

Joey thought you were Asian.

I told him I was Asian. Can I take off your pants?

Let's do it at the same time. Okay, first the button. Now, unzip. Now, start to pull down. Okay, bend your knees. Slowly. Okay, let your pants fall to the floor. Kiss me. Step forward. Yes, we did it.

What about underwear?

Let's switch. Turn around. Okay, hand me yours and I'll hand you mine. Turn around again.

You look good in briefs.

You look good in boxer briefs.

I feel fat.

You're not fat. You're really hot. Can I put my hands in your underwear?

Can I put my hands in yours? I mean mine. Can I hold you from behind? I remember you liked that last time. See. Your breathing. That's the first thing. And then you lean back. I could hold you like this forever. I just want to keep holding you.

Let's go in my room. Here, hold my hand. Oh, let me pull the curtains shut. We don't want everyone to see.

I want everyone to see.

That's hot. That's really hot.

Except.

I know. Don't worry. The curtains are shut. Should we turn the light on?

Yes. I want to see you. Lie down. I want to give you a massage. Oh, this comforter is so soft.

I know. But should we pull it back? And get under the covers?

Here. You lean back. You lean back, and I'll sit on top of you.

You want me to lean back? Can I tell you something?

Sure.

I think I'm getting hard.

I don't think I'm going to get hard. I'm too high.

That's okay. I just wanted you to know. We don't have to do anything.

I want to. I really want to. Let me sit on your lap. Can I sit on your lap?

Can I tell you something?

What?

I really want to fuck you.

Oh.

I don't have to. I don't have to fuck you.

How did you get so hard? How did you get so hard on X?

It's because of you. It's because you're so hot.

Do you think you'll stay hard? I mean do you think you'll stay hard in a condom? I get nervous. I get nervous because.

Because what?

I don't want to ruin it.

You won't. You can't. You can't ruin it. Kiss me. Kiss me again.

I get nervous because of my father. Do you know what I mean?

I know what you mean.

Are you sure?

Joey told me. Joey told me about your father. It's okay.

What time is it?

Ten thirty. Ten thirty in the morning. Is your clock right?

It's thirty-two minutes fast.

Then we have an extra thirty-two minutes. Do you want to take a shower? Or maybe a bath. Should we take a shower or a bath?

We took a bath earlier.

Was that today?

Do you want to smoke pot first?

Oh, yes, pot. You're turning into a pothead. Wait—we can't open the blinds because it's light out. We can't smoke with the windows closed. Should we wait until we get to Joey's? Or, okay—how about this? We can blow the smoke into the washing machine, and then before it comes out, we'll run the laundry. Do you think that would work? Or, never mind—let's just smoke in Nate's office in back, but make sure you lean your head all the way out the window, okay?

Okay. I just need a little bit. I might be crashing.

Don't say that.

What?

Don't say you might be crashing. Let's smoke some pot, and then you'll be fine.

Do you have any coke?

I don't want coke right now, do you?

I was just thinking about it, because I'm always thinking about it.

Always?

I don't know.

Do you do a lot of coke?

The same as you. Or Joey.

Joey does a lot more than me. I do coke every day, but not a lot. Except when I'm with Joey.

Me too. Like coffee. Maybe a gram a day. Except when I'm with Joey.

A gram a day? That's a lot.

Do you think so?

I don't know. Let's take a shower. Here, you go first, you look cold. I'll call Joey, and tell her we're running late.

I'll miss you.

I'll miss you too.

Can I ask you something?

What is it?

Can I borrow a shirt? Mine's all sweaty.

Oh, yes, let me pick something out for you. How about a sweater? Something soft. Something really soft.

When we finally get to Joey's, she opens the door with a kazoo in her mouth. Happy birthday, happy birthday, happy birthday—me, she says, and she looks totally crazed. ABBA's playing in the background. Oh, oh, Joey says—I forgot. Alexa's here. I forgot. And she rushes over to the stereo before I have time to say it's okay, it's your birthday, I can deal with ABBA, but then she switches it to something so good it makes the whole room vibrate. What is this?

Richie, she says, Richie Rich. The one and only. Sure, we all know about the one in New York with bleached hair and roller skates but that cunt doesn't have those fabulous cheeks. Our Richie has those cheeks. She's cheeky and she can spin. Boston's one and only.

Girls, Joey says, take off your coats. Make yourselves comfortable. A lot has happened since you've been gone. A lot. Has. Happened. First of all, another hit. Another hit of ecstasy. Ecstasy you know me as—sextasy. Oh—who has a bigger cock? Tell me, who has a bigger cock? Wait—wait—don't tell me, Miss

Alexa. I have a ruler. I have a ruler here. Somewhere. I want to know. Everyone wants to know. The whole world wants to know. Who. Has. A. Bigger. Cock. Hold on—I need to vomit my guts out. I need to vomit my guts out again. I'll be right back.

Avery reaches for my hand. Joey's clothes are piled up on the floor, suitcases on the sofa. Where do we sit? Joey comes back from the bathroom.

Much better. Much, much better. I shouldn't have eaten that pizza. Now, where was I? Right—which one's the man, and which one's the woman? Wait, wait, let me guess—all you did was bump pussies. Scratch and sniff. Go ahead—say it. The world is waiting. *National Enquirer. Star. National Lampoon's Vacation.* Pussy Tourette says, "He drives a Karmann Ghia," but I say the world can't wait for pussy. Whose snatch smells like donuts, and whose snatch smells like skunk? Never mind. You're both bottoms. Come in the bedroom. On the left table, Marge Simpson's ketamine connection. On the right table, cuckoo for Cocoa Puffs old-school blow school. Blow, bitches it's time to blow—it's time to blow your fucking hearts out. It's my birthday, and I'll cry if I want to. I'll cry if I fucking want to. Go ahead—sing it, sing it, sing it! Sing it, bitches, sing it for Miss Joey Severe. Joey Severina. Joey Sever Vivinia. Congratulations—Miss Alexa, don't play coy with me. You did the deed. How was it? Wait—wait. Don't tell me—don't tell me. First I need another line. No, really, I'm happy for you. I'm happy for you both. You're too smart for your own good, and he's too stupid. I'm sorry. I'm getting out of hand. I'm getting out of arm. I'm getting out of chest. I'm getting out of tits. I'm getting out of tits and ass. I'm getting out of sass. I'm getting out of grass. Grass. That's what's missing—did you bring the grass? Why didn't you say something before? You two take a walk down lovers' lane, and I will pause for a moment to catch my breath.

Avery does a line of coke, and when she looks at me she looks like Avery again, and I don't know what I mean exactly I mean maybe I'm just being mean.

And you? And you, Miss Alexa? What will it be? Cat tranquilizer, or Colombian couscous? Don't tell me you need to sleep—it's my birthday. You can't leave me. You can't leave me, yet.

I do a line of coke, and as soon as it hits my head I think shit, I just fucked up my high. So then I do some K. Better to balance it out. Avery's right behind me. Your turn, I say, and this time I like watching her eyes change.

We smoke pot. Joey gets a little calmer. The music is really good.

What's going on, Avery says.

What's going on, Joey says. What's. Going. On? Let me take you in the other room and show you.

Joey leads us into the kitchen. The whole table is filled with vials—this really is a drugstore.

Okay, Joey says. Everything is set up. I counted it. Ninety-four vials. Thirty quarters. Forty-three halves. Twenty-one—no, twenty-two grams. That makes ninety-four. A hundred and twenty-five vials total. Thirty-one are empty. I bet you didn't know I was good at math. Do you see how I have it all arranged? Before, when all the vials were the same size, I had to go in the bathroom and take them out of my pocket to look. Now I can just feel with my fingers. That's what you'll do, you'll just feel with your fingers.

Alexacunt, Avarice, please pay attention. Pretend this is *Masterpiece Theatre. The Twilight Zone.* You are about to enter ... *Xanadu. The City of Lost Children. Pee-wee's Playhouse.* My name is Dawn Davenport. And I'm a shitkicker. And a thief. Or is it a thief and a shitkicker? Only John Waters knows. But back to business. Listen to my directions. Ask questions later. Wait, I'll be right back. I need another line.

Avery leans over and kisses me, just like that, the bitter taste in his mouth and I'm starting to feel the X again, or maybe it's the K, and then Joey comes back in.

Oh. I caught you. I caught you in the act. Did I mention I love it? Love. It. But, back to business. I'm a shitkicker and a thief. Ask questions later.

My name is Dawn Davenport, Avery giggles.

No, my name is Dawn Davenport. Okay, I explained the vials. Step two: this is my pager. You know how to work it, work it, work it you know I know you know you know how to work it. It's still in my name. Contract on the table. Pay with a money order, and no one will know. Same thing with the apartment. No one knows I'm leaving. Here are the spare keys. What else? What else? You've seen all the gadgets. Waist belt, ankle, shoulder, in case you want to hide anything. If you don't, you can use this one as a headband. Or a cock ring. If it's really big. What else? What else? Oh—how it works. You know that little cabinet door by the entrance, I know you thought that was for munchkins. But actually it leads right to the cabinet in my entryway—it was sealed when I moved in, but I fixed that. There's a bag of cat litter inside. Meow. Let me show you. See? Better than coffee grounds, someone might want coffee. You buzz them in downstairs, they replace that cat litter with the new cat litter. Oh—oh—you leave the money in the old one. Obviously, the drugs are in the new one. I mean the same one—you don't need to change it, unless you get a cat. You just open the door, and the drugs will be in a little bag inside the big bag. You never even see each other. I can't tell you whose idea it was, but it's flawless. Fabulous. Fierce. So I'm leaving you the business. It's a lot of money. A lot. Of money.

Questions, Joey is saying, questions—does anyone have questions?

Avery says are you telling us you don't want to sell anymore?

Ten points, ten points for my biggest customer.

And you want us to take over the business?

Ten points—tens across the board. Keep going, keep going.

But why?

Oh—a stumper. Let's go back in the bedroom. I need another line. Let's celebrate. It's my birthday. I'm two hundred and one. I'm making cocktails. I know you like orange juice. Does anyone want a cocktail? No, no—the real question: Does anyone need a cocktail?

We go in the kitchen—there's something buzzing, or is it my head. Joey says oh, oh—I have to flip the tape. Let's go in the other room. And she grabs her bottle of Absolut and takes a swig. Sorry, ladies, she says, I hope you don't mind backwash.

We follow Joey into the bedroom and she does another line of coke. I'm dying, she says.

You're not dying.

No, she says, that's where you're wrong, Miss Alexa. You're not usually wrong. For example, I am a racist, you were right about that. And I hate women. Most of the time. Except Traci Lords. And Betty White. And CeCe Peniston. This room is a mess. Let's go back in the kitchen and sit down. I'll make cocktails. What was I saying? Oh—I'm a liar. But I'm not lying right now. I have five T cells. That's right—five. You know what that means, Alexa—you're the activist. And Mother Teresa doesn't have a bed big enough for this bitch. I'm going home tomorrow. My parents are picking me up. But you both look so serious—I didn't mean to fuck up the party.

BETWEEN YOUR HEART
AND THE FABRIC

I would never have imagined reading this book with Nate, but he came home one night and I was sitting at the dining room table, sobbing. No, I'd already stopped sobbing—I was just looking at the wall. Or, not at the wall really, but in that direction—you know how you can look right at something, but you don't see it.

I was thinking about when I first heard about AIDS, maybe I was twelve and it was Rock Hudson in the *Enquirer* and I didn't even know who that was, a famous actor my mother said and the headline told me he died of AIDS.

Liberace too—pictures of him really scared me, I didn't know what to do with those pictures. I just knew that I was going to die, if anyone knew, knew about me, and they did know, so I knew I was going to die.

In *The Gifts of the Body*, the narrator is a home care worker for people dying of AIDS, and when I opened it up the first time I got scared because the writing was so simple and I wondered if all these deaths had changed Rebecca Brown's writing. When Nate asked what was wrong, I handed him the book and he said we should read it together.

So now I'm already crying again on page 2, which is numbered 4—the narrator's talking about leaving little surprises under the pillow of the person she's taking care of. Or rearranging his toys so the toys are kissing. "Rick loved surprises," Rebecca Brown writes.

And then, on the next page, Rick is on the floor, or no, I guess it's not the floor it's the futon in the living room where he's curled up in fetal position, writhing in pain. The narrator says to Rick: "I'm sorry you hurt so much," and I'm thinking about how much I hurt. How much everyone I've ever known hurts, or everyone I've ever known who's meant something to me, and what about the ones who act like they don't hurt, like nothing's affecting them at all, like Joey, look what happened to Joey.

And then the narrator does something that I can hardly believe. She gets on the futon with Rick. She gets on the futon and lies on her side and puts her arms around him as he's sweating and in pain.

I'm kind of relieved that I can still cry like this, in spite of the coke cure. I'm only on page 7, and this book already means so much to me. The home care worker is cleaning the apartment while Rick is in the hospital—she wants Rick to come home to a place that's soothing. She avoids the kitchen table, there's something she saw there and when we find out what it is, when I find out what it is, that's where I'm crying again.

Rick had gone out to get cinnamon rolls like he used to, after his lover died but before he'd also gotten sick. He'd gone out to choose the softest rolls, one for himself and one for the home care worker. And now he's in the hospital. The narrator closes her eyes and lowers her head toward the table and I'm thinking of tears, tears at this table with Nate and how he's still not looking up, which helps me not try to change anything and I wonder if he knows that.

"There's something about no one else knowing someone is

taking care of you," Rebecca Brown writes—if Mrs. Lindstrom pretends the attendant is just there on a visit, on a visit saying hi, maybe if she just pretends, all this can become pretend. I look at Nate again, and I wonder what we're pretending. Ever since I told him about Joey, he says he's not in the mood for sex so I cook dinner because Nate says he's trying to get healthy, though I'm sure he's eating bacon and eggs for breakfast, and a hamburger for lunch, but it's almost cute how he asks all these questions about my cooking and forgets everything I say. We sit down and talk like husband and wife or father and son or maybe just friends, that's the best part, when it actually feels like we're friends. Every now and then, Nate wants me to give him a massage, and then when I get hard he says oh, let me see that, and then he jerks me off until I come on his chest. And then I hate him again.

I should be reading this book with Avery, but he doesn't like reading, and anyway he said he didn't want to read a book about AIDS. But what about Joey, I asked, don't you want to think about Joey?

Joey's gone, Avery said—Joey's gone, and he's not coming back—what's there to think about now?

It's so surprising, when you cry and when you don't. The narrator tells Ed that he can check into the hospice and then leave if he wants to, even though she's never seen anyone leave. Is this an act of kindness? The narrator is so caring and detached, she feels so deeply for these people she only knows through their illness, and I wonder if this is what community means.

Ed turns down the hospice. He's enraged, making contra-dictory demands. He's a child, and an adult. He wants to have a garage sale. He wants the option to leave his house again on his own. The chapter is called "The Gift of Tears."

I'm getting used to the light of this chandelier. Nate is behind me, placing another cocktail to my right, thank you. I wonder if I want him to touch my shoulder, but then he doesn't.

I'm thinking about the way death brings you closer to childhood, does that mean into or away from pain? The way the narrator washes Carlos's hands, arms, armpits, feet. His innocence at experiencing touch, with and without its impli-cations. And then the fear—that's the childhood I remember. Can there ever be innocence with so much fear?

Mrs. Lindstrom, who asks the attendant to call her Con-nie—she seroconverted from a blood transfusion when she had a mastectomy. Before blood was tested for HIV. She has a gay son, Joe, who feels guilty because he thinks he should be the one dying—his mother never did anything wrong.

I'm thinking about this shame we all carry, the shame that means we deserve to die.

Connie, holding onto her routine and hoping that if she doesn't mention she can't eat, maybe she'll be able to. Ed says: "There won't be anyone left to remember us when we all die." And I wonder if that's already true. How Avery has taken Jo-ey's place at the clubs with all the different-sized vials, and no one even asks, no one even asks about Joey. We sit in his apartment, and it's like we're ghosts.

These people want so much. This attendant, she tries to provide what she can. Maybe more. "When the epidemic started there was a shorter time between when people got sick and when they died." That's a line that really gets me, because this isn't the beginning of the epidemic anymore, but one minute Joey was telling us—and I didn't believe her, I really didn't believe her, I thought it was some cruel joke. It's all frozen in my head now, like we're still standing on the Esplanade in the snow and Joey says: I'm dying. I'm dying. And the next day she went home to her parents' house in Brandywine, Delaware.

I thought we were going to visit. She told us we could visit. She told us there were castles there. I thought we were going to visit the castles.

I remember that queen who came to our house in San Francisco to look at a room, and she wanted to do touch healing on everyone. I was appalled. I saw her around a few times, and she always acted like we were really close, and at first I was annoyed but then I started to like seeing her. Then the next time I heard about her it was for her memorial.

Or Thomas who arranged all these candles on the bathtub before we had sex in the bath, and I was like what are you doing, we don't need candles. But he wanted it to be romantic. It was romantic. In six months he was dead.

I had one friend who went to every memorial he heard about, even for people he didn't know. But I didn't want to steal other people's grief. As if there was a limited amount. Now I wonder if I should have gone to all those memorials. Maybe reading this book with Nate at the dining room table is some kind of memorial, but what are we going to say when we're done?

"Like a bunch of ninety-five-year-olds watching their generation end." I close the book for a moment and drink the rest of my cocktail, and I notice Nate's shifted his body to the left, and I've shifted to the right, so we're not directly across from one another anymore.

What is a lie, and what isn't? Like when the narrator tells a new client that his former attendant misses him, even though she's never actually met that attendant. And when the new client says: I miss him too. That place between your heart and the fabric on your chest, the fabric on your chest and the world beyond.

The narrator learns that her supervisor is leaving. She's leaving because she's sick. Another of these moments that feels like a shock—a shock to the narrator, a shock to me at this table with Nate where I keep crying and he doesn't look up, except this time he does, just briefly, and then he reaches over for my hand and I reach for his, this gesture that happens so often in the book and maybe it feels nice here too. Although it's hard to reach that far across the table, I mean reach that far and keep reading at the same time. So I pull my hand back, softly, and I smile—Nate smiles too, and then we both go back to reading.

It's not that this book doesn't have flaws, it's just that there are so few of them. I'm getting to the end of my third cocktail, and there's that feeling in my head that must be chemical, the perfect combination of liquor and coke, invulnerability on ice. It's what I need to channel in order to fuck Nate—right now I could easily bend him over that white sofa. He would laugh in that drunk old guy way and say let's go upstairs.

Maybe I'll never have to do that again.

The book ends with Connie's death. The ending is nothing but sobs until I have to put the book down and go upstairs to piss, I've been holding it for too long. I study my face in the mirror—under my eyes there's a rash, and my lips are pressed up into a child's frown.

I can't decide whether I need a bump of coke, but I do one anyway, and then I wonder whether closing the book with the death of an old straight woman is dishonest. I go up to my room and lie on top of the velvet comforter and stare at the chandelier, floating in a way but also sinking. Eventually Nate comes upstairs and stands in my doorway. He looks like he's in shock. I sit up, and he sits down next to me on the bed. For a moment it feels like we're in the same place.

TOO SEXY

Avery calls me up and says Alexa, I figured it out.

You figured what out?

I figured it out, Alexa, I figured it out I figured it out I figured it out!

Honey, you are coked out of your mind.

Alexa, who isn't? But listen up, I know you're always talking about how everyone in Boston is totally apathetic and I'm like the worst example, I mean I don't even have a political bone in my body—I know I was a poli-sci major for like ten minutes but I didn't even know what was going on I thought poli-sci was science. Alexa, there are so many problems, so many problems and I know you know that I know I know I know, Alexa. But what was I saying, what was I saying? Oh—I still don't fucking know what's going on, but I thought of something we can do together— oh, maybe I shouldn't say it on the phone. Alexa, it's true, I have to wait at the haunted house for a few deliveries, but I'll tell you my idea later, when I see you. I think you'll like it. I think you'll really like it. Really really. I'm sure. I'm really sure. Okay?

Later, Avery and I are at Bertucci's and she looks around to make sure no one's paying attention and then says listen, Alexa, listen: Remember when we went to Star Market last night to get contact lens solution? Yes, last night, that was last night! Okay, so I was looking around at everyone looking at you. Everyone. And no one, no one at all, no one was looking at me. You see what I mean?

Not exactly.

Alexa, don't play coy with me, coy decoy, you're the one who likes to call it bargain shopping. No one was looking at me, get it?

Oh, okay, yes, yes, I get it. Bargain shopping realness.

I knew it, Alexa, I knew it! And you're right about something else—I should smoke more pot, I didn't realize I could be so hungry, even though there isn't any fucking cheese in this pizza it's yummy, almost as yummy as you, and here's my example, it's cold out, right? Really fucking freezing-your-ass-off cold. So what do people need, people outside? People stuck the fuck outside in this fucking freezing cold. Sleeping bags, right?

Usually I'm so focused on my own bargain shopping, studying everyone's reactions while I yawn and pretend to be oh-so-relaxed. Wait, did I tell you how relaxed I am? Honey, I could almost fall asleep right here. Everyone looks at my hair, but then there's the moment when they look away and that's when I liberate those seventy-dollar vitamins.

But it's so much easier when all I have to do is take in the attention, bask in it, glow. Whenever someone glances in Avery's direction, I ask some idiotic question or act like I'm about to slip a Hula Hoop into my purse and boom, all eyes are on me. Eight sleeping bags in one afternoon—we can't help adding up the prices on the labels, just to see. Okay, goodbye evidence. Hello homeless shelter. Let's just drop these off outside.

Remember *The Unbelievable Truth*, where in the beginning two girls are lying in the grass looking up at the sky while talking to one another and that's kind of how I feel in the car with Avery, doing another bump of coke and this is our movie, shot from inside a cream-colored Mercedes. It's probably not called cream. Avery, what do they call this color?

Breathe deep and let your head roll back and then step outside like you don't even notice the camera's on you, yes, you. Every store has plenty of mirrors, even if they're selling sporting goods in Allston, Cambridge, Brookline—and everybody knows mirrors are for runway. High-level undercover stunway. Honey, what is all this gear for? Bug smearer. Rain fearer. Forty-degrees-below-zero dream gear hair smear bug fear right here, turn.

Think about waving, waving for the cameras. Especially when they're playing "Highway to Hell." Think, but don't look. Yawn again. Turn. Avery's out the door. Pose. Let the lights blend into your eyes. Walk.

Another bump? Of course, darling, of course—you always know how to provide.

The good thing about the coke cure is that it helps with my cough. No, seriously. Just a little bump and I'm fine. Another bump and I'm even better. A third bump and the cough is practically gone. Or if not, what a perfect distraction—AIDS alert in aisle four. "Camera's ready, prepare to flash." Runway runaway.

Avery, you're right, you're right, this is fun. Fun for the whole family. Whose family? Brighter days brighter days brighter days! Wait, what am I making for dinner yes dinner, do you want to come over? Oh, probably not a good idea, I mean not right at this moment.

Why not at this moment—you don't want Sugar Daddy to see you with your bitchy boyfriend?

I don't want him to see me with my bitchy boyfriend when we're both coked out of our minds.

I am not coked out of my mind, I'm coked into my mind.

Girl, that's brilliant, but wait, today's the day we get our test results.

Here we are on Boylston, opening the door in the wind tunnel and then checking in at the front desk, where the receptionist gives us that fake smile and then waves us into the waiting room dungeon. Clinics are so depressing. It's like they're just waiting for you to die. Why can't they at least play good music, something with a beat, maybe a DJ and a dance floor, they could easily fit a disco ball over there in that corner by the dusty plastic flowers.

What about real flowers—even something cheap, carnations, what about carnations? What about art on the walls, I'm sure there are plenty of rich bitches who would be glad to donate art, or if not, then give me a couple of twenties and I'll go to Goodwill to find some wacky glamour. Or at least paint the walls bright colors instead of this atrocious faded gray-and-tan wallpaper—we're here to take care of ourselves, not to fade into nothingness. What about velvet sofas and herbal tea and steamed vegetables and brown rice and maybe something to read besides pamphlets about STDs?

What if the clinic was like a café where you could hang out and gossip and cruise or even read a good book, there could be a library or free massage or acupuncture or hugs, right, what about hugs? Instead of hugs we just get sterile beige carpet and hand-me-down office chairs and a few boring ads for safe sex.

What about makeup lessons or a reading group? If no one wants to read, we could practice all Kevyn Aucoin's makeup tricks, I wouldn't mind practicing makeup tricks with a bunch of queens at the STD clinic. What about a deejaying workshop, I would love a deejaying workshop. Art supplies—what about art supplies?

They call my number and Avery's still holding my hand and I'm thinking about colored pencils and crayons and magic markers and oil pastels. Or what about making collages? The clinic would be such a great place to make a collage—it wouldn't even cost anything. Everyone could just bring in their old magazines and cut and paste and get to know one another. It would be fun.

Avery's squeezing my hand tighter—I can't believe she's twenty-three, but she's never been tested before. They call my number again and then I'm in another sterile room, this one feels like they sucked out all the air and some blonde woman in a powder-blue cardigan with pearly buttons asks me what I would do if I tested positive.

I have nothing against powder-blue cardigans, especially not powder-blue cardigans with pearly buttons, I mean I have a lavender one just like it. But that strand of pearls around her neck. Real pearls.

Those pearls, I want to say. What are you trying to say with those pearls?

How would you react if you tested positive, she asks me again.

Honey, I'm thinking—I would jump off a bridge. Can you take me to the highest bridge? I need a ride. You don't drive? Then at least give me directions.

I want to say that I would go out and do so many drugs that

I wouldn't even know my name. "My name is Luka. I live on the second floor. I live upstairs from you. Yes, I think you've seen me before." But instead I just say I don't know.

She asks me about my risks. I don't ask about hers. Is she going to give me my results?

After she suggests condoms for oral sex—yeah, already tried that—she finally looks down at the piece of paper and says: You tested negative for HIV. Thank you for coming in today. Do you have any questions for me?

Back in the waiting room, now I'm nervous waiting for Avery, until he comes out with a smile. I can't believe how hot it is in here, I'm totally covered in sweat.

We get to Avery's and she pours a bunch of coke on the mirror without even taking off her coat, snorts way too much and then shakes her head back and forth and starts jumping up and down. She hands me the mirror, says let me hold you while you do it—come on, come on, hurry up, catch up with me—and then I'll bend you over and fuck you over the sink.

I thought you never wanted to have sex again.

That was before.

I wake up the next day singing "I think I love you, what am I so afraid of, I'm afraid that there's no cure for ..."—what are the rest of the words? "No cure for ... No cure for ..." Avery, do you know that song, who sings it? "I think I love you ..."

"What am I so afraid of ..."

Yeah, yeah—that's the one.

I'm just imitating you.

The way it all blends together, one day and then the next.

One store and then the next. One line and then the next. The day we wheel a whole shopping cart full of canned food out of Star Market—hello, food drive. And then the next Star Market. And the next. Honey, we're getting a tour of all the Star Markets, who's the star now?

That feeling in my head, where am I, that feeling when I'm sitting with Nate and he's speaking and I'm trying to pay attention—oh, right, another cocktail, thank you. That feeling in my head, so warm and cool at the same time, blending these pills and powders and potions and yes, that feeling in my head, hold me.

The way my eyes can be blue but really that's white and blue and a circle of green, sparkly brown spots on the left I never realized brown could sparkle is it really purple in disguise like the way the white of the eyes is the part that shines the most and you never realize that from far away. Or the way skin is really all these little holes, some dry and some greasy even after the apricot facial scrub and oil-free moisturizer it's never just smooth except from far away and I guess that's why so many people wear so much makeup. But even the bags under my eyes can become pretty when I stare long enough and let everything blur. Look, look how my lower lip is bigger and puffier and redder than the upper lip.

And now, our special guests for the evening: teeth—that's just the way you are—teeth. We think of you as white, but that's only compared to night. So much closer to yellow, hello—unless you've been bleached. Bleached, leeched, and impeached.

No, don't impeach my teeth—I swear they didn't mean to lie when they said they were light-bright spite fright mighty fighty tighty-whitey, I swear.

Really, stop looking for stains, okay? Stop pulling back skin to disguise structure. Focus on the way the water pours over your hands in little tiny waterfalls, all this hot water for my hands, oatmeal soap a massage until I'm ready to take out my contacts, right, I'm taking out my contacts. And then, time for magical Marinol, oh yes.

Avery rings the bell and when I get to the door in my robe he's standing there with sunflowers, what a great way to start the day. Then she reaches down and picks up a boom box— where'd you get that boom box?

I'm bringing back the eighties.

Oh, no, please, not the eighties. Anything but the eighties. Even the seventies, I mean you know how much I hate disco but anything's better than Michael Jackson. Thank you for the flowers, they're beautiful.

Okay, 1991. It was only four years ago, but wait until you hear this. You're beautiful. Too sexy.

Avery wants to watch the sunset, and when we get to the Esplanade it's almost warm out—I mean it's freezing, but at least there's no wind. Look at those pink clouds over there, someone's finally lighting the Citgo sign on fire. Avery puts the boom box down and says are you ready? And she presses play.

No way. The beat starts and I can't help it, I'm flinging myself into the air and around, falling to the ground and rolling in the frozen grass toward water and then jumping across the paved part and back again for more space, give her, give her what, give her the river, deliver, shiver, my liver, and Avery's clapping and I'm throwing my arms everywhere, hands flying up and back, head in every direction, yes there are a few tourists and joggers who look scared, too sexy for my, too sexy for my, too sexy for my, and then I do the big kick in the air as high as possible and I land with one leg straight out and the other crossed underneath like I'm just sitting there so calmly. Avery comes over to fan me with her hand, and that's when I jump up and twist around her, is this another mix, how many mixes are there?

And there's that beat like one of those movie songs—girl, where the hell did you find "I'm Too Sexy" anyway? Okay, okay, here I go, running down the Esplanade and Avery's cackling and I start to twirl around and around and around until I'm dizzy enough that doing the falling-over runway really is falling, bending side to side and taking the tight rope into fight rope, light rope, blight rope, smash the glass and jump-up-and-down delight rope, and Avery runs in front of me and I stop, turn, put my hand on her face and then we turn around together, I'm holding onto her back like I could hold on forever but then I push her aside and she laughs and what is this mix, I don't remember this mix and now I'm leaning back against Avery like a prop or a wall or treasure or the end of the line or sustenance.

COME IN THE CURTAINS

I tried to take a break from the coke cure because I got really sick and the coke wasn't helping. Avery was taking care of me, which was kind of romantic since Nate was away so the palace was ours. Avery even insisted on getting in bed with me and my phlegm and bloody noses and night sweats—she said if she was going to get that cough she would've gotten it already, and it did feel nice with her holding me so close. Eventually she convinced me to go to the clinic and of course they gave me antibiotics even though they didn't know what was going on and the antibiotics made me shit for a week but then I did get better.

So then I thought maybe I would keep going with the break from drugs and even alcohol, though it was quite an endurance test eating dinner with Nate without cocktails, and Avery was starting to annoy me again. We even ended up arguing about the word snatch—she said she was reclaiming it, which is the stupidest thing I've ever heard and then I went from that argument to dinner with Nate, who kept saying Tyler, you don't seem like yourself. So I figured it was time for a cocktail—I took one sip of that first drink and thought oh, this is it, my life, hello. After the third cocktail I went upstairs and did a bump and when I came back downstairs Nate said you're in a good mood.

That's when he asked me if I wanted to read another book together and I was feeling pretty daring so I said *Close to the Knives*, I'm always ready for *Close to the Knives*. So, here we go, "Self-Portrait in Twenty-Three Rounds," and there's that feeling in the back of my head, how do I describe that feeling? Listen: "So my heritage is a calculated fuck on some faraway sun-filled bed while the curtains are being sucked in and out of an open window by a passing breeze."

I finish the first chapter way before Nate so I sit there and wait, sipping my cocktail and looking at his face until he looks at me and says: It's a little much, Tyler—it's a lot to look at. And I think about how reading *Close to the Knives* was the first time I ever felt my own rage in print, and whether Nate thinks that's what's too much.

Chapter 2, and I realize that when it's this quiet I can hear the sound of the refrigerator in the other room. I look up at the chandelier, and the way the light goes in all directions. I think about my breathing—is it shallow or deep? And then Nate clears his throat, and when I look at him he says: I think I'd like to start with the other one.

He means *Memories That Smell Like Gasoline*. He saw it in my room. I actually have two copies because I used to give them out to people in San Francisco, new friends, anyone I wanted to get to know. Okay, I say to Nate, though I'm pretty sure he doesn't know what he's getting himself into. Back downstairs Nate opens the book to the table of contents and says would it be okay if we read one chapter at a time?

And that's a little weird because this book is so short, but also it's kind of fun now that I'm studying the cover—the blurred headlights of a truck on the highway in a soft teal blue and then the title in yellow, David's name in black, black-and-white stripes on the side that lead to the spine and onto the back cover, which otherwise is orange. I never thought of this before, but maybe the stripes are supposed to represent a prison jumpsuit? A piano. A hospital.

And then you open the book and on the inside cover there's David's handwriting, just a few enlarged words and phrases—"8th Avenue and hands and," and then a word I can't figure out, plus some partial words and then "wouldn't sucking him he come in the curtains."

On to the first page, which means the first image, I would call it a watercolor, but on the back of the book it says these are ink paintings. What's spooky about this picture is the look on the face of the one guy you can see—it's like he's grinding his teeth and furrowing his brow, looking down or deep inside and not at either of the cocks in front of him. The only desire is the way his left arm wraps around one guy's calf, hand disappearing into the floor. I mean there's no hand, just an arm that goes away. You can see the way darkness frames light in the brushstrokes that almost look like fingerprints, gray and black and then white—the white is what makes it look like the flash of a camera has just gone off.

And then, just when I feel like I'm reading too much into the expression in that one guy's face, there's the first line of text: "Sometimes it gets dark in here behind these eyes I feel like the physical equivalent of a scream."

The way driving becomes sex becomes imagination becomes intimacy becomes loneliness, you turn the page past the rest stop and the silhouette of a man, to an image of a guy jerking off in the top left corner of the page, but it's the next page where

I see myself in this guy who leans forward to suck someone off. Someone's resting his hand on my head as he leans back in something so close to pain while the background looks like smoke billowing up—the theater the truck stop the bathroom the park, wherever it makes sense and doesn't make sense this hope for connection. That's what David first gave me, a language for talking about my own desires that before I still thought I needed to overcome. Because when I went to those bathrooms as a teenager I was trying not to feel, over and over again these old guys, guys like Nate with pasty skin and pink sweaty bodies, over and over again these guys sucking the drive I hated but couldn't stop. And then afterward, once I remembered about my father, I thought oh, I wanted to beat him, to win, to win over these desires that meant I was evil, deserved to die, I would never be anything else.

And when I first read David's words, is it okay that I call him David, David because he feels so close even though I discovered his words through his death. And I thought oh, this is what sex could mean, should mean—a flash, an explosion, a connection so rare, so possible, so hopeful, so empty.

And here David talks about looking at the light fixture on the ceiling through a puddle in between bathroom stalls, and I'm thinking about how I used to stare at the tiles on the floor of the bathroom at Mazza Gallerie after school, looking for the movement of shadow that meant jerking off, that meant maybe someone would hand me a note on toilet paper wrapped around a pen, and we would head off to the back stairwell and down into the mall parking lot.

I was on the way to my father's office, and doesn't that make so much sense now. Because first I was trying not to feel anything in these interactions that I craved in spite of all my shame, and then I was aware of something else, I didn't know what exactly, but there was a way that this secret world felt like a trap but also a place I could escape to.

I will never be on the way to my father's office again, but maybe I'm still looking for the place I can escape to. It's the end of the chapter, as this guy is grabbing or maybe holding, I think he's holding David's head and saying go ahead, enjoy it, and then: "His fingers and face scattered into shards of light." That line in red, the way it goes into my eyes suddenly light too, and I'm wondering if David was able to plan out the layout of this text, the layout of the text and images before he died.

And when I look up at Nate he's smiling, and so I smile too, and there's something like desire between us. Or maybe not desire exactly, what is it?

And Nate says: I want to give you a hug. Is that okay?

And I say yeah, that would be sweet, and I'm wondering if it really could be sweet, maybe in this moment—it feels kind of nice to rest my head on his shoulder and drift away except then I'm thinking oh no, now he's going to say let's go in the bedroom, I don't want to go in the bedroom now.

I don't get to Paradise until one a.m., but then right away I'm dancing with some muscly blond guy with swept-back hair who's kind of tacky but he really knows how to work the moves, I mean really. His name's Calvin. He says don't you remember me, you know I used to be friends with Brian, I was in the coast guard, I stayed at your house, we did coke together, you were making a spinach salad. He's wired. Those glassy blue eyes. And I'm just laughing my ass off because I guess now he's a fag.

After a while he's got me in his arms—I don't know how it happens exactly because first we're practically flying into one another but stopping in the way you do on the dance floor, but then somehow it moves into something else and he says do you want to go home with me? So then we're outside, getting into that same red sports car, and I'm trying to remember if I've ever gone home with anyone from Paradise.

We do coke in the car and then when we get to Calvin's place he offers me K and I get kind of excited since I haven't done K in a while, somehow I forgot all about it. But then I do too much and suddenly I can feel my heart beating in my skin is that really my heart I mean how do I know this is really the same Calvin I mean how does he remember so much, and I'm staring at the door behind his face like someone else is there and I can feel the ground beneath the ground but also it's like I'm on a roller coaster. So we just sit there for a while and then eventually I go home.

I forgot that chapter 2 of *Memories That Smell Like Gasoline* was about rape, rape and the way you remember, the way it stays in your body and keeps you so scared and helpless. I didn't remember until now, now when I'm sitting here at the dinner table with Nate and he looks so concerned, which makes me cry more, and then he says did something like that happen to you?

But does he mean a trick gone wrong, turned into rape in a truck on the side of a road you don't know, like in the book, or does he mean a trick gone wrong, turned into a rape that you see again, when you see him or when you don't, or does he just mean a trick gone wrong? Or does he mean rape in general, and is rape ever general, or just rape, does he mean have you ever been raped, and who hasn't been raped?

I haven't told Nate about my father, I mean I told him I hate my father, that when I was thirteen I decided I had no respect for my parents at all but still I was trapped and now I don't want to talk to them ever again. But I haven't told him why. I don't know if I want to.

But now Nate's saying has that ever happened to you, and I just nod my head and continue sobbing. He comes over and rubs my back. I'm sorry, he says, I'm sorry that happened to you—I don't want it to happen to you again. And I can't believe I'm crying this much, when was the last time I cried this much, I mean I can't believe I'm crying again with Nate, who hands me another cocktail, and do I want this cocktail, yes.

Later I'm with Avery—he was so present for me when I was sick, but now he's all over the place. Avery, I say, I need you to listen to me. But he's still not listening.

I want to tell him about crying with Nate, and what does it mean? I want to tell him about David Wojnarowicz, about rage, about powerlessness, about childhood, about all this emotion I'm starting to feel, even with the coke, I want to tell Avery that she's part of this emotion, this feeling, this opening up. But I can't get her to pay attention so I just tell her about Calvin, and she looks really scared.

You went home with someone? She says it twice. Almost

three times—two and a half—because the third time she just says you went home.

Yeah, with some guy who used to be straight, I mean he was in the coast guard and he passed out in my room but now he's a fag and we went back to his place and did K but then I felt weird and walked home.

You went home with someone?

Avery, why are you freaking out?

Back at the dinner table with Nate, we've reached the place in the book where the drawings become less ink and more line. These are the ones that made me anxious the first time, made me feel gross. Right before I remembered I was sexually abused.

I think it was this first drawing in particular: black lines on a white page with a hard dick in the center. Face cut off. The chest is just a box, arms without hands, and it's a drawing of a Polaroid a guy took when David was nine or ten. It freaks me out to look at it now too. Nine or ten, when I was nine or ten.

Then there's something so disgusting about looking at the line drawing of this old guy with a receding hairline staring into those white briefs to look for signs of an STD. In the narrative underneath, David writes that the guy is with his son, they picked David up together, and somehow this guy reminds me of my father, even though my father's hair isn't receding. I remember when I was nine or ten, and I would take my father's underwear out of his dresser and smell it while I was jerking off. There's a chill going through my body until I finish my cocktail, and then Nate stands right up to get me another.

It's strange how when I thought about this book before it was all about AIDS, but now we're two-thirds of the way through and David hasn't even mentioned AIDS. Except then there's page 39: "The beautiful view and my overwhelming urge to puke." The view from a friend's hospital room, right across from the guy looking into ten-year-old David's underwear. And then after the image of the hospital and the smell of human shit, and some guy telling David-as-a-kid not to worry, he won't come in his mouth, while the wind in the picture blows everything in the room to the left, I turn the page and it's a guy covered in lesions. And I don't know if I'm ready, I mean I don't know if I'm ready to read this with Nate. So I close the book, and I say what do you think of the drawings? And Nate closes his book too and says: I think they're pornography, child pornography.

There's something about having sex with someone who knows you, who knows you so well, who knows you so well in this particular way. Avery and I are on Joey's bed, Avery's fucking me from behind and I don't have to ask him to put his hands underneath my thighs, to rub softly, really softly. When I move his hand away from my dick he doesn't move it back, I don't have to keep pushing him away. When I pull his arms around me he keeps them there, holding me with his dick still in my ass, until I relax and then he moves his hands all over my head and face and down to my neck like he's going to choke me and I feel so safe.

And he pushes me onto the bed, face down, I know this is a game we're both playing until ouch, I pull away, and he pulls out, turns me over, grabs my head again and we're making out in that way that makes me forget there's anything else except this tongue and those eyes so close to my eyes I can feel his eye-lashes, my hands all over his back, squeezing his armpits, there's his dick at my asshole again, inside as he puts all his weight right on my chest, yes, spits in my face the way he was afraid to before and I'm laughing because there's a lot of spit, I'm laughing with all this spit and Avery on top of me, now he's biting my neck and pumping, grabbing me all around, I can tell he's going to come so I grab his head and feel the pressure of his belly against my dick, and after he comes and pulls out and throws the condom to the side he lies down beside me and I get on top of him, move one of his hands under my balls and then I squeeze him tight, that stickiness between us and now Avery's laughing and saying how did you come so much?

So when Nate says child pornography I feel defensive, like he's criticizing my life. How we were so close yesterday or the day before, and what does it mean to feel that close, when you're not really close? Maybe I need another cocktail.

And then Avery pulls the sheets off the bed, opens the linen closet and there are all different colors—paisley, plaid, bright yellow—at first I wonder what happened to Joey's sheets, but there they are on the bottom shelf. Avery pulls out the paisley sheets and drapes one over me, it's soft but stiff in that new-sheet kind of way. They're for you, he says, us, and when I go to the bathroom to look at myself in the mirror, wrapping the sheet around my head, I see there are new towels too, paisley towels that almost match the paisley sheets, such beautiful colors and I feel like a little kid twirling around in one of my mother's dresses, I mean I was never allowed to do that but now.

In *Memories That Smell Like Gasoline,* the Gulf War is play-ing on hundreds of TV screens at St. Vincent's Hospital—I'm thinking about senior year of high school when I was studying for finals at the American University cafeteria and I looked up at the TV screens and there it was, the bombs were dropping: I couldn't study anymore.

Then on the next page there's that drawing of the guy with lesions all over his body, everywhere, there's nowhere without lesions and his eyes are closed like maybe he can imagine this away. Something so simple can feel so scary. And I'm thinking about how I hardly ever see anyone with lesions anymore, and where have they all gone?

And then I hear Nate gasp, and when I look up I see his hand over his mouth. He doesn't look at me. We both go back to read-ing. There's a drawing of a guy with blood all over his clothes from cruising the waterfront for hustlers: "Maybe I did some-thing wrong," he says, on one side, and then on the other we learn for the first time about the virus inside David's body.

BOYS IN THE SAND

So now here I am, wired to all hell, at the party picnic table in the Fens. I'm not even horny, or I don't think I'm horny, but Avery and I were arguing again about Calvin, who asked me out on a date, and I said why is this date such a big deal, I mean I don't even have any friends. And Avery said why do you need friends?

So now I'm in the Fens, smoking pot to try to calm down— Avery doesn't care about the Fens, since I'm never going to meet any friends here. Some guy wearing a big floppy hat comes up and sits down across from me, I figure he just wants pot so I hand it to him and he says oh, oh, manners, remember manners, don't we? Don't we? I hold out my lighter and then he takes a big hit.

Ooh, ooh, that's right, he says, and smiles at me. What's your name, he says, and holds out his hand.

Ooh, that's a good one—what's your real name, the one your mother gave you? Ooh, ooh, I'm sorry, I didn't mean to offend you. That's the last thing I wanted to do. You know you're an awfully attractive boy. Boy-girl. Girl-boy. I like a girl boy boy-girl girl-boy girly girly cutie hot-tot hottie tottie hottie, yeah! Yeah! Do you like to party?

So then I'm on my way to his house, wondering if this counts as a date. He lives in one of those big old buildings right on the Fens that I've always thought were kind of glamorous, but we don't go inside, we go around back behind the gas station next to the Ramrod, and his apartment has its own entrance on the ground level. He makes a big show of saying welcome, welcome to Pee-wee's playhouse, but when he opens the door it's pitch dark and he says don't worry, don't worry 'bout a thing.

He turns the lights on, red bulbs in some kind of retro fixture and Christmas lights all over the walls which are covered in splatter paint and the sofas too, almost like the paint poured down from the walls and then there's a tacky brass four-poster bed in one corner, puffy white comforter and white sheets, I don't know why gay men love white sheets so much. White carpet too, or maybe it's beige, I can't tell if it's clean or dirty in this light. He flicks another switch, and there goes the disco ball—with the splatter paint and the lights I'm already feeling high and then he takes a vial out of his pocket and pours the whole thing onto the coffee table, some big mirrored thing from the eighties. Special K, he says, just like the cereal, do you know about Special K? And he throws down a few straws.

Somehow he already has his shirt off, muscular arms and a big tattoo of a snake on his belly. Want to see the rest, he says, and starts to pull down his pants, but then he says just kidding, Miss-ter Alexa—I'm not trying to rape ya. Although I bet you've got a nice ass. Oops—hope you don't mind my humor, it's in the gutter. Do you like my playhouse? Ooh, ooh—I forgot to introduce myself. Bobby, like the bar, that was my bar, Bobby's. Did you ever go there?

Bobby's?

Ha, ha—stumped you on that one. Lots of hot boys there, right? I miss Bobby's. Lots of hot boys. I could see you at Bobby's, dancing to the latest hits.

I don't like the latest hits.

Ooh, ooh, I bet you like disco—I've got lots of disco—I re-member disco, don't I remember disco? How old are ya? No, no, don't tell me—just a baby, my baby, young enough to be my baby. Do ya like ecstasy, I've got ecstasy. How 'bout music, do you like music? I'll put on something real nice that we can dance to.

I don't really like disco.

Are you kidding me? Where did I pick this one up? I bet you don't even like ecstasy.

I do like ecstasy.

Well, why don't you pick out some music, maybe do some more K-K-ketamine, and I'll be right back, pussycat.

Bobby comes back with a glass of orange juice, and I'm sit-ting on the sofa watching the lights. Just when I think he forgot about the ecstasy he hands me a hit. You do drink orange juice, don't ya, he says. What did ya pick?

I can't decide.

Ooh, never mind, you're too young—don't get me wrong, I like 'em young, and you're a beauty, aren't you? Aren't you? What about ESG, do you know about ESG? Black girls from the Bronx, sisters who jammed in their backyard in the late seventies—it'll blow you away. Blow, blow, blow—let me do some more of this here K, 'kay? Ooh, yeah, ooh, ooh, that's right, listen to this. Do you want to watch some porn?

Not really.

A cocktail, do you want a cocktail?

Sure.

What'll ya have, dearie?

A screwdriver.

Yeah, baby, screw, that's the way I like it. Did anyone ever ask you if that hair was real?

Never.

Ooh, yeah, ooh baby yeah. Help yourself to more of that K.

I do another line, and this music is great, I can't tell if they're playing synthesizers or actual drums. This sofa is my new best friend. And that disco ball—I should get one at home. It would look great with the chandeliers. Nate's always saying he wishes he knew more about gay culture.

Bobby comes back with a cocktail in a huge glass, something ridiculous, it's almost too heavy to hold. I think the ecstasy is starting to kick in, seems pretty fast so maybe it's the K. Bobby's running all over the room—I can't tell what he's doing but it's pretty fun to watch.

You get really calm, he says, you get really calm on it, you just calm the fuck down like it's all so easy, yeah, so easy, you just calm the fuck down.

The lights are starting to go in and out of my eyes and Bobby's doing that thing where he moves his hand back and forth in front of my face like a tunnel and then when I do it to him he goes whoa, whoa, so I go whoa, whoa, and I guess now we're kind of at the same level, level forty-two, what does that mean, why forty-two?

Forty-two, he says, how did ya know—yeah, boy, I'm forty-two. Old enough to be your father. Except, wait a second here, I'm fifty-two—how does that make you feel? Whoa, whoa, let's go for a ride. Is there anything you've always wanted to do, but never had the balls to?

I hate it when someone says balls so I just sit there watching Bobby going whoa, ooh, ooh, whoa, and I can't tell if he's making fun of me but then he says wait, wait, have you ever seen *Boys in the Sand*? It's porn from when porn was art. The seventies. Before you were born. I've got it on Super 8, I can take out my projector and set it up.

Bobby doesn't wait for my answer, he just starts setting up the projector so I figure it's a good time to do more K and take off my shoes. Bobby says you go boy, you go, you go, you go, and I realize the carpet is like a sponge. A really soft sponge. Feels so good with the disco ball lights taking the paint off the walls and swirling it around the room. Make yourself comfortable, Bobby keeps saying, and it's kind of hot in here, maybe I will take off my shirt. Yeah, Bobby says, yeah, you go. I lean back on the sofa, the fabric so cool on my skin and I really want to take off my pants but I'm way too high to have sex so I say Bobby, and he says yes, yes, and I say Bobby, I'm having so much fun.

He says ooh boy that's great, that's why you're here, and I say I think I'm going to take my pants off, but I don't want to have sex, is that okay, and he says of course, of course that's okay, dearie, why don't we get naked and make ourselves comfortable? And I say I think I'm going to keep my boxers on, and Bobby says okay, I'll keep my Jockeys on.

Oh, I love this movie already, the titles written in the sand— if I sit down on the carpet I can pretend I'm writing in the sand too. What should I write?

HELLO. HELLO. It takes longer than I thought it would to write in the sand sponge carpet.

How about HO, like Polly wrote in the sand on her birthday when we went to Revere Beach. Where's Polly?

Pretend I'm at the beach with the lights swirling around the splatter-paint sky and this movie, the way you hear the birds in the trees as leaves alternate between light and dark and what beach is this?

Fire Island, Bobby says, and now I understand why people go there. But what is this awful music, can we turn the other music back on? HELLO. HELLO. Wait, now it's night already, that was fast. Night on the beach, this guy in the sky with his shiny chest glowing, okay, daytime again and the ocean, I love the ocean, green and blue and wait, now it's night again I'm getting confused so I look at Bobby to see if he notices and oh, his eyes, now he's behind me, rubbing my back, this guy's back, shaved head, before I thought he was kind of cheesy with the seventies denim look but now, now Bobby's rubbing his back, this is fun.

Some boy's running toward us from the ocean and then we just see his hand feeling that guy up I'm feeling that guy up and now his head goes down, before I wasn't sure about facial hair but he's much hotter than the guy from the ocean a mermaid but without scales I miss the scales and oh, Bobby's on his knees with my dick in his mouth and how did this happen? Bobby has a shaved head too, how come I didn't notice that before, I guess his hat, where did the hat go, was it red?

Now I'm laughing because it's funny with Bobby down there between my legs the way he's grinding into the carpet and trying to get me hard I'm not going to get hard I already told you that but he puts my hands on his skin so warm as these guys step into the woods and they're making out, wow, I love it when the blond one rubs his hand through the back of the other guy's head, down his chest but it makes me nervous that neither of them is hard, maybe they're on ecstasy too and here's Bobby's mouth like a fish I kind of want to lie down but now Bobby's standing up with his dick in my face, wow it's huge but Bobby, stop, I told you I'm too high. Okay, Bobby says, and goes into the kitchen.

Oh, the blond guy in this lighting, now I get it, here's where he's hot, the sun illuminating space through the trees and now it's his ass pumping away and oh, okay, now he's hard but his dick isn't as big as Bobby's, what would I do with a dick that big it's too big and the camera keeps going back into the trees sparkling with the sun and now someone's getting fucked but I can't tell who it is and then the trees.

Oh, wait, now the blond guy's jerking off on the other guy's face, mouth open to take all that come so much come and then he rubs it all over his face, wow, the seventies, now they're making out again and then the one with the shaved head is getting his dick sucked and the music is really religious, like a choir or *The Sound of Music* or the Mormon Tabernacle. When I was in fourth grade I wrote a report on the Mormon temple, like a fairy castle except they wanted you to convert and oh, Bobby's sucking my dick again I'm in the movie with the disco lights and splatter paint and this guy's jerking off while everything flashes, we're flashing on the disco ball rolling down the beach and he takes his cock ring off I don't like cock rings anyway but he puts it on the other guy's arm and then runs away. But where are you going—oh, into the water, wait, you disappeared, I miss you, now Bobby stop, stop, you're going to miss the movie.

The blond guy puts on his clothes and walks down the beach, what a pretty beach with trees right at the water and here's another wave, let's go swimming. But now the blond guy's dressed, why did he get dressed? He's by the harbor in white jeans, he must bleach those jeans a lot it's hard to find white jeans without stains, grass or dirt or ketchup and mustard, oil and vinegar or car oil oily handprints wine egg yolk dog shit dead bugs or chewing gum or melted chocolate or come, someone else's or your own or what about sand, maybe the ocean doesn't stain. Where is he now I ask Bobby who's behind me again though I can still feel his lips at my crotch but how does he do that, now that he's behind me, Bobby, where are we now?

Still Fire Island—I want to take you there sometime.

I'm on a ride, a ride on the boardwalk like the teacups not something scary—Bobby, I haven't even made it to Provincetown. Now the guy in the movie's petting a dog so I can pet my legs woof woof and Bobby's moving my hands, whose hands, look, my hands—and this guy's reading a newspaper called GAY, is that a real paper, and Bobby says have some more K.

I like the sound of the projector more than this music, and Bobby says ooh, ooh, I have something special for you, just what you need to relax, and he runs back into the kitchen, now this guy's writing a letter and is that a wedding ring, why would anyone get married? A mineral on the table, pyrite like gold, fool's gold my grandmother said but I always thought it was prettier than gold and now this guy's walking around naked, we can walk around naked together on the carpet beach swimming pool sand smooth feet I like the feeling of your feet so soft and bouncy and cool.

But now he puts on pants to send a letter, I don't want to put on pants this is confusing and Bobby's back with a big glass of orange juice for me just me, now he has his briefs on again, that's better. Where are my boxers? What a pretty purple glass, purple and orange and I'm watching the lights on the glass in the juice and this guy's swimming as the calendar starts to burn, why is the calendar burning?

You're beautiful, Bobby says, like one of those sculptures, a Michelangelo, did anyone ever tell you that? And now there's a kid running on the beach with a dog, just after sunset and the calendar's floating in the water I wish we could go swimming the water is purple bubbles and Bobby says go ahead, drink your orange juice, fresh squeezed but there's so so much and I'm finally in the water I can feel it pouring through me so warm I love this music through the path in the trees where does this path lead, oh, back to the beach and I'm in the water floating away, the heat from the sun on my skin I'm floating away a kid with a kite at the post office I'm running naked through the woods and the drums, the matches, fire in the woods and a glass case I'm bubbling in the water swimming through my skin in the music whose heart pumping so fast in the dark with the lights I'm spinning everything's red in the shadows of the trees in the sand in the ocean.

We're in a sauna, sweating in the bubbles floating through the tunnel the music my body and Bobby's saying yes, that's the sound of his hands, the tunnel so bright and dark, inside and outside I'm a gymnast bending into new shapes, rolling on the beach over and around the pole where's the pole I think I can stay balanced my body opening the water and through the woods and into the softest wave I've ever felt yes I want to stay here with the water flowing through me.

And when I wake up, wait, have I been sleeping, Bobby's kissing me and saying yes, yes, and I look for the movie again oh it's upside down—someone's reading the newspaper called GAY, everyone reads that paper now I close my eyes and Bobby's saying yes, yes, and is he fucking me, wait, I'm on a deck, reading the paper, inside the paper is more paper, I keep opening and opening until the water comes through the sky the stars so bright and night, this tunnel through the trees and oh a little window I'm climbing through the window into the other side of the sky another window, something in my mouth, bubbles—blow bubbles blow I'm on the elevator going backward fast through the stars and on the other side is light, the sun on the beach and now the water, backward through the water the waves my body shaking in the waves and how am I breathing the elevator shooting through the water, backstroke, sidestroke, fancy diving too, oh wouldn't it be so lovely to be with you. To be with you. To be with you. And I never noticed before how if you let everything go, if you let everything go in the water you can feel the way it becomes a pump your heart.

I wake up in a bed, a soft bed but something hurts, maybe my stomach and how did it get so dark? I start to sit up but I'm too dizzy. I need water and then sleep, more sleep, please more sleep, but can I get up? I close my eyes.

I'm doing backflips on the beach in the sun—I never realized my body could do this before, I just keep flipping my legs over and over and over and over and over and even though it hurts it also feels like I'm flying, why don't I try this more often, maybe because I never go to the beach anymore. But then I hit a wall. It doesn't hurt like I thought it would, it just feels like diving into the water and forgetting to put your hands out in the right position and the current is pushing me back, I'm swimming but I'm not getting anywhere and then I let go.

Now I'm awake again, how long has it been? My mouth so dry is this my mouth? Tongue, that's my tongue. There's no one else in bed, should I get up? Oh, this carpet, I remember this carpet, I need water. Here's the light switch in the kitchen, ouch too bright turn that off. There aren't any windows in here. A glass. I need a glass, should I drink this orange juice, wait now I need to shit.

Oh my God. Shooting pain going right through my body when will it end. Diarrhea. Blood on the toilet paper, I can't tell if it's a lot or a little but it's definitely blood. I need something to eat, is there anything in the refrigerator? Gross—what's that smell?

Okay, Wonder Bread, I guess I can eat Wonder Bread. Iceberg lettuce? Mustard. I'll make a mustard sandwich, with iceberg lettuce. Here's the toaster. Maybe it will talk to me, oh, the toast is already burning.

I need more water. This isn't that bad, this, this sandwich. Chewing hurts. I guess I'm alone, alone in this apartment, but why? I need more water. Ouch ouch ouch ouch ouch I better sit down. Oh, a shower, yes, a shower. Red, I do like all the red in here, except, you know: blood. A shower of blood, no don't exaggerate. But yes, the water pressure is really strong. The only soap is Dial, but I need to get this smell off of me. Should I write a note? What would I say? How come you kept saying you're so beautiful, I know you kept saying that because otherwise I wouldn't have it in my head.

Soft towels, at least he has soft towels. There's no condom in the trash. But actually there's nothing in this trash can. Maybe it's in the kitchen. I can't find the trash in the kitchen, but I'm not turning that light back on. Maybe the lights in the other room—oh, these splatter paint walls, this is awful. There's nothing on the floor, under the bed, in the sheets, okay maybe I can turn that light on in the kitchen. Here's the trash: it's empty. Maybe he took it out in the morning. Is it morning? I don't know what to do. There are condoms in the drawer by the bed, but how can I tell if he uses them? K-Y Jelly, of course he uses K-Y, why would anyone use K-Y?

Oh, this bed is so comfortable, I hate how comfortable this bed feels. Should I just sleep a little longer? No. I need to get out of here before he gets back. Should I make another sandwich? I need to shit, but I don't want to, it's going to hurt too much.

Avery, something awful happened. Avery, I left you and I went to the Fens, I went to the Fens and then something awful happened. Avery, I don't know what happened, but I need to talk to you. Avery, I'm really scared. Avery, I can't find the phone, where's the phone, I want to call you. I want to call you, to ask for help. I just want you to hold me. Okay, will you hold me?

Oh, here's the phone, covered in splatter paint, what is this place?

Avery picks up the phone: Domino's Pizza, we deliver. She's really high.

Avery.

Alexa, there's a lot going on here, a lot.

Oh.

Alexa, are you ready, are you ready for this story?

I don't know.

Alexa, you sound nervous, are you nervous? I just want you to know that you've got a nice asshole, but I found something even better, ha ha ha, even better.

Avery.

Alexa, I called this guy from *The Phoenix*. You used to have an ad in *The Phoenix*. Well, I called this other guy from *The Phoenix*, Chad, I mean I know that's not his real name, but Chad, Chad has an amazing ass. Chad, don't you have an amazing ass? And we have a lot in common, you know, we both like powder so that's what we've been doing. Don't worry, I paid him first, I fucked him for an hour and then he decided to stay over because of my, well, you know, just to hang out, and we've been hanging out ever since—I don't know, fifteen hours, twenty-five hours, how many hours? No, wait, maybe we slept, and then we fucked, and then we slept again?

Avery.

Alexa, what's wrong, are you okay? Where've you been, are you coming over? Are you coming over soon?

I hang up the phone. My heart, I hope it doesn't break

through the skin. Now I need to shit again, ouch. I'm not dying. I'm not dying. I'm not dying yet.

Oh, he folded my clothes. I can't believe he folded my clothes. I can't believe I have to shit again.

Okay, don't think about how when we were little we would sit on the toilet trying to shit and then there was always blood, always blood, don't think about it. How many stairs, how many stairs to the top? He's not going to open the door before I get there.

Oh, there aren't any stairs.

SOME ARE HERE, AND SOME ARE MISSING

I used to love churches—I never loved what they stood for, but I loved the architecture. I fantasized about the cathedral at Ulm, which was always blue or green in the pictures in *National Geographic*. Or that cathedral in France that's on a tiny island and when the tide comes in it's basically rising out of the water, what is that one called? Saint something-or-other. Or Neuschwanstein, with the mountains in the background. But I guess that's a castle.

This church is kind of pretty in that overstated understated New England way but oh, these assholes—standing outside smoking themselves to death and then going inside to talk about addiction. I really want a bump, just one bump, just one, okay? Just one before this fucking meeting—that would totally make it bearable. Maybe I should call Avery. Fuck Avery. I'm never calling Avery again.

Of course the meeting is in the basement, and what the fuck are they thinking with those fluorescent lights? Everything smells like instant coffee and cigarettes and cologne—oh, my sense of smell—please take it away. Someone else is late too, and someone else, and someone else—I guess quitting drinking doesn't make you punctual. But no one looks upset. They actually look kind of friendly, curious even, maybe a bit confused. I take off my sunglasses, to see if I can handle it.

There's a lot of clapping. I'm George, and I'm an alcoholic.

Everyone claps. I'm Aaron, and I'm an alcoholic. Everyone claps. Someone says it's his thirty-second birthday, but honey he is way older than thirty-two. Oh—he means he's been going to AA for thirty-two years, are you kidding? I thought AA was supposed to cure addiction.

Someone reads from the Big Book, that's what they call it. He even mentions the page and chapter numbers. People are nodding their heads already, some are speaking along from memory and I guess we are in church.

Apparently the topic is fellowship—how you ask for help, how you let people help you. This guy says he tends to isolate and think he can do things on his own, so he ends up sitting at home feeling sorry for himself. He says asking for help is not my strong suit.

I'm looking around the room at people nodding their heads and at first I'm thinking they're all idiots but then something strange happens, I get kind of emotional, what the hell is going on? I better put my sunglasses back on—this light is hurting my eyes. Now the facilitator is calling on people—it seems like he's just picking names at random. He better not call on me, there's no way in hell I'm going to say I'm an alcoholic. I don't even like cocktails that much.

Someone says something about having a pity party—that's the kind of language they use, baby language, is that part of the program? Someone says something about the mentality of the user, always thinking what can I get from you and what can you get for me. That's kind of true. Someone else says: I still think I'm so unique, I'm so fucking unique.

What's wrong with unique?

Now he's saying: I isolate myself but now I have tools, I can make choices about whether to use them, I need to just get over myself.

I don't want to get over myself.

Is there organ music in the background—yes, there is organ music, somewhere in this church. Someone says: I couldn't have made it without the fellowship—I need to keep doing things that make me uncomfortable, reach out instead of reaching for the bottle—there are so many of us who don't manage to do this.

Yes, this is cheesy, but all these gay men in a room, speaking to one another. And at the end the facilitator asks if anyone is available to sponsor—half the guys in the room stand right up and look so proud, so proud of what they're doing and I'm wondering if I've ever been in a room full of gay men who are trying to take care of one another.

Self-seeking will slip away, someone says, and I hate that phrase but somehow I don't hate being in this room like I thought I would, I mean the lighting is depressing but it's better than the Ramrod with its fucking leather dress code. I definitely don't know how to ask for help—who the hell would I ask? Now I hardly even go outside because I don't want to run into anyone, but then I don't want to run into Nate either, so I just lie in bed and pretend I'm taking a nap.

I don't even act like I'm in school anymore, what would be the point? Ever since I realized Nate cut me off, cut me off without telling me. I was such an idiot that I never checked the balance until there wasn't any balance left. Then when I asked him about it and suddenly he looked so distant like we were at a business meeting: Tyler, you haven't been so active in the bedroom, have you?

And then this headache. It started the day after I got back, or no, the day after I just slept, so I mean the day after that. I know I'm saying I got back, like I went on a trip or something, but it was just down the street. Just down the street, I mean that was only a few weeks ago, right, but already everything's different.

Anyway, I was at Bread & Circus with Nate and suddenly it felt like there were pins going into my forehead and I didn't know what to do except close my eyes and Nate said it was a migraine. So he got me an appointment with his eye doctor, and one of the doctor's standard questions was have you experienced any recent trauma? And I just started crying. But he wasn't the kind of doctor who knew what to do about that.

So the doctor gave me these glasses people use after cataract surgery, like blind person's glasses, big and square and dark and they wrap all the way around like a box on your face. They're the only glasses that work—even inside I have to wear them if the light's too bright. The only time I can take them off outside is right at dusk, but it's hard to figure out when that is because right before dusk doesn't work. And then, after it gets dark, the streetlights, the stoplights, car headlights, anything bright or uneven makes me feel this ache behind my eyes like someone's trying to pop them.

I can hardly even read. I get halfway through an article or a few pages into a book and then I find myself squinting because the words won't stay still, I mean it literally looks like some of the letters are big and some of them are small and then there's the headache again, gnawing into my eyebrows and what the fuck am I supposed to do? All I can think about is drugs and Avery and how I used to love the Fens and what if I'm positive, I mean I'm not getting tested for six months because otherwise I won't know if it's accurate but every time I get even slightly sweaty in bed I wonder if it's seroconversion fever.

But I haven't had a real fever yet—do you always get a fever when you seroconvert, I'm not sure.

It's the end of the meeting so everyone stands up. Oh, we're holding hands, holding hands in a circle and I'm crying, I'm crying a little behind my sunglasses even though everyone's reciting the Lord's Prayer.

I'm surprised I don't want to run right outside and get cocktails, I guess I'm still standing there because some guy who's staring at me actually comes up and says hi, I haven't seen you here before. His name is Tyler. I almost laugh because I guess that's what a real Tyler looks like—he even lives in Newton. He asks me how long I've been in the program.

Oh, you're a newbie, he says, it's nice to see another young guy here—there's a great meeting in Newton on Mondays if you ever find yourself there.

Walking home, I wonder why I didn't think of ACT UP earlier—that was a room full of gay men taking care of one another, right? Dykes too, there were as many dykes as fags. But every meeting felt like a battle.

Back at home, can I really call it home, back wherever I live,

Nate asks how the meeting went. I'm still kind of confused, because I actually liked it, some of it. Nate says I thought you would find something there, and I look at his eyes to see what he knows but I don't see anything. He found me passed out on the floor of the bathroom, at first I was scared because I really couldn't remember how the hell I ended up there, and I could tell by Nate's voice that he was scared too.

That's when I noticed the blood, but luckily it was only my nose, and Nate asked what happened. I couldn't think of what to say, so I said something about drinking too much at the Ramrod, and that's when he said maybe I should consider going to AA, and I tried to laugh, but my whole body hurt, and I didn't want him to notice that I'd shit in my pants, so I just sat up slowly, and he said Tyler, I'm worried about you.

That night Nate didn't pour me a cocktail, and I didn't ask for one. The next night he brought up AA again, and I still felt so horrible that I told him I would try going to a meeting, except then I ended up on the other end of Newbury buying hair dye at Allston Beat with the money Nate gave me for a cab. Now that I've actually made it, Nate hands me a booklet with all the meetings—he got it from his friend, he has a lot of friends in AA. I guess his friend even circled the gay ones, that's what it looks like. For the first time I'm sort of curious about his friends.

I already like the second meeting less than the first one. This room smells like cigars and mold, another basement. Oh, it's not the Lord's Prayer—it's the Serenity Prayer. Someone is reading the steps and all I can think is: We admitted we needed a power vacuum.

The speaker tells us he went to a party when he was sixteen and didn't come home until he was forty-five. He was living a wasted life, the police started recognizing him, the judge was sick of listening, he faced the possibility of a lifetime in prison but his life already was prison.

He's not reading from the book, but it sounds like he is. All that mattered was me me me—this disease I suffer from, he says, and at first I think he's actually going to talk about AIDS. But I guess he means low self-esteem. My life began when I got sober, he says—drugs never made me feel this good. A bike ride on a sunny day, the feeling of the wind on my skin—I feel like I've gotten a reprieve from this disease called alcoholism.

Oh, shit—alcoholism is the disease. Now I just want to get high, I can feel it all through my body, like the rush is starting now so I close my eyes, and this guy is saying he surrounds himself with winners, the guys who go to conventions. There are winners and losers and it's your fault if you're the wrong one.

I open my eyes. I'm still in the same moldy basement. Moldy basement and God, what's God doing going to conventions and smoking cigars in this moldy basement? Someone's talking about the victims of King Alcohol, and the four horsemen: terror, unhappiness, bewilderment and something else. My biggest enemy is me, someone says. Really heavy step work, some else is saying, like he's on a StairMaster pushing hard, harder, hardest—he says I used to feel like I was atrocious and weird, but now my life is filled with such gratitude because I know I'm normal.

But what could be worse than normal?

I didn't know how to show up for people, someone says, I'm so grateful to be in this church basement thirty-two years after I started my recovery. I love being an alcoholic today, just because I get to be me.

It's that same guy from the other meeting. Is he joking? No one's laughing.

Someone visiting from Schenectady tells us he was in the psych ward, delirium tremens, sixteen hours a day drinking for twenty years, and he ended up with wet brain—I didn't think I would make it, he says, and when I got out I thought I would lose everything—I hid my alcoholism from my partner and I can't believe he didn't leave me.

I go to the bathroom: more mold. Some gym queen says they're out of paper towels, I guess I'll just use my boyfriend. Gross.

Back in the meeting, someone says the Big Book tells us that rarely do we see a person who fails if he follows the steps. That left me an out, he says—I thought I would be that person who fails.

Okay, that's a joke—people are smiling. Now he's reading the promises, something about serenity, peace and self-pity and then finally it's over. Now we're moving into a circle to hold hands and look at one another—I wish we could do this the whole time. But then we have to recite that stupid prayer again, and then there's a cheer that I don't quite catch. Then it's done, and I'm thinking about the feeling of the guys' hands next to me, and why are hands so comforting?

Oh, here's the guy who says he's been sober for thirty-two

years, here he is introducing himself. Alexa, he says, I'm so glad you made it tonight.

And I know this is ridiculous, but it actually feels like he means it.

Back at home with Nate, he says he got me a little gift. He's always getting me little gifts now, ever since I realized he cut me off. Oh no—it's the Big Book. It really does look like a Bible, a gift from God. I try to smile, then I go to the bathroom to do a bump. I mean I go to the bathroom, not to do a bump. Oh my God I can almost feel it going to my head. Close your eyes. Don't look in the mirror. Go back downstairs.

Nate asks me for a hug—are you fucking kidding? Then he's hugging me and I get hard, just like that, maybe because I haven't had sex in so long, haven't even thought about it really, I've just been so overwhelmed by figuring out how to survive this horrible headache, how to digest anything, how to sleep for more than a few minutes instead of just lying in bed with my head racing in all directions. Nate squeezes my dick through my pants, he's got that hungry look in his eyes.

Maybe now I won't have to take out an ad, that's what I'm thinking as we walk upstairs. Nate unzips my pants, and it almost feels like too much when he puts his hand under my balls so I reach in the drawer for a condom and lube right away. He's already undressed, all that baby oil flab waiting for my cock, he bends over and I stick it in just like that.

He moans, and I can't tell if it's pleasure or pain—who cares. I grab the back of his scratchy hair—I really don't understand why he never takes that thing off. I'm looking at the black-and-white ass outlined in the white light of the sun on the wall, somehow it feels so far away and I spit on Nate's back. Yes, he says, yes, so I start smacking him, light at first and then harder, harder until it's red more than pink and how could this be so hot, that's what I'm wondering.

Another meeting and it already feels like I've been here for years. Someone's talking about how some people are constitutionally incapable of being honest. No one is perfect, he adds, as if we didn't all learn that in second grade. Someone says he was the only black guy when he first started going to meetings, he didn't believe he would ever fit in, he just wanted to get his slip signed because his probation officer told him to go. But I saw all these healthy faces, he says, I wanted what you had.

One of the women in the room says everywhere she goes, she runs into people she knows from recovery, all her friends want to know how she knows so many people, so many gay men. I don't know what they think I'm doing, she says. This guy says: My world got really small, because I went through everyone's jewelry boxes, medicine cabinets, glove compartments and people didn't invite me back.

My world is really small, that's what I'm thinking. And I didn't even go through people's jewelry boxes. Maybe medicine cabinets.

Time is not recovery, someone says. I guess that means you can stop doing drugs but still be an asshole. There are definitely a lot of assholes in this room. Like the guy who says he finds so much love here, but then he has to go outside and face the people that aren't us.

The people that aren't us.

Someone says he has to figure out what thoughts in his head are alcohol and what are real. And I guess that's like when I get up and I want to smash everything in Nate's house, starting with the chandeliers, all the chandeliers, every single one though those crystals probably don't shatter easily so I could use the chandeliers to smash all the windows into tiny pieces, and what would that sound like with real crystal? I could take all the dishes and throw them onto the marble floors, and then anything that doesn't break the first time, take that and throw it through the shattered windows and onto the street. Or onto Nate's bed. I could take all the Oriental rugs and white sheets and towels and pillowcases and comforters and burn them on the white sofas until everything became a charred mess. And then go upstairs and take a nap under my burgundy velvet comforter.

It's time for the promises. There's something about work, and everyone in the room yells you work! Something about gaining interest in our fellows, and everyone yells fellows. Someone is telling us about being allergic to alcohol, any drinking at all leads to bad behavior. One drink leads to another, leads to another. My story is the story of relapse, the next person says—you can't cure yourself without a psychic change. And then someone says: I did not have a relationship with a power greater than myself, and when I finally found that moment of grace I was able to be at peace.

Tonight is the night for moments of grace. And psychic change.

Or death: the next guy says several people died at work this week. Today it was this guy who always seemed happy, he never seemed to have problems, he was always smiling, he was the one everyone loved. And then today he killed himself and left a suicide note.

I'm so grateful for the love in these rooms, this guy says.

Relapse is something I'm very familiar with, someone else says—my relapse carried into sobriety for the first five years— sometimes I would even show up drunk. But you can't pick and choose the steps, that's what I was doing. I've learned that if I drink again it's not going to be a good time, I'm just going to end up feeling dead inside.

And that's what hits me. Because I always end up feeling dead inside. At home I flip through the pages of the Big Book to find moments of temptation, escape from disaster, midnight, cynicism, dividends, guidance, the defects, stirring spiritual experience, treatment, the medical profession, determination, money, desperation, a dozen bottles, a mild bender, coffee, Florida sunshine, inconsiderate habits, withdrawal, a position to be hurt, belligerent denial, a glass of beer, a friendly taxicab driver, absolute proof, reformers, skilled guidance, Easter Sunday, a duplex, post-operative day, Christ's injunction, a one-way street, the asylum, a real stinker, Good Samaritans, New Delhi, people in Akron, gay young Bohemians, optimism, central heating, my marriage, completely blacked out, a domestic standpoint, God's hands, the Eighteenth Amendment, a reformer, obsession, proper respect, floating away, a drugstore, mail-order business, that midget, desperation, emphasizing alcoholism, sneaking my drinks, dollar hotels, a skull, waste, a jackrabbit, a Cleveland group, daily living, my drinking career, Uncle Sam, a dandy, that sanitarium, closed meetings, inner freedom, a vigorous campaign, spirits recharged, the pokey, eighteen years, our crowd, your husband, psychologists, a daily reprieve, the Spirit, Ku Klux Klan, interpretation, a Sunday supplement, resentment, professional men, Ohio Edison Building, $5,000, scandalous gossip, a rabbi, a technical education, reality, spring of 1939, blacking out, heartsickness, apprenticeship, the wreckage, your wife, his Creator, the head cook, Vietnam, a fine Christian mother, a psycho ward, Beverly Hills, John Barleycorn, spiritual hunger, the Navy, that first drink, my son's illness, a teaspoon of brandy, restitution, merry-go-round, DuPont, ruinous slander, Champlain Street Station, bitterly-hated business rival, my children, a minister, character removed, school publications, a gangster's moll, ribaldry, this bare room, Texas, sneaking drinks, a heel, mutual trust, the Kingdom, to swallow me, mechanical drawing, Suez Canal, that hospital bed, blame, outsiders, volume, old sweet selves, the bums, Dr. Bob, Jekyll-and-Hyde, bottle after bottle, PTA, mere cessation, a rummage sale, another six months, Christian Science, bootleggers, helping other alcoholics, God goes deep, the New Land, we never apologize, Bridge of Reason, a grim jest, fleshpots of Egypt, Boozeville, the West Coast, Venus, an upset stomach, YMCA, the Commanding Officer, the theater, mental twists, boyhood, Hitler's war, our marriage, a Midas touch, two girls hitchhiking, law school, Prohibition, Atlantic City, Mother's Day, a goner, the Chicago area, wisecracking sneerer, my sponsor, incapacitated father, foolish decisions, a nut, a stickler, design for living, alcoholics field, pagan mystic, a happy childhood, early July, God's handiwork, a two-fisted drinker, the South, the first Christmas, a telephone booth, grammar school, morning coffee, borrowed sum, the strange hospital, belligerent denial, a psychiatrist, John D. Rockefeller, non-meeting nights, Priscilla, my husband, a cocker spaniel, the water wagon, San Diego, commercial banks, the cocktail hour, hard knocks, my wash day, a fashionable suburb, popping pills, my relatives, lost time, every alcoholic, the Mount, he's a sissy, a salesman, poison, a loaf of bread, a big potted plant, her house, shocking things, another principle, untold grief, seed, an ambulance, a mattress, nothingness, a mental fog, an early morning truck, pneumonia, Boxer Rebellion, Tijuana, Washington State, the mirror, wet canteens, Tall Man, Pittsburgh, two drinking societies, necessary escapism, the clergy, the rugs, hilarious life, basis of love, Heavenly Father, indispensable, we cannot subscribe, lack of control, simple cornerstone, emotional disturbances, cancer, crack-pot, take it easy, now about sex, my associates, a quart, fashion design, vicissitude, insanity, fatal illness, agnostics, permanent brain injury, heartening success, the dishes, a churchgoing wallflower, Nevada City, corn liquor, radio broadcasts, Detroit, elderberry blossom wine, membership, a corker, nurses, hooch, wild oats, my sick ego, a tough Irishman, reformers, 8th and L, reputation, Serenity Prayer, humiliation, moonshine, material goods, Alsations, saloons, foolish martyr, Boss Universal, the Far East, high road, the vacuum, a new freedom, this dry spell, outside, splinters.

And here I am again, I still can't believe I'm here but I'm

here. Apparently today's the day when people celebrate anniversaries: thirty days, sixty days, ninety, six months, nine months, one year, eighteen months—twenty-four hours? There are a lot of cheers, and everyone gets chips—I'm not sure what you do with these chips.

Today is a speaker's meeting, which I guess means the speaker takes as long as he wants. He says he grew up in the suburbs, went to Catholic school and hated it—Catholicism was a huge part of my family, he says, we all lived together in the same neighborhood. And eventually I did learn from the Catholic Church: I learned how to lie. I knew I wouldn't be supported if anyone found out I was gay—I was not a popular kid. The first time I got drunk it was Grand Marnier and I got really sick and vomited and I never tried that again. But I remembered that warm wash all over me.

That warm wash all over me—this guy's actually a good speaker.

He says: I went to high school in the late sixties and early seventies and those were the counterculture days but you wouldn't have known it in the community where I grew up—alcohol and drugs became a means to escape. I looked for the others who were like me—there was another guy in my high school and we started venturing out to the big discotheque in Boston at the time. It was magical—I almost couldn't believe all the beauty and excitement there. But there was a lie woven in with that magic, the lie of so much shame and self-hatred covered up by drugs and alcohol. Like the Pet Shop Boys say, "Some are here, and some are missing."

The Pet Shop Boys. It's funny that he's quoting the Pet Shop Boys to talk about the seventies.

I developed all these relationships with older gay men after I was kicked out of my house. It was like one of those scenes in a movie where everyone found out I was gay in less than five minutes, and I'd like to tell you that story sometime so feel free to ask me about it but I don't want to get off track. Let's just say it was a catastrophe, and these older gay men plucked me off the streets and nurtured me. I really owe everything to them.

Sometimes it was a secret mentorship, like when I lived in Central Square in a big old Victorian with eight other gay men and they told me that the kind of drinking I did, it couldn't go on in the house. But I didn't listen. The men in that household were some of the first people on my list for amends. It seems like this went on for a while—I witnessed the sexual revolution as it unfolded, it was like people suddenly came out of their shells and blossomed. Sex was everywhere, and it still felt so magical to connect in this way. I had relationships that lasted a week, and relationships that lasted years. And it felt like an idyllic life until somewhere around 1982, when there were the first rumblings about a gay cancer and suddenly I found that idyllic life unraveling.

Eventually I had to stop going to funerals because it was too depressing. I still had the ability to use drugs to shut off everything around me, in fact I was getting better and better—I was taking every pill and powder and substance available. But I started a love affair with Scotch, that secret embrace. I would go to the bar before and after work, and I always had a bottle at home.

I moved to Orlando for two years for work—to open a hotel at Disney World, and I hated it. Everyone had a tan and the sun was always setting and it was so hot and grimy, even the prettiest things had a slime underneath. And I was the one who kept the party going, I was the one who made it pretty on the outside. A lot of you don't know this, but I was a DJ all up and down the East Coast. I was always in demand. But eventually the hemorrhaging of pain and despair started impacting my health. I kept moving from house to house, but I wasn't ready to look at my addiction.

When I first got back to Boston, I was selling coke on the side, and I got a call from my housemate that the feds were arriving in twenty-four hours and I had to get everything out of the house. Then my partner died, he killed himself because he didn't want AIDS to kill him. I went on a bender—drunkenness became a sport, a way to pick on people, I thought I was smarter than everyone, I would get in fights and say I bet I know how to make you cry. And then I would do it, I would make people cry, and I would laugh so hard—I felt like I was better than everyone.

Eventually I ended up in the hospital, all the doctors were wearing hazmat suits, I'll spare you the details, but let's just say I was near death. And you know how people talk about spiritual experiences, I had a spiritual experience in that hospital. I called a former drug dealer friend of mine who was working at Fenway Community Health, and he came right over. Actually he came to the hospital room every day for the next six months. He gave me so much nurturing, compassion, empathy, love, immense courage and strength. And that's where I began my long road of recovery.

I entered a one-year program, there were twenty-six of us at the beginning and I was in so much pain I had to lie on pillows on the floor. At the end of the program, only two of us were left: everyone else was dead. I don't know why I'm still here, unless it's to speak to you here in this room still alive. Disease has affected my community in so many ways, but my pain has become a great motivator to help others. Pain, and trauma— because I experienced such huge amounts of trauma growing up. We're all experiencing that trauma again now, the trauma of losing so many people we care about, and who's next—it could be me. Or you.

I didn't come to twelve-step meetings for a year. I thought it was a cult. I had so much contempt for you in this room, in all of these rooms, meeting in such dark and unattractive places. Although when you think about it, don't we often meet in dark and unattractive places?

It might sound funny, but I always say that the most important people in my recovery are the quiet ones who hide within our rooms, who dart in and out, who sit in the corner and don't have the courage or strength to participate fully. Those are the people I'm drawn to. I wanted to read some excerpts from the Big Book, but I'm aware that I'm running out of time and I want to hear some of the newcomers speak. Let me just quote from Quentin Crisp, who says: "Your profession is being."

And just like that, we're out of time. Someone's reading the promises, and now we stand for the serenity prayer.

I rush over to talk to Sammy, that the speaker's name. I say I always thought AA was a cult too, I mean I never imagined I'd be here except as a joke—I've always been suspicious of mentors, and no one has ever reached out to me anyway but if they did I probably would have laughed at them. Anyway, I just wanted to thank you for being so honest. My name's Alexa.

Alexa? What a beautiful name. Do you want to go to coffee?

What a beautiful name—no one ever says that. I go to coffee, and I'm hooked.

CAMERA'S READY

Breakfast at Tiffany's starts with "Moon River" and a taxi ride in the morning in New York—I guess that must be Audrey Hepburn getting out of the cab in a black Givenchy gown, we know it's Givenchy because they played the credits first.

Oh, hilarious—she's eating a pastry out of a paper bag, with black evening gloves, coffee in a to-go cup, this is much better than I thought. Especially those costume jewelry pearls with a huge fake diamond clasp, I wouldn't mind an accessory like that.

But what is this horrible Asian landlord stereotype—the whole audience bursts out laughing. Luckily I'm in the aisle, should I just leave? I could tell the AA girls that the movie was hurting my eyes. Maybe I'll go on a walk and come back for the ending.

I don't know what to do, so I end up walking through the Urban Outfitters mall, and how could there be this many college sweatshirts in the world? Not just Harvard or MIT or BU or Tufts, but Worcester Polytechnic. Amherst. Johns Hopkins. Cornell. Stanford—are you kidding? Is it really that exciting to go to Au Bon Pain and a few bad Indian restaurants and then wander around on the fake cobblestone sidewalks, looking for the best jock bar—I don't get it.

I end up sitting in Harvard Square, staring at the punk kids staring at me. My hair is better, just admit it. Maybe I'll go to that thrift store where I found the checkered polyester pants, that was a good thrift store. But I can't find it.

Eventually I'm back in the theater. Audrey's sitting on a white sofa made out of a bathtub, with magenta pillows—I'll take that sofa, Nate doesn't have one of those yet. Now Audrey's at Tiffany with her new boyfriend, and she says: "Nothing bad could ever happen to you in a place like this." So I'm waiting for something really bad to happen.

But this isn't that kind of movie—eventually Audrey gets busted for drugs so then she's smoking in the entrance of the police station as the paparazzi conduct interviews. An organized crime kingpin is on the phone saying: "She's a phony. But she's a real phony." I guess that's where that line comes from.

Her not-quite-boyfriend pronounces his love in the taxi, tells her that no matter where she runs, she'll just end up running into herself. Sounds like something from AA. Then the two lovebirds are getting drenched by the rain machine in matching trench coats, kind of like the coat Joey used to wear, maybe this was where she got the idea.

Everything started with *Breakfast at Tiffany's*, that's what Allen said at our last AA coffee so then we ended up here. But I guess now she notices this wasn't exactly my type of entertainment, because afterward she asks me about my favorite movie. I don't have a favorite movie. Well, pick one, she says, and we'll all go over Mama Cass's and watch it together.

So here we are, three days later, chez Mama Cass—it's like a cross between the Thirteen Colonies and Marie Antoinette's spare cottage—there's so much going on in that wallpaper that it could be an entire magazine spread. Of course Cass collects dolls—everywhere, dolls in glass cases. Decaying wooden dolls with scraggly hair, Cabbage Patch Kids, Barbies, geisha dolls, Hollywood celebrities, even papier-mâché dolls.

We're watching *Poison*—right at the beginning a seven-year-old shoots his abusive father and then flies away. Richie Beacon, gotta love that name—did I see this movie before or after I remembered about my father? It must have been before, that's why I don't remember this part.

Dr Nancy Olson, from Boston, arrives to assist Dr Graves, who has captured the sex drive in liquid form in some campy laboratory, and Allen starts clapping and laughing and then she delivers one of her favorite phrases: I've always depended on the kindness of strangers. I say what movie is that from again, but Bud says shh.

Dr Nancy Olson, from Boston, Allen says in her exaggerated Woburn accent even though Nancy Olson's accent is more blueblood than Boston realness.

Dr Graves drinks the potion when Nancy leaves, he's watching her walk away with lust in his eyes and then he's a monster. The movie shifts from black-and-white noir to 1980s pastel kitsch as Richie Beacon's mother is being interviewed, she says his father hit him, just like any other kid.

Back to Dr Graves in black and white with sores all over his face, sores that transfer to the woman he kisses in a bar, and Cass says: That'll definitely keep me from drinking.

And we all laugh—it's fun to watch this movie here.

And then McGovern's Bar: LEPER SEX KILLER ON THE LOOSE, Nancy sees the headline after kissing Dr Graves—why didn't you tell me you're contagious?

Blue light, this is the part I remember best: John Broom, the smaller guy, reaching out to touch Jack Bolton's broad chest while he's sleeping. They use last names because they're in prison, and Broom's hand creeps along Bolton's skin, down to his crotch. Bud gulps, and Allen says wow, full frontal, can you believe that?

A doctor who treated young Richie, saying he was suspicious because Richie had an infectious discharge—a six-year-old with an STD, but still this doctor didn't intervene. I wonder what would've happened if I'd gotten an STD when I was six.

Nancy dies in Dr Graves's arms, and I don't remember this part being so sad before, is it because I'm watching it now with Allen, who names her KS lesions, and Sammy, whose T cells are plummeting again? Dr Graves tries to run from society and persecution and then Richie's mother is back in color saying: "My child was an angel of judgment."

Broom provokes a fight so he can get closer to Bolton, and I'm thinking about that Barbara Kruger poster about how men create intricate rituals to touch one another's skin. In this case the ritual is rape as Broom fucks Bolton from behind and we see him bobbing up and down—even though Bolton is crying, we still focus on Broom. I focus on Broom. Watching this scene was when I first realized I wanted to get fucked—I didn't know why then but I do now.

At the end of the movie Dr Graves is outside, sores covering his face, and I'm thinking about that drawing in *Memories That Smell Like Gasoline*. Dr Graves jumps from his window onto the screaming crowd outside—people back away and he falls to the ground. We watch his whole face disintegrate in the hospital as he dies. Broom listens to Bolton getting shot while trying to escape prison, and Richie's mother says her husband was beating her and she thought she was going to die. Until Richie shot him. Before jumping out the window. And flying away.

Cass refills our mocktails, and says baby doll, we know there's a lot going on in your head if that's your favorite movie. And then it's one of those nights: I wake up, which should be good news because that means I was sleeping, right? But I didn't even notice—in my dream I was still trying to fall asleep. And then that feeling in the room, a shaking in my breath, an extra dimension of fear—he's here somewhere, my father, is he here? This is so old, this panic, why now?

Maybe I sleep and maybe I don't, but somehow I make it back to a meeting. K-Street is so much better than those churches, I can't believe I ever went to those churches—at K-Street there's no cross in sight, and we sit in a circle, lounging on sofas. I guess I'm early, so I go outside, and there's Joanna. Now her hair has grown out and she basically looks like your average Red Sox fan. I can tell she's shocked to see me here, but then she holds out her arms for a big hug, and I realize how much she still means to me. She says oh, I miss you, I really miss you, I'm so glad you're here, is that why you're here? Oh—I'm so glad. I'm going to smoke, and I'll see you inside.

I go inside, sit down on my favorite turquoise armchair, and Allen says you're in a good mood. And he's right, I am in a good mood. But then the meeting starts, and Joanna isn't there. And she didn't give me her number.

Bud is presenting tonight and he looks really nervous. What I want to talk about isn't pretty, he says, but I know I have to dig deep into the hardest places, otherwise why am I here? So let me begin by saying that I've been sober for twelve years, but now I have to start over. Let me check the time, six fifteen, that means it's been approximately sixteen hours since I stumbled into bed drunk as a skunk after twelve years, twelve years of sobriety and I'm so grateful I knew I had to come in tonight because otherwise I'm not sure what would have happened.

Listen, this isn't a pity party—I've got it all going for me—great job, just renovated my house in the South End. I bought a new car six months ago, a Beamer convertible, and look at this, I just got myself a Rolex. I'm not telling you any of this to brag, I just want you to know that I fucked up, I really fucked up this time. You see, I got tired, I got tired of working the steps, thought I had it all, thought I had it all figured out. I got tired of the same old, same old. Listen, I might be highly successful in financial matters, but I'm fat and old and ugly and even a whole fleet of Beamers isn't going to cover that up.

One night I was driving by one of my old haunts, the 1270, I'm sure most of us know it, what's it called now? Quest. What a name. So I was scoping it out from outside, no harm in that, remembering the good old, bad old days, some kind of nostalgia sinking into my pits but I kept driving. Sometimes I drive around like this, looking at the bars from outside so I found myself at Chaps—I like to pull over by the entrance just to see what the young guys are wearing these days, and I don't know what possessed me this time but I decided to go in. I know what you're thinking—how many times have I gone through the steps? But the program can't do everything for you. It was that same old godforsaken loneliness.

This one pretty young thing at Chaps, he wasn't the most attractive but he was blond, strong bone structure, nice chest and he couldn't have been much older than twenty-one—he saw the old guy looking so he came over and asked me to buy him a drink. Of course I knew I shouldn't be enabling anyone, but that smile, those crooked teeth just crying out for braces. I bought him a drink, a Long Island iced tea. And then another. And a third one, and he's telling me about his time in the service, you know, how hard it was to live without pussy, and I'm trying to figure out where he's going with that, since we all know there's no pussy at Chaps. Excuse my language.

Anyone with a few hundred brain cells can tell he's working me for drinks—I'm old now but I was young once too. I'll probably always remember those eyes, gray like a puddle in the street after a big storm. Tells me he wants to go home with me so of course I thought he might rob me. I thought about calling my sponsor—I've got plenty of numbers but I sure as hell knew what everyone would say. So we get to my place, and he asks me what I have to drink. I tell him I'm sober, and he starts grinning like that's the best joke he's ever heard. I tell him he can leave if he wants to.

But I guess he didn't want to leave because we ended up in the bedroom every night for practically two weeks—I felt like I was sixteen again. Except when I was sixteen I didn't have the courage. Of course I kept going to work, kept up appearances, but all I could think about was Jimmy, who was staying in my apartment—he said he needed a vacation. I said take your time, I've got time. All the time in the world. He was one of those butch guys who likes to clean, I would get home and everything would be neat and tidy. I called and canceled my maid service, said I was going away on a business trip, not sure how long, I'd call again when I got back.

I started to fantasize that this would go on forever, just me and my military buddy, fucking like rabbits. Then one day I was alone again. But I was still sober. That was the important thing. Except there was something else. I was taking care of my sobriety, but I wasn't taking care, I wasn't. I wasn't. I don't know if I can say it. You know, this straight guy, this straight guy and he was so young, I just thought I didn't have anything to worry about.

Bud doesn't look like he's fifty-six anymore, he looks like a little boy. A little boy who can't say the rest. There's an awkward pause, and then people are clapping—is that what's happening, people are clapping? Someone's saying he really appreciated Bud's share, he really appreciated his willingness to look so deeply at himself, and Bud, pay attention to the studies, there are new drugs now, the new drugs are working.

I really want to stand up and yell at that guy, but instead I go to the bathroom. If I start pounding on the walls, everyone will hear me so instead I press my face into my hands, and open my mouth like I'm screaming. I look in the mirror: my eyes are red, but I'm not crying, why can't I cry, I want to cry. That fucking asshole—the new drugs are not working, how could anyone believe the new drugs are working? I feel like I'm trapped, like I can't go back out there. But then I open the bathroom door anyway, walk right past Bud and everyone else, and I notice Allen is looking at me so I try to smile. Then I open the front door and I'm outside.

I kind of want someone to come after me, so I wait a minute, but no one does so I start walking. There's the Fens and it's not that cold tonight but I don't want to go to the Fens so I take the road through the middle. I'm thinking about how no one talks about it until they're dying. And that asshole, who was that asshole? Telling us the new drugs are working. I'm thinking about when Avery showed me those new sheets, all those new sheets and we barely had a chance to use them.

I start walking. I start walking toward Avery's.

I get to the door, and I can't decide what to do. I ring the buzzer and he answers: Peter Pan's house of homos.

I hang up.

Breathe, Alexa, breathe. I pick up the receiver again and dial the apartment.

Hello, Avery says. Are you going to say something?

It's Alexa.

Alexa?

She buzzes me in. I like the sound of her voice. She opens the door and I smell that cologne, or maybe it's a different one.

I'm trying to figure out if she's angry or pretending to be angry. Her hair is curled with some kind of cream, almost a Jazz Age look. The apartment is all designy now, sleek European leather sofas and chrome lamps.

What do you need, Avery says.

I don't know if I need anything.

Oh, Alexa, I know you're not here to smell my snatch. How about this? I'll give you a special, twenty for a gram, the purest shit you'll ever do. You caught me at the right moment, I haven't even gotten around to cutting it yet. A special, just for you. I'm not even making a profit.

She holds out her hand. I reach in my pocket for a twenty, and she hands me the vial.

Always a pleasure to see you, she says. I lean over to kiss her, and she turns her cheek.

I step outside with the vial in my pocket. I need to throw this in the river, I need to throw this in the river right away—where am I? Oh, I'm right here, right here outside Joey's apartment. Joey's apartment. Shit. That's when I start crying. They've got new drugs, the new drugs are working. Working the steps. Working the steps with the new drugs.

I get home and I put the vial in the center of the table like it's a tiny sculpture. The river, I was supposed to throw it in the river. Instead I open it, and look inside. Nate isn't coming home tonight, another business trip, Singapore. Maybe I'll do a little, just a little.

Oh my God it's not what I expected. The pain. My nose. That burn.

Oh, I love that burn.

I need to go out. I need to dance.

Avalon. Tonight's Avalon. But what will I wear?

Oh, that dress I was making out of torn-up prom dresses

from Dollar-A-Pound, yes, that dress. All the wedding gowns Polly and I used to collect, pinned together over that tight gold Contempo Casuals Lycra number, all the wedding gowns forming one big train—I never wore that dress.

A shower. I need to take a shower first.

Oh, this was such a good idea. I love this bathroom. I fucking love this bathroom.

And now for the dress of dresses—shiny magenta shoulder pad top covered in rhinestones, glistening green sequins over the chest, something blue and silky down to the waist in tatters over the gold underneath and then yellow, red, more magenta, all the biggest bows torn off and pinned back together and then at the bottom are all those anorexic weddings, passing out and dragging below. Should I pin it up further, or let it drag on the ground and get ruined?

Ruined, of course. Ruined.

But I need something around my neck. Everything, I need everything. My bag of pearl necklaces, all of them—and then the silver balls, the big plastic clear beads, the purple square beads, the lime-green oval ones—oh, here's my hotel chandelier crystal collection.

Quick—let's make these into earrings. Minimalism is so overrated.

Lipstick, yes, lipstick. All over my face. More lipstick. Shape my hair into perfect green-and-orange swirls, spray to keep it in place, no one's seen the green and orange yet. Smear the purple eyeshadow from eyes down to cheeks and over to ears, and then add the gold glitter, the silver glitter, the big chunky white glitter. Oh, honey, now these sunglasses are perfect—this is what I should have been wearing the whole time.

Combat boots, definitely combat boots. Jellybean tights. Of course the pipe-clamp bracelets to keep me grounded. Wrap all these lace garter belts up my arms, oh that looks amazing. I can't believe this came together so fast.

I need another line. Just a little. Downstairs at the dining room table—this is what chandeliers were made for.

I step outside and there's a cab waiting for me, just up the block. All the windows are open and I think of asking the driver to close them a little so my hair doesn't get messed up, but then I just lean back and we're already there.

I can't believe how early I am—it's not even midnight. Jason's at the door—she waves me in, girl it's been a while.

I step inside and yes, runway through the spinning lights and past the stupid strippers and everyone staring and all the way to the back bar at Axis for a vodka sour with grenadine, tonight I need grenadine, yes the disease called alcoholism, oh it tastes so good.

Some drunk tells me my lipstick is smeared. Oh, really? I should have brought a mirror.

Sage and Juniper save me—Alexa, we thought you were dead. Undead.

Well, you certainly look better than ever. That dress is fierce. You should go into fashion. Do you need anything?

I need everything. Fashion. This music. Another vodka sour with grenadine, please, and the magic pill, so tart.

Oh, that drumroll—it's "Camera's ready, prepare to flash"

and honey I am flashing on the dance floor, twirling around in my tangle of dresses, bending over the beat into jump rope, skip and kick, leap into the fall down rip skip and kick turn skip and kick turn.

Yes, I'm throwing down all my tricks and Juniper and Sage are on the sidelines delivering high kicks in their platforms and, yes, this jump, twirl, kick and swirl, shriek and unfurl, girl, sure, I can feel the dress ripping again—I'll just pull this part up and pin it closer to my waist, turn, and people are backing up to give me space yes space give me space I'll take all the space I can get.

There's Lady Dionne, waving her fan like she's been here the whole time, she owns the place and she couldn't give a damn, couldn't give a damn about anything, I've always loved Lady Dionne.

Work, mama, work is the sound of everyone yelling because we're feeling our drugs, and we're feeling the music, and we're feeling Lady Dionne, yes, I'm yelling too. And she shakes her finger in my direction, and then points right at me I can hardly believe it I'm shrieking so loud and everyone's yelling work and I'm literally rolling on the floor, jump up into more and more and more and more until I realize I lost my sunglasses, where are my sunglasses, dammit.

Oh, who cares—now I'm in a world of softness and light.

Time to check in on my eyes—oh, yes, my eyes, I've been waiting so long.

Welcome, Alexa. Welcome.

Welcome back.

We're here in the bathroom with a stack of paper towels to

absorb the sweat, listening to the music through the walls—the music of everyone doing bumps, toilet flush, do I need a bump, save that for later, I'm prepared, always prepared, another bump, another flush, runny nose, I'll take that rose, but should I leave the bathroom?

Oh, but the mirror—it's kind of comfortable watching the show from this angle. Someone wearing head-to-toe designer garbage comes in and stops in the doorway like she's seen an accident, hand to her chest, and she says girl! And I say girl! And she says girl! And now we're best friends.

I'm studying the colors of my hair, the way the glitter changes with my eyes yes my eyes and lipstick and those crystals in my ears, all the necklaces piled around my neck, what a collar. People flowing in and out as I say welcome, welcome, you're welcome, thank you, glorious, fantastic, fabulous, phenomenal, philosophical, fierce.

Yes, fierce and flaunting it in your fabulous phlebotomy.

Flawless. Fantabulous. Tantalizing. Mesmerizing. Marvelous. Magnificent. Magna Carta. Carte blanche. Blanche Dubois. W.E.B. DuBois. Boise, Idaho. Don't call me ho I prefer hooker.

Where did I get this? Oh, Louis Boston—I get everything there, so reasonable. This is just a little resort wear for a dip in the Charles—yes, my makeup, thank you. I managed to slip in for a consultation at Neiman Marcus just before last call.

Of course—oh, yes, never leave home without Chanel. Never leave home, sweet home—oh, darling, not a wig at all. Sorry, my hair just grows like this. I know, it's soft.

Welcome, you're welcome—yes, I live here. All the time.

Just need to decorate—oh, a bump? No, but thank you—maybe later.

X? You mean X-trava. X-traterrestrial. X-tra sensational. Extra Sensenbrenner. Extra Saltines. Extra sass. Extra pass the sugar. Extra pour some sugar on me.

Yes, I know you mean Excalibur—just look for the girls in platforms, tell them Alexa sent you. Alexa Arrivederci. My pleasure.

Oh, maybe I should go out there too—this is Miss Alexa Avalanche, reporting from Axis on Sunday.

Louder Than I Thought, on News 11. At eleven.

No, News 9. At eleven.

News News, at News.

Upstairs: the Photo Booth. A totally different crowd. Tell us, Miss Avalanche, tell us about the crowd.

The crowd looks scandalized.

Behold Miss Avalanche as she falls against the bar, flings herself gently on the surface and then slides to the floor while Phil Collins croons one of his soulful tunes.

Prunes. Because we care about your digestion.

Should I get another cocktail? Just to look at that grenadine—grenade, Granada, champagne, tostada.

So much prettier than diamonds, who needs diamonds when you can have garnet, ruby, carnelian—nothing does Queen Grenadine justice. Drumroll, please.

And then somehow I'm alone in the secret bathroom and there's no more music, but that's okay—we've got lights, a mirror, toilet paper and hot water, what more could we need?

Yes, Alexa, yes, that's the perfect temperature—now, give us another pose, up against the wall, yes, arms in the air, just like that. Welcome.

Now, lean in and kiss the mirror. Yes, just like that. Lick it, honey, lick it.

Wait, there's someone banging on the door. This is the only bathroom that locks—I thought maybe I could stay here forever, talking to that girl in the mirror. Yes?

Oh, it's security. I could do without security, but I open the door anyway. The security guard looks shocked, but it's not like I haven't been here the whole time. I let him escort me down the stairs—royalty, for sure.

The lights are on and the place looks desolate. He takes me through the back door and then I'm outside and oh, it's the best weather in the history of the world, soft, chilly air on my face and the streets are deserted—Boston is fucking gorgeous when everything's deserted. Should I go to the Fens?

Of course, darling, what this dress needs is that subtle hint of mud for spring '96. Sneak. Preview.

It's so easy to walk through the grass because the wind is pulling me toward the stars yes the stars and I'm floating between gardens to the reeds oh look at the way the reeds are dancing with Miss Prudential, there she is, we're dancing with Miss Prudential. I'm twirling in the grass like that scene in *The Sound of Music* or maybe it's *Wonder Woman* because I take the shortcut through the lights in the sky and then I'm already on Commonwealth, I mean what happened to Mass. Ave. but wait, is it starting to get light out? I need to control the lights.

Oh no, am I crashing?

Don't worry, honey, we have plenty of powder at the palace.

Nate's not home, but we still don't want to drag mud through the house so let's just rip the wedding dresses off the bottom of the gown and leave them in the street for the cars to run over. It's time for daywear anyway.

Oh, the palace, here I am. I just need a refresher.

I sit down and pour the coke onto the table, all of it, should I do all of it at once?

Alexa, don't get ahead of yourself, maybe just half.

The curtain is rising, honey—get ready for the biggest line of your life.

Oh my fucking God my nose oh my nose it's burning down the house I'm a mouse, gobbling up the poison where's my heart.

Alexa, don't be ridiculous. Stop leaning your head over the sink, it's time. It's time to take over the world.

But first I need sunglasses, where are my sunglasses?

Oh, I left them at Avalon. I'll have to use another pair. Two pairs.

Okay, I'm fine. Just take the stairs.

Oh, the stairs, yes, I love these white stairs. Let's see, where do I keep all my sunglasses? Yes, the closet. Here I am. In the most beautiful closet the world has ever seen, gritting my teeth—Alexa, stop gritting your teeth, everything will be fine. You just need a little Xanax, where's the Xanax, oh, Nate took it from me, never mind.

Let's take a look in the mirror. More lipstick, that's what we need, yes, just bite off a few chunks, perfect. Let's add the rainbow glitter, yes, let's add the rainbow glitter to the lipstick. Love it. Now, let's get the hair back in place and freeze those curls for the world, the world needs those curls. Here's the sunglasses drawer.

Oh, my camera, camera's ready, yes, let's take out the camera.

But Colin's ashes. They're still here in that paper cup. I need to do something with Colin's ashes.

Alexa, you're mumbling. Mumbling and fumbling, no crumbling.

I need to hear that song.

Oh, that's better. So much better. "Good evening parents, tonight I'm going to take you on a tour ..."

Yes, a tour, honey, a tour—why didn't I think of that sooner? And which purse should I bring?

The red one, darling, of course the red one, there's always a red purse.

Alexa, don't forget the sunglasses, can we fit three pairs on at once?

Maybe if I take the lenses on the middle ones out.

Perfect. It's the hottest look for winter, spring, fall.

Sprinter, wring, sprawl.

Orange juice. We need orange juice. Yes. The colors. Bring back the colors.

Maybe a little more coke, just a little, and I'll leave the rest here on the table for Nate.

Morning. It's morning. I'm mourning. But I'm leaving the house for a reason, I finally found a reason.

Ignore. Ignore. Ignore. Them. All.

Splinter, minter, mawl.

Printer, dinger, brawl.

Blur. It. All.

Except for the runway. Funway. Stunway. Mesmerizing get-done way. Obliter-one-way. Xtrava-spunway.

Okay, are we ready for one glance toward the hordes of beige and navy and, yes, everybody's in awe. Turn the head, slowly. Then the shoulders. Then the hips and feet. Brilliant. Now we're back to where we started.

And there she is, the queen of all runways, Miss Jeannine Hancockatiel, rising above the rabble as the office drones stream out of the T, yes, let me pour some of these ashes right here, under your perfectly shined loafers and sensible heels, oh, the runway of our destiny, grinding ash into cement.

Yes, it's a bit hard to see through three pairs of sunglasses but I think that woman in beige just stepped on a bit of bone and why hasn't anyone made a house song out of WE DIE, YOU DO NOTHING?

It would just be perfect, everyone could dance all day and all night.

But house music is never about you, is it? It's always about us.

WE DIE, WE DO NOTHING—yes, I need to take some of these ashes back to Avalon. Or someone's ashes—there will be more, there will always be more ashes over our runway. Runway over our ashes.

Doesn't Jeannine look beautiful in this light? That's because she looks beautiful in every light.

They're all snapping photos, I'm sure. Don't worry, Jeannine,

I won't steal too much attention. I'm just sprinkling some ashes in the park, so I can find my way back past the wolves, a trail of bone fragments to guide me.

Here I am at the entrance, all those mirrored doors and the office drones are streaming in. Are the cameras ready? I've got the ashes, please bring the sashes.

Rashes. Rashes for us all.

Last call.

ACKNOWLEDGMENTS

As always, I want to thank the wonderful critics and friends, friends and critics who gave me detailed analyses of the manuscript: Mairead Case, Jennifer Natalya Fink, Gabriel Hedemann, Michael Lowenthal, Jory Mickelson and Katia Noyes.

For tangibles and intangibles: Kevin Coleman, Andy Slaght, Joey Carducci, Adrian Lambert, Tony Radovich, Sarah Schulman, Jesse Mann, Jessica Lawless, Dana Garza, Yasmin Nair, Steve Zeeland, Jason Sellards, Kate Zambreno, Porochista Khakpour, Alyssa Harad, Mel Flashman, Nick Arvin, Jessica Hoffmann, Alexander Chee, Julie Buntin, Masie Cochran, Kristen Radtke, Lauren Goldstein, Hedi El Kholti, Randa Jarrar, Jessa Crispin, Stephen Kent Jusick, Sara Jaffe, Corinne Manning, Cari Luna, Jed Walsh, Matthew Schnirmann, Jacob Olson, Eric Stanley, Ananda La Vita, John Criscitello, Karin Goldstein, Peter Mountford, Chavisa Woods, Michael Bronski, Libby Bouvier at the History Project: Documenting LGBTQ Boston, everyone at Hugo House, Karen Maeda Allman, everyone at Elliott Bay Book Company, Rebecca Brown, Amy Scholder, Richie Rich, Michael Sheehan, Elissa Washuta, Seth Haldeman, Wakefield Poole and anyone else I may have inadvertently forgotten—in spite of the length of this list, I'm sure there are many.

For publishing excerpts of this book, in various forms: *Denver Quarterly*, *great weather for MEDIA A Night in the Barracks*, and *The Spectacle*.

Thanks to Brian Lam for taking this book on—it was when I was living in Boston in 1995 that Arsenal published my first short story, so the circle is complete! You are one of the very few publishers consistently publishing challenging queer work, for decades now, and I'm honored to be part of the trouble. Thanks to Shirarose Wilensky for keen line edits, Oliver McPartlin for the stunning cover design, and Cynara Geissler and Alyson Sinclair for publicity magic and mayhem, here we go ... And, to Amanda Annis, as we embark on our journey together ... To more!!!

No writer is a writer without other writers, and so I'm thankful for all of you, really. Let's do this together.

MATTILDA BERNSTEIN SYCAMORE  is the award-winning author of a memoir and three novels, and the editor of five nonfiction anthologies. Her memoir, *The End of San Francisco*, won a Lambda Literary Award, and her previous title, *Why Are Faggots So Afraid of Faggots?: Flaming Challenges to Masculinity, Objectification, and the Desire to Conform*, was an American Library Association Stonewall Honor Book. Sycamore's novels include *So Many Ways to Sleep Badly* and *Pulling Taffy*, and her anthologies include *Nobody Passes: Rejecting the Rules of Gender and Conformity* and *That's Revolting! Queer Strategies for Resisting Assimilation*.

Sycamore writes for a variety of publications, including the *San Francisco Chronicle*, *Bookforum*, *BOMB*, the *Baffler*, *Truthout*, *Bitch*, and *the Los Angeles Review of Books*. She recently finished a book on desire and its impossibility called *The Freezer Door* and is working on a book about her fraught relationship with her late grandmother, a visual artist, tentatively titled *Touching the Art*. Mattilda lives in Seattle, where she loves the rain almost as much as she loves the sun.

mattildabernsteinsycamore.com